Someone Is Watching

Gay Youth Chronicles

Someone Is Watching

Mark A. Roeder

Writers Club Press
New York Lincoln Shanghai

Someone Is Watching

Writers Club Press
an imprint of iUniverse, Inc.

For information address:
iUniverse
2021 Pine Lake Road, Suite 100
Lincoln, NE 68512
www.iuniverse.com

ISBN: 0-595-26073-X

Printed in the United States of America

This book is dedicated to all those boys who struggle to be true to themselves.

Contents

Other Books by Mark A. Roeder Listed in Suggested Reading Order

Gay Youth Chronicles:

Ancient Prejudice Break to New Mutiny

Mark is a boy who wants what we all want: to love and be loved. His dreams are realized when he meets Taylor, the boy of his dreams. The boys struggle to keep their love hidden from a world that cannot understand, but ultimately, no secret is safe in a small Mid-western town.

Ancient Prejudice is a story of love, friendship, understanding, and an age-old prejudice that still has the power to kill. It is a story for young and old, gay and straight. It reminds us all that everyone should be treated with dignity and respect and that there is nothing greater than the power of love.

The Soccer Field Is Empty

The Soccer Field Is Empty is a revised and much expanded edition of *Ancient Prejudice.* It is more than 50% longer and views events from the point of view of Taylor, as well as Mark. There is so much new in the revised edition that it is being published as a separate novel. *Soccer Field* delves more deeply into the events of Mark and Taylor's lives and reveals previously hidden aspects of Taylor's personality.

Authors note: I suggest readers new to my books start with *Soccer Field* instead of *Ancient Prejudice* as it gives a more complete picture of the lives of Mark and Taylor. For those who wish to read the original version, *Ancient Prejudice* will remain available for at least the time being.

Someone Is Watching

It's hard hiding a secret. It's even harder keeping that secret when someone else knows.

Someone Is Watching is the story of Ethan, a young high school wrestler who must come to terms with being gay. He struggles first with himself, then with an unknown classmate that hounds his every step. While struggling to discover the identity of his tormentor, Ethan must discover his own identity and learn to live his life as his true self. He must choose whether to give up what he wants the most, or face his greatest fear of all.

A Better Place

High school football, a hospital of horrors, a long journey, and an unlikely love await Brendan and Casper as they search for a better place…

Casper is the poorest boy in school. Brendan is the captain of the football team. Casper has nothing. Brendan has it all; looks, money, popularity, but he lacks the deepest desire of his heart. The boys come from different worlds, but have one thing in common that no one would guess.

Casper goes through life as the "invisible boy"; invisible to the boys that pick on him in school, invisible to his abusive father, and invisible most of all to his older brother, who makes his life a living hell. He can't believe his good luck when Brendan, the most popular boy in school, takes an interest in him and becomes his friend. That friendship soon travels in a direction that Casper would never have guessed.

A Better Place is the story of an unlikely pair, who struggle through friendship and betrayal, hardships and heartbreaks, to find the desire of their hearts, to find a better place.

Someone Is Killing The Gay Boys of Verona

Someone is killing the gay boys of Verona, Indiana, and only one gay youth stands in the way. He finds himself pitted against powerful foes, but finds allies in places he did not expect.

A brutal murder. Gay ghosts. A Haunted Victorian-Mansion. A cult of hate. A hundred year old ax murder. All this, and more, await sixteen-year-old Sean as he delves into the supernatural and races to discover the murderer before he strikes again.

Someone is Killing the Gay Boys of Verona is a supernatural murder mystery that goes where no gay novel has set foot before. It is a tale of love, hate, friendship, and revenge.

Do You Know That I Love You

The lead singer of the most popular boy band in the world has a secret. A tabloid willing to tell all turns his world upside down.

In *Do You Know That I Love You*, Ralph, a young gay teen living on a farm in Indiana, has an aching crush on a rock star and wants nothing more than to see his idol in concert. Meanwhile, Jordan, the rock star, is lonely and sometimes confused with his success, because all he wants is someone to love him and feels he will never find the love he craves. *Do You Know* is the story of two teenage boys, their lives, desires, loves, and a shared destiny that allows them both to find peace.

Keeper of Secrets

Sixteen-year-old Avery is in trouble, yet again, but this time he's in over his head. On the run, Avery is faced with hardships and fear. He must become what he's always hated, just to survive. He discovers new reasons to hate, until fate brings him to Graymoor Mansion and he discovers a disturbing connection to the past. Through the eyes of a boy, murdered more than a century before, Avery discovers that all is not as he thought. Avery is soon forced to face the greatest challenge of all; looking into his own heart.

Sean is head over heels in love with his new boyfriend, Nick. There is trouble in paradise, however. Could a boy so beautiful really love plain, ordinary Sean? Sean cannot believe it and desperately tries to transform himself into the ideal young hunk, only to learn that it's what's inside that matters.

Keeper of Secrets is the story of two boys, one a gay youth, the other an adolescent gay basher. Fate and the pages of a hundred year old journal bring them together and their lives are forever changed.

The Vampire's Heart

Ever wonder what it would be like to be fifteen-years-old forever? Ever wonder how it would feel to find out your best friend is not what he seems? Graham Granger is intrigued by the new boy in school. Graham's heart aches for a friend, and maybe a boyfriend, but is Josiah the answer to his dreams? Why is Bry Hartnett, the school hunk, taking an interest in Graham as well? When strange happenings begin to occur at Griswold Jr./Sr. High, Graham's once boring life becomes more exciting than he can handle. Mystery, intrigue, and danger await Graham as he sets out on an adventure he never dreamed possible.

The Vampire's Heart is not part of the Gay Youth Chronicles, but readers will find much in the novel to enjoy.

Preface

I wrote *Someone Is Watching* because of the many gay boys out there who have such a hard time dealing with their homosexuality. I believe that it helps to see how others have handled the situation. Fiction allows us to explore who we are, especially when the characters are "real.".

In my novels I strive to leave behind homosexual stereotypes and feature characters that are realistic. *Someone Is Watching* is the story of a struggle with a secret tormentor, but it's even more about a boys struggle with himself. It is these inner battles that are the most difficult and all of us must face them. I think every gay boy can identify with Ethan and his struggle, there is a little of him in all of us.

In this revised edition, I've added new material, including the last chapter "Do Not Open Until Christmas." The new scenes are meant to flesh out the story a bit more and give a stronger connection to the other novels in the series. I've also taken this opportunity to correct errors that crept into the original work.

Acknowledgements

I'd like to thank Dave for his suggestions and criticisms of all the early drafts of *Someone Is Watching*. I'd also like to thank Ken Clark and Jim Hertwig for their useful suggestions and the many errors they pointed out. I'd finally like to thank all those who have written me, sharing their own thoughts and feelings. A special thanks goes out to Brandon for his insightful thoughts on *Ancient Prejudice*.

Chronology

This novel takes place at the same time as ***The Soccer Field is Empty*** *and just before* ***A Better Place..***

August 1980

Prologue

I rested on the handle of my shovel for a moment, allowing Nathan to take a turn at digging the posthole. We'd already set eight posts for the new section of fence and it was barely noon. Even with the two dozen or more we'd set after school through the week, we were far from done. That seemed to be the way of farm-work, it was always far from finished. No matter how I strained my back or worked my muscles until they were sore, there was always another task that lay before me. It was the eternity of the farm.

I wiped my sweaty brow and chest with my shirt, and then hung it from my belt loop once more. I raised my hand to my eyes, shading them from the sun, and could just make out the figure of my uncle, driving the tractor along the edge of the huge cornfield to the north of the house. My uncle, or Jack as I called him, was always demanding, but he put in every bit as much time on the farm as I did, and more. Jack was a little rough on the edges and often pissed me off, but he was my only real family and there was a special bond between us. Both my parents had been killed in an accident when I was only ten and I'd lived the last seven years of my life on my uncle's farm.

I watched Nathan as he worked. His slim muscles tensed and flexed as he jammed the post-hole-digger deep into the earth, drew the handles apart, and lifted the dark soil out of the hole. Nathan had only been working for my uncle for three or four weeks, but the hard work was already thickening his muscles and increasing his strength. He needed it. Nathan was a scrawny little guy. He was a good four inches shorter than me, standing at only 5'6" and was underweight for his height. His slim body looked better now that it was tanned, but his ribs still poked out, giving him the look of someone who didn't get enough to eat. Nathan's family was dirt poor and I wondered if maybe he didn't go without sometimes.

"Break time," I said.

The sun was hot overhead and I was drenched in sweat. Nathan's hair was plastered to the sides of his face, making it look almost brown instead of blond. Nathan was a cute boy, despite his slight build. His face possessed an innocent beauty that was set off by his light blond hair and blue eyes. I pulled my mind away from such thoughts—I didn't like it that I noticed.

Nathan and I walked to a great, spreading maple tree that offered plenty of cool shade. Not far away was an ancient water pump that still worked, despite years of rust. I pumped the handle several times and chilly water rushed out the spout. Nathan leaned over and dowsed his entire upper body, washing away the sweat and grime. Nathan pumped the handle while I took my turn under the water. It was cool and refreshing, a pure delight on such a hot August day. I gathered a few mouthfuls in my hands and drank. The water felt as good sliding down my throat as it did coursing over my sweaty body.

We sat down under the maple, much refreshed. I pulled a couple of sandwiches out of a pack I always carried to the fields and handed one to Nathan. He gladly accepted. His eyes really lit up when I pulled out big slices of chocolate cake and a couple of cold soft drinks. Nathan and I shared a love of all things chocolate.

There was something special about eating outside. I couldn't quite put my finger on it, but the sandwich just tasted better and the soda was sweeter and colder. I leaned back against the trunk of the tree and relaxed. It was a beautiful day and the sky was a brilliant blue. I loved being outdoors.

One would think that being outside wouldn't have been such a big deal to me. After all, I was outside more often than not. There were times I didn't like it, especially during the icy Indiana winters when the temperatures dropped to near zero. Most of the time I reveled in it. I loved the summer best. There was nothing better than pulling my shirt off and getting all hot and sweaty on a steamy summer's day, unless perhaps it was diving into a cool pond a little later to cool off, or dowsing myself under the water pump. I enjoyed the fresh smell of spring too, when everything was new and green and the lambs were beginning to walk on wobbly legs. The autumn I liked also with its cool crisp days when a flannel shirt felt so warm against my skin. Even winter had its attractions. There was no snow quite so beautiful as the snow that fell on Uncle Jack's farm. It lay in a giant carpet, undisturbed, as far as the eye could see. Of all the seasons, summer was my favorite, however. It could never get too hot for me.

As we ate and talked, my eyes roamed over Nathan's jeans and the worn shirt that hung at his side. He wore the same clothes every day. I'd even seen him in those same jeans at school. They had a sizable tear on the right thigh that revealed Nathan's tanned flesh. The knees were worn nearly through and even the belt loops looked like they'd seen better days. I'd have automatically assigned them as work clothes, or just tossed them out, but they seemed to be Nathan's only pair. He always wore the same shoes too, a pair of work shoes that resembled hiking boots.

Nathan and I never discussed his life at home, but I wondered what it was like. His tattered clothes and voracious appetite spoke of poverty. Of course, everyone knew his family was poor. There were few secrets in Verona, Indiana. Everyone pretty much knew the business of everyone else, whether they wanted it that way or not.

Nathan wolfed down his sandwich, making me wonder if he'd had any breakfast. I wondered if he'd get anything else to eat when he went home. I made a mental note to make sure I gave him something before he left for the day. His protruding ribs spoke of many missed meals.

"Crappy way to spend a Saturday, huh?" I asked.

"It's not so bad," said Nathan.

"Wouldn't you rather be swimming, or watching a movie, or just hanging out, or doing anything?"

"Yeah," Nathan admitted, "but this is okay too. Besides working for your uncle is like joining a health club. I get a workout here every day, and he pays me!"

I laughed. "I guess you could look at it that way."

"I'm a lot stronger than I was when I started."

"Yeah, I can tell," I said. I felt myself turning a little red, but my face was so flushed with heat I doubt Nathan could detect the change.

"Really?" Nathan was clearly pleased that I'd noticed the improvement in his musculature.

"Sure, you're a little broader in the shoulders and chest, and your arms look a little thicker. Just a little, but I can see a difference."

"That mean someday I'll look like you?" Nathan spoke with such open admiration that I was embarrassed. I'd never learned to take compliments well. Nathan's eyes roved over my torso, admiring the thick muscles of my chest, my baseball sized biceps, and my flat, hard stomach. He had a look of hero worship in his eyes that kind of made me feel proud of myself.

"Sure," I answered. "I've been doing this stuff for seven years. Of course, I also lift weights to train for wrestling, when I get the chance." I looked at Nathan's slim form again. "How old are you anyway, Nathan?"

"Guess."

I was a junior at school and Nathan was a sophomore. He looked about fourteen, but he couldn't possibly be that young. I took a stab at it.

"Fifteen."

"Nope, sixteen, almost seventeen. I'm surprised you guessed even that high. Most people think I'm just a little kid."

I didn't know what to say to that. Nathan was kind of small. Instead of responding, I unwrapped my cake. The plastic wrap stuck to the icing and pulled a good deal of it off. I licked it clean before dumping it back in the pack. Nathan did the same and laughed.

"You know, I think it just might be a sin to waste good chocolate," he said. I couldn't have agreed more.

Nathan looked at me thoughtfully.

"Don't you like it here?" he asked.

"Sure I do. It's just that I'd like to have more time to do other things. I'd like to be able to go out with my friends, have some fun, and just hang out like most of the guys I know. I have to spend most of my free time working."

"I don't have many friends," said Nathan quietly. I could tell the words issuing from his lips saddened him a great deal.

"You have me," I said. Nathan jerked his head up. He looked more than anything like a dog that had just been invited for a walk.

"You mean it?"

"Sure I do. You didn't know we were friends?"

"I just thought we worked together was all," said Nathan.

"Well, we do that sure, but I like you. I enjoy your company and I like talking to you. It's a lot more fun when you're here. Sounds like we're friends to me."

Nathan smiled. It was good to see him smile; he did it all too infrequently.

"We can do something together sometime, away from the farm," I said. "If you want."

"I'd sure like that," said Nathan.

"We'll do it. As soon as we get the time."

All too soon it was time to get back to work. Uncle Jack would have a cow if we took too long a break.

"Here," I said, tossing Nathan a couple of apples. "I'm stuffed. If you don't want them you can feed them to the horses later." Nathan made a bag of his shirt and secreted them away. I knew the horses would never see those apples.

CHAPTER 1

A Fatal Glance

I awoke at five a.m. on Monday morning, just like I did practically every morning. Farm work was always staring me in the face as soon as I opened my eyes. I sat up and stretched my arms above my head, then stood, allowing the sheets to fall from my naked body. My morning hard-on swung between my legs as I walked into the bathroom to take a leak. I splashed cold water on my face to bring myself to consciousness, and then walked back into my room to dress.

As I did every morning, I walked to the barn, fed the chickens, gathered eggs, slopped the hogs, filled all the troughs with water, and performed an endless series of tasks. In the winter my chores were even worse. In addition to everything else, I had to feed the horses and cattle and break up the ice that formed in the troughs. The cold of the northern Indiana winters could be almost unbearable, too, adding to my discomfort. It was late August, however, and winter was far away. The cattle grazed in the pasture and the horses ate sweet grasses on the hilltops. Still, I had more than enough tasks to perform.

Once done, I headed back inside, undressed, showered, shaved, dressed for school, then made myself some toast for breakfast. I liked my toast best with plum or blueberry jam. It was a routine I knew only too well. Occasionally the pattern was broken—sometimes Uncle Jack made breakfast, and sometimes I didn't need to shave.

❧ ❧ ❧

I was still a little tired when second period P.E. rolled around, despite a restful Sunday. My body never seemed to quite recuperate from the rounds of farm work and wrestling practice. Juniors didn't have to the take P.E., but it was something I enjoyed. There were only about five of us juniors in a class of twenty-eight, the rest were sophomores. It was the one class I shared with Nathan. It was a little odd, but Nathan and I didn't talk much at school. Of course, he was a sophomore and I was a junior. Few juniors would degrade themselves by talking to a lowly sophomore. We all tended to hang out with people in our own class. It wasn't even an unspoken rule or anything; it's just the way it seemed to work out.

Second period was also the only class I shared with Jon, my best friend. I was so busy I rarely got to see him outside of gym, lunch, and a few minutes before I had wrestling practice and he had soccer practice. We went out on Friday nights quite a bit too, since that was the one night I was usually spared from farm work. There was also the occasional Sunday together, but I didn't get to see Jon nearly as much as I liked.

I caught sight of Jon in the locker room as he was undressing. Jon was one good-looking boy. In fact, he was almost too good looking to be a guy, although I'd never have told him that. Hell, I'd never remark on his looks at all. I didn't fail to notice them, however. Jon had coal black hair, which he wore kind of long in the back. His eyes were brown and that, combined with his finely arched eyebrows, made him look both cute and serious at the same time.

My eyes roved over Jon's chest. He didn't have quite the build I did, but his torso looked like some artist had sculpted it to perfection. He pulled off his briefs as he was facing away from me. Jon had a real cute little butt. I tore my eyes away and focused on changing into my gym uniform. I felt guilty about looking at Jon the way I did sometimes. I wasn't even sure what it was all about. I just knew that I liked looking at him, just like I enjoyed being with him. Jon was a lot of fun and hilarious as hell, especially if he'd been drinking a little. I was always happy when I was with him.

I found my eyes drawn to him once more as we did calisthenics. Jon looked good in the blue and white colors of our school. Hell, Jon looked good in anything. I couldn't help but watch as his biceps bulged while he did push ups. We took turns holding each other's ankles while we did sit-ups. Jon's shirt was a little short and exposed his mid-rift. He had a hard, six-pack stomach and a thin trail of dark hair just below his navel that dipped into his shorts. Looking up his shirt made me breathe a little funny. Sometimes I got a weird feeling when I looked at Jon; a feeling I didn't quite understand. I wasn't so sure I wanted to understand.

I knew I shouldn't be looking at the Jon the way I did, but I couldn't help it. My eyes seemed drawn to him as if guided by some unknown power. Perhaps it was just our close friendship. Just looking at Jon made me remember all the laughs we'd had, all the crazy shit we'd pulled. Jon was a wild boy; well, so was I. We were forever doing something crazy (and quite often stupid). Any Sunday might find us exploring an abandoned house, scaling a cliff, or climbing high enough in trees to break our necks if we ever fell. I could go on forever just listing the many ways we risked our lives. I loved it; it made me feel so alive and was such a departure from the routine of the farm.

Still, there was something more about Jon, something that drew me to him. I pushed the thoughts out of mind, as I always did when I started to think too much about Jon. Sometimes too much thinking wasn't a good thing. Some thoughts were better left un-thought.

CHAPTER 2

The Varsity Wrestling Squad

I had a nervous feeling in my gut all day. It was the beginning of the second week of school, and the day we found out if we'd made the wrestling team. Coach Zeglis didn't like to make snap decisions; everyone who tried out for wrestling had a full week to prove himself. Our school wasn't all that large and the number of guys who tried out wasn't that big. Not making the team was almost an impossibility. The real challenge came in making the varsity squad. That's what I'd my sights set on, and that's what was tying my guts in a knot. I loved wrestling. I was good at it, too. At the end of last years season Coach Zeglis had pulled me to the side and told me I could make varsity soon if I kept myself in shape. I took him at his word and had lifted weights all summer long. My farm work kept me toned, and added muscle, but I strove to build myself up that much more.

I did more than just work out to improve my wrestling skills. Throughout middle and high school, most of the boys on my team wrestled "down." They wrestled in the lowest possible weight class. I always wrestled "up", competing in the next higher weight class. In the sixth grade I weighed 102 pounds. I could've easily cut my weight down enough to wrestle in the 98-pound class, but I chose to wrestle in the 105-pound class instead. By doing so, I was matched against boys that were bigger than me, some of them were as much as nine pounds heavier. That may not sound like a lot, but believe me, it can make a big difference, especially if that nine pounds is all muscle. I made the same choice every year. I always wrestled "up." It forced me to work hard and really hone my wrestling skills. Always wrestling someone bigger than me made for some tough competition and more losses than I would've liked. It also made me a much better wrestler. Taking the hard road had really paid off.

Uncle Jack wasn't so hot on the idea of my being on the wrestling team. Each year he resisted it more, saying it was a waste of time. Each year I had to swear not to let my chores slip before he would let me join the team. He hadn't said anything specific about it recently, but he'd been hinting around that he didn't want me on the wrestling team this year. If I made varsity, it might change his mind. If I didn't, I was afraid that would be it for wrestling. Jack would say I'd wasted enough time on it, time that could've been better spent working on the farm. He wasn't being unreasonable because there was more than enough work to do. We even had acreage we couldn't use because there just weren't enough hours in the day.

I couldn't bear the thought of life without wrestling. It meant the world to me. I can't quite describe just what it was about the sport that I so loved, but love it I did. It was something I enjoyed immensely and I was good at it. There was just something about pitting myself against another guy, with no one to help me, with only my own brains and brawn to depend upon. I thrived on the competition. Winning gave me a real sense of accomplishment. It meant that all my hard work was paying off. I was usually proud of myself even when I lost. If I could do well against a tough opponent, that was as good as a win. Wrestling gave me such a rush too. When I was struggling against another guy, the sheer power and strength I felt coursing through my body made me feel so vital and alive.

Wrestling was my life. I couldn't even imagine what I'd do without it. I just had to make it! I had to make the varsity squad! If I didn't, wrestling was over for me and that was something I simply could not bear.

I was a little shaky after school and just barely managed to work the combination on my locker. It was tricky at all times, but especially so since my hands were none too steady. I had to stop and take a deep breath to calm myself. I was really worked up and it wasn't like me to get all nervous about something. Wrestling was that important to me, however, and I was determined to make varsity. I had to laugh at myself. I acted as if I was trying out for the Olympics and not a high school team.

"Ethan!" Jon slapped me on the back as I dumped my books in my locker and slammed it shut.

I followed him out of habit. Every day after school, we each bought a Coke and sat together until it was time for practice. Jon was a soccer player and not a wrestler, but our practices were at about the same time. I always enjoyed our little talks. Jon had the ability to make every moment fun. I was usually content just to be near him and watch his face. Being close to Jon brought me a peace and contentment I seldom experienced. I certainly needed a little peace on that day. I had myself so worked up my stomach was grumbling. A stomach-ache was not what I needed.

"Ethan, when are you going to teach me to ride like you promised?" asked Jon.

"Huh? Oh yeah!" I smiled at the thought. "Uhm, I'm taking Kim out Friday night, then…"

"Hold it, back up there, you're what?"

"I'm taking Kim out. Oh yeah, I didn't tell you about her, did I?"

"No-o-o-o!" said Jon with great exaggeration.

"Well, just before school started, I saw her out at Koontz Lake, you know, that day your parents made you go to your aunts in Ohio? Anyway, we were talking and she was kinda giving me the eye…"

"Hot for your bod, huh?"

I smiled and turned a little red, but chose not to answer.

"I could tell she had a thing for me, so I asked her if I could buy her a milkshake. We went to that little burger place near the lake, you know the one. Anyway, we had fun. We've been talking a lot on the phone since then and this Friday, we're going on a date."

"Why didn't you take her out last Friday?"

"I was with you."

"Yeah, but I would've understood if you wanted to go out with her instead. What are friends for?"

"Well, uh..." I didn't really know what to say. The truth was, I enjoyed spending time with Jon more than I did with Kim, or anyone else for that matter. Something told me it wouldn't be wise to admit that, so I kept my mouth shut about it. I knew girls were supposed to be the number one priority of every teenaged boy, but they weren't that high on my list. I guess I was a "late bloomer." I was excited about going out with Kim, I guessed, but I'd really rather have been spending time with Jon.

"Anyway," I said, to get the conversation back on track. "I have to work all day Saturday, but you could come over on Sunday. I'll probably have some stuff to do in the morning, but if you got there about noon, we'd have the rest of the day to goof around."

"Sounds good. Now tell me more about Kim!"

"There's nothing to tell. We just talk on the phone."

"Come on, give! She's got a hot bod. You gotta feel of it yet, huh?"

"There's nothin' to tell, man. Really! Hey, I can make up some shit if you like, but nothing's happened—so far."

"Okay, I'll believe you—for now." Jon looked at his watch. "Shit! We'd better get going or we'll be late. See ya!"

Jon was gone in a flash. Even though we hadn't discussed wrestling, I still felt a little more at ease, about making the varsity team that is. My conversation with Jon had created a whole new anxiety over Kim. I pushed it from my mind. *One thing at a time,* I told myself. I made my way to the locker room and changed for practice.

❧ ❧ ❧

Steve stood waiting on the mat. He was one of the finest wrestlers on the team. Not only did he have muscle, he had skill. He was like a wildcat; sleek, strong, and quick. I'd always had a certain admiration for him. He had a bit of an attitude and was kind of a punk, but his skill as a wrestler couldn't be denied. Anyone could tell, just by looking at him, how powerful he was. His shoulders and chest were broad and thick; his arms were knotted with muscle. He had tremendous upper body strength, as well as powerful legs. He was a force to be reckoned with on the mat.

"Ethan!" Coach Zeglis called me forward.

Mentally, I thought, *Oh shit! Not me!* Outwardly, I approached the mat with calm and confidence. I could feel the other guys looking at me with relief that *they* didn't have to take on Steve. I was an excellent wrestler and had some slick moves, but Steve was a match for anyone. My heart beat a little faster in my chest. I knew this was it. This was where I proved myself to coach. How well I did against Steve would determine if I made varsity or if my uncle would force me off the team. I didn't necessarily have to win to make the varsity squad, but I needed to make a good showing against Steve.

We shook hands. Steve eyed me cautiously. He knew I was no pansy. One of the things that made him so damned good was that he never let his guard down. He never allowed himself to get overconfident. He treated each opponent as someone who could take him down.

Coach put me in the defensive position. I got down on my hands and knees and Steve took his position with one arm around my waist. I could sense Steve's watchfulness as we waited for the whistle. I could feel his body just waiting to spring into action. All eyes were on us. Everyone knew it would be an exciting match to watch. I narrowed my focus to just Steve. No one else mattered. I concentrated on his arm encircling my waist. I was keenly aware of my own muscles, tensed and ready to act. The gym grew still. I could hear nothing but the sound of my own breath and that of Steve. It was as if time had slowed.

Coach blew the whistle and I snapped into motion, fast as lightning. Steve was ready for me. His strong arms held me, muscles bulging. I struggled to break free, channeling every ounce of power in my body to escape. I shifted my weight, but Steve followed me, kept his balance. His arm still encircled me, holding me prisoner. I couldn't break free. I concentrated on his stance in my mind, pictured where his feet were, and calculated his center of balance. I surged sideways, causing him shift position to maintain control. Steve was ready for me, but he wasn't ready for the next move. I shifted straight back, a position he could not accommodate in his new stance. I broke free and jumped to my feet!

In a real match, my escape would have been worth a point. During my tryout, it was worth much more. I was exhilarated that I'd accomplished an escape from Steve, but our match was far from over. We circled one another like two lions; muscles tensed, ready to pounce. Our eyes searched for weakness and error. We collided, each with his own agenda, each with his own moves and counter moves. It was a game of strength and skill, ever changing, ever shifting. Both of us knew there was far more than mere strength involved. This was a contest of wit as much as of muscle.

I feinted; Steve ignored me, crushing my ploy, swatting me down like an annoying insect. I didn't let it bother me. I just tried a new tact. Steve came after me. I was ready. My shoulders weren't going down on the mat. I feinted again, Steve countered in a way I'd not expected, opening himself in a manner I had not considered. I adapted and slammed him to the mat. I fell on him, using my weight to subdue him. He lifted me into the air. I forced his powerful arms back down. Our muscles bulged and strained. It was a show of pure brute strength, then skill, and then strength yet again. It was an ever-shifting contest.

If it'd been a scored match, I would have had three points to Steve's zero. My escape was worth one and the takedown was worth another two. I was gaining more confidence. I was beating him. I knew that anything could happen, however. The situation could change with lightning speed in a wrestling match. I'd seen more than a few wrestlers get beat when it looked like they clearly had the upper hand. All Steve had to do to win was pin me to the mat. If he did that, my points wouldn't matter. And if there was one thing Steve was known for, it was pinning his opponents. I was doing well, but it was far from over.

Steve and I wrestled on the mat, each of us seeking the advantage. I'd taken him down, but I couldn't pin him. I couldn't quite force his shoulders to the mat. He twisted and turned, all the while grappling with me, trying to get me on my back. I was glad I'd wrestled "up" all those years. I was thankful for every workout. I needed every ounce of strength and experience I had to wrestle Steve. I was proud that I was doing so well against him. I hoped my good showing would earn me a spot on the varsity squad. It was a fleeting thought, one that just zipped through my mind in a heartbeat. I didn't dare think about anything but Steve.

I perceived my chance, dangerous, possibly fatal, but I took it. I slammed Steve to the mat. He wasn't quick enough to counter me, to make the move that would easily have put him on top of me. If he'd seen his chance and taken it, I would've been doomed. He missed the opportunity, however. Instead, he squirmed beneath me, unable to break my hold, his powerful body impotent against my maneuver. I leaned into him, pressing his shoulders to the mat. Closer, closer…almost there. We strained against each other with everything we had. Steve's shoulders touched the mat. Coach pounded his fist down near us. I'd done it! I'd won!

Steve and I rose from the mat, heart's pounding, breath coming in gasps. I smiled, thrilled with my victory. Steve smiled too, knowing the source of my happiness was the great respect I held for his prowess. I'd conquered him, just as he'd conquered me in the past. It wasn't over; we'd meet again, to test our skill against one another. I looked into Steve's eyes and read the same love of wrestling that I felt within me. It was the contest that mattered, the struggle—winning was the goal, but losing only meant the chance to try again. Steve patted me on the back, and sat down on the bench. I looked over at coach. He gave me a thumbs up. I'd done it! I was in!

❧ ❧ ❧

I slammed the screen door and ran upstairs to my bedroom whooping like a maniac. I couldn't restrain my joy at making the varsity squad. Uncle Jack would almost have to let me wrestle. Even he had to recognize that making varsity was a big deal.

I stripped off my shirt and jeans and changed into my work clothes. This was one day that I wanted to get to work fast. Being on the varsity team would take up a little extra time and I wanted to prove to Uncle Jack that I could handle both that and my work on the farm.

I ran back downstairs and grabbed the orange juice from the fridge. I took a few quick gulps from the carton, then set it back on the shelf. I closed the door. There was a note stuck to it with a magnet, "Ethan, your girl called, she wants you to call her back as soon as you get home." I looked at the phone, then thought better of it. I was half an hour late already—Kim would have to wait. I raced out the door and sprinted into the barn.

I repeated most of the chores I'd performed in the morning. My life was a never-ending circle of feeding chickens, watering cattle, and performing an endless succession of similar tasks. I didn't really mind it all that much. I liked being around all the animals, especially the horses. I derived a certain satisfaction from straining my muscles and pushing my body to its limits. It was just that, sometimes, I felt like all I ever did was farm work; everything else took a back seat to it, and more often than not, my work kept me from doing other things that most boys took for granted. I don't know how many times I'd passed up invitations to parties, movies, cookouts, and the like, because I had to work on the farm.

I lifted a hundred pound feed sack, dumping it into the feed bin. It didn't feel like it weighed a hundred pounds to me. It wasn't light, but most of my friends couldn't have lifted it, and I whipped it around like it was a five-pound bag of sugar. I watched my biceps as they flexed. That's one thing I got from farming. If I'd been a city boy, I probably wouldn't have been half the wrestler I was. I surely wouldn't have had nearly as good of a build. I was proud of my body. I worked hard on it, and took great pains to take care of it. After all, what was I but my body? Sure, I valued my thoughts, my personality, and all that, but the truth was that most of what I could do, I was able to do because of my body. My mind was important to me too, but I saw even it in physical terms. Weren't thinking, studying, and all that like working out? Reading a book or figuring out a math problem strengthened my brain, just like lifting heavy sacks of grain strengthened my back and arms. I didn't ignore my mind, I just thought of it as another muscle.

I brushed the feed dust off my shirt and headed for the new fencerow. I knew Nathan would be there setting poles. We'd been working on that particular task for days, and still would be for days to come. I felt a little sorry for Nathan. Digging all those postholes seemed like too big a task for him. I couldn't help but think of him as a kid, even though he was less than six months younger than me.

I was eager to see Nathan; I couldn't wait to tell him about wrestling practice. I enjoyed talking to Nathan. He was a good listener. He seemed to hang on my every word, taking it as gospel. I remember when he first starting working for Uncle Jack. He was quiet and shy; he spoke little, but he listened intently as I explained how to hoe the garden, how to drive the tractor, and how to do the thousand other things that a farm required. Nathan knew next to nothing about farming, but he was a quick study. His bright eyes sucked in every detail and his sharp ears committed every instruction to memory. It was a rare day when I ever had to explain anything to him twice.

When I caught up with him he was hard at it. His chest and back were covered with sweat mixed with grime. There were little trails down his torso where the sweat had streamed down, washing away the dirt that had adhered to his slim body. Nathan was red faced and breathing hard, but doggedly attacking the earth with the post-hole digger. One thing was for sure about Nathan—he was a good worker. Even Uncle Jack had remarked on that a time or two. If Uncle Jack thought someone was a hard worker, they were without question.

"The cavalry has arrived," I announced, taking the post-hole digger from him. Nathan dropped down on his butt, clearly grateful for the break.

"Where ya been, Ethan?"

"Wrestling."

"Yeah, how'd that go?"

"I made varsity!" I started talking a mile a minute. Making varsity had me all excited and I was just bursting to talk to someone about it. Nathan smiled and listened as I went on and on while sinking the digger into the hole.

In just a few minutes, I was sweating up a storm. The sunlight was practically gone and evening was settling over the farm, but it was still hot as blazes. I paused for a moment and pulled off my shirt, before attacking the posthole once again. Nathan and I talked for a long time about wrestling, and then went on to other topics. We seemed to have discussed everything in the few weeks he'd been working on the farm, but there was always something else to talk about just around the corner. I'd never found anyone who was half as easy to talk to as Nathan. I even found myself telling him things I wouldn't have shared with anyone else. Nathan was always interested in whatever I had to say. It didn't seem to matter one bit what I talked about, he listened like I was telling him the secrets of the universe. I liked that.

"What's your little brother like?" I asked.

"He's cool, seems pretty smart for a nine year old."

"You'll have to bring him with you sometime. He might like seeing the farm."

"Yeah, I think he'd like that."

I'd never met Nathan's little brother, Dave, but I'd seen him walking with Nathan after school a couple of times. He had blond hair just like his brother and seemed almost like a miniature version of him. He had the same gaunt, underfed look, the same serious expression on his little face. He was smiling when I saw him, however. He seemed a happy boy, which was more that I could say for his big brother.

"How are your parents?" I asked. Nathan suddenly grew quiet. I knew I'd said something I shouldn't have, but it seemed an innocent enough question. There was silence for a few moments as I dug out the final inches of dirt.

"Here, help me with this pole," I said.

Nathan and I lifted up the heavy, creosote soaked pole and let the end slide into the hole. It fell away from our hands and dropped straight in until it hit bottom. Nathan held it level while I shoveled dirt around the sides and stomped it down. It was one more fence pole in an endless line. I felt like the railway workers must have when they were laying the transcontinental railroad.

"Come on, let's see if we can finish another before it gets completely dark."

Nathan followed me, measuring out the distance to the next pole. When he selected the spot, I started digging again. He hadn't said much at all since I'd asked about his parents. I made a mental note to avoid that topic in the future, but I wondered what bothered him about it.

It was dark before we finished setting the next pole in place. It was too dark to do it properly, so we left the filling and leveling until the next day. We stood and talked for a little bit more. It was a clear night, with the stars shining bright and beautiful. I could see a gentle glow to the east that was the little town of Verona. Its streetlights lit up the night sky. On the farm, all was dark and no light obscured the heavens. I gazed at the stars, wondering what was out there. The immense vastness above me made me feel small and insignificant. What was my life when compared to all that? I was just a tiny speck in the universe. Somehow I found that comforting.

It was growing late. Nathan bid me farewell, gathered up his sweaty shirt, and walked towards home. I strolled across the pasture to the house, still looking at the stars.

🍁 🍁 🍁

Uncle Jack still wasn't in from the fields yet, so I grabbed a quick shower, pulled on a pair of boxers, then walked downstairs. Being able to walk around practically naked sure felt good on a hot August night. Even so, I was still a little warm. I looked at the note on the refrigerator. I knew I needed to call Kim, but I wasn't exactly looking forward to the conversation. I still wasn't quite sure how she'd ended up becoming my girlfriend.

I should've known I was headed in that direction that day at Koontz Lake. I could tell by the way Kim's eyes drifted down over my body that she was interested in me. A lot of girls looked me over, especially when I wasn't wearing a shirt. Sometimes I even liked to check myself out in the mirror. Anyway, Kim was kind of checking me out as we talked and I noticed some of the guys watching us. She was pretty and had a nice body, but I wasn't really all that interested in her. She was certainly interested in me, however, that much was obvious. The guys were watching us and listening in on our conversation. They knew as well as I did that Kim had a thing for me. I knew they'd think there was something wrong with me if I didn't do something, so I asked her out. She said, "yes" almost before I was done asking.

I hadn't planned to have a girlfriend. I hadn't even really thought about it. But, all of the sudden, I had one. We went to this little burger place not far from the lake and I bought her a milkshake. We sat there and talked a long time. I did enjoy her company, but I wondered what I'd gotten myself into. The way she kept looking at me made me a little uncomfortable. I felt like I was a juicy steak and she was a dog drooling over me. I know Kim wouldn't have appreciated the comparison, but that's how I felt.

She called me that very evening, and then twice that night. She made me promise to call her the next day. I did. Later the same day she called me again. Just before I went to sleep, I called her. I thought it was the thing to do. I felt like I lived on the phone. Uncle Jack had even taken to teasing me about it. Why did Kim have this need to talk to me every five minutes? What was it about girls? We hadn't been on our first real date yet and she had to be reassured constantly that I liked her. Arrrrrrrggggggggggggggggggh!

I dialed her number. I sighed. I already knew it by heart.

"Kim, hi, it's Ethan."

"Ethan!" I could almost hear the swoon in her voice. I must admit, it kind of made me feel good about myself.

"My uncle said you called. I was out working."

"Yeah, you just get my message?"

"Yep," I lied. "I called you the very first thing."

"Really?"

"Of course." I wasn't big on lying, but what did it hurt in such a case? It was just a little lie to make her feel good.

"How were tryouts?"

"I made the varsity squad!" I was getting enthused. The thing was, I wasn't nearly as excited telling Kim about it as I was telling Nathan.

"Great, I knew you would. I bet you look great in your uniform." Oh geesh! I ignored her last comment.

"Want to come watch one of my matches sometime?"

"I want to watch all of them, at least the home meets."

"We won't have one for a couple of weeks, but I'll let you know when it is."

"I'm really looking forward to Friday night," she said.

"Me too." I couldn't figure out if I was lying or not this time. Part of me was looking forward to Friday night, part of me wasn't. It would've been cool going with Kim just as friends, but I wasn't too keen on the whole boyfriend-girlfriend idea. It was all new territory for me, and kind of scary.

The rest of our conversation was pretty dull, not that it had been too exciting up to that point. I thought I'd never get off that phone. Every time I tried to end the conversation, Kim started in on a new topic. Girls!

❦ ❦ ❦

When Uncle Jack came in he was bone tired and kind of grumpy. I decided not to say anything about varsity until I could catch him in a better mood. I was on the brink of exhaustion myself. Wrestling practice, then a few hours of digging, had siphoned away my strength. I closed myself in my room and did my homework. It was midnight before I finally got to bed. My muscles ached. I think I fell asleep before my head even touched the pillow.

I didn't get a chance to talk with Uncle Jack for two days. That wasn't surprising. Uncle Jack was generally little more than a profile in the distance, riding a tractor or checking on fields of corn, wheat, or soybeans. Sometimes I almost felt as if I lived alone, unless I wanted to be alone. Then Uncle Jack was right there. He seemed to have a knack for being around just when I wanted him elsewhere.

I was apprehensive about talking to Jack about wrestling, but at the same time I wanted to get things settled. I didn't like not knowing if I'd be allowed to continue wrestling or not. Despite making varsity, I felt a cloud of doom over my head. I didn't know why I felt that way, but I did. I hoped it wasn't some kind of bad omen.

Just after returning from practice, I found Jack in the kitchen, fixing himself a sandwich.

"Little late, aren't you, Ethan?"

"Yes, sir, I had wrestling practice. I made the varsity team."

It was the first chance I'd had to tell him. He paused for a moment, but gave no hint of his reaction to my news. I swallowed hard. I had that queasy feeling in the pit of my stomach that sometimes appeared when I was in a difficult situation.

"So this varsity team takes up even more time than junior varsity?"

I didn't like the sound of that. I thought, *Oh shit, here it comes.* I just knew I'd be getting the "I need you here" lecture.

"It doesn't take up much more time, just half an hour a day, sometimes less."

"I see." Jack took a bite of his sandwich and chewed slowly. My heart was pounding in my chest. I didn't say anything.

"You know I had to hire Nathan to take up some of the slack created by you being at school."

"Yes, sir. I appreciate that. And I know that wrestling keeps me away even more, but…"

Jack held up his hand. I waited for the ax to fall. I could see where this was going.

"Just don't let it interfere with your work."

That was it, that was all there was to it. As simple as that I could stay on the team. I was elated; especially after thinking I was on the verge of losing wrestling. I was practically walking on air.

"Thanks, Uncle Jack!"

I detected the slightest hint of a smile on Jack's face; it was practically an emotional outburst for him. Jack wasn't much on showing feelings. He had a good heart, though.

"Nathan's out working on that fence row. Get your butt out there and see if you two can get something done this evening."

"Yes, sir!"

I ran upstairs and changed as fast as I could manage. Moments later I was running across the pasture as if my feet had wings. I felt as if I could dig a hundred postholes before dark.

CHAPTER 3

My First Date

I arrived to pick up Kim for our date, but she wasn't ready. I had to sit in the living room with her father. His eyes bored into me as we sat there in silence. He looked at me like he was sizing up some kind of threat. I felt like I was a murder suspect or something, instead of a boy who had come to take out his daughter.

The silence was nearly unbearable, but when it was broken, I found myself longing for its return. Kim's father asked me all kinds of questions. It was like the Spanish Inquisition or something. He acted like all I wanted from Kim was sex. He never came out and said it, but I could tell from what he did say, and his tone of voice, that I was being warned. His message was clear, "Keep your dick in your pants boy." Of course, he didn't say that either, but I knew that's what he meant.

I was distinctly uncomfortable in there. It was hot and stuffy and smelled funny. I bet they hadn't cracked a window in that place since Kennedy was President. I kept looking at the stairs, willing Kim to get down there so we could go. I wanted nothing more than just to get the hell out of there. Kim's father grilled me about wrestling, then moved on to other subjects. I thought I was taking some kind of test or something.

"How about baseball? You like baseball?"

"Not really, it's kind of boring." That was the wrong thing to say. I knew it immediately from the look on his face.

"What's wrong with you, boy? Everyone likes baseball." I just shrugged my shoulders. I didn't like baseball because nothing ever seemed to happen. The few times I'd watched it, all I did was sit there and wait for the guy to hit the ball. When he did, he just ran a little bit and then I waited for the next guy to hit the ball, and so on. Like I said—boring. I didn't like it and I wasn't about to say I did.

Things were going from bad to worse and then he noticed the earring in my left ear.

"Why are you wearing an earring, son?"

"A lot of my friends have earrings," I said. It was true.

"They must be girls then, or fancy boys. When I was in school only girls wore earrings, girls and queers." I swallowed hard. I really, really wanted out of there. First this guy all but accused me of planning to fuck his daughter as soon as we were out the door; next he starts acting like he thinks I'm gay. I thought to myself, *Make up your mind dude*. It didn't seem fair that I should be accused of both.

I wondered what block of ice this guy had been frozen in. When he was in school! That was probably a hundred years ago or something.

"A lot of the other wrestlers wear them, the football players too." That was kind of a lie, but I didn't care if I lied to that old geezer or not.

I was wearing a gold chain around my neck. I saw his eyes light on it and thought, *Oh fuck, what now?* Just then Kim made her appearance. I practically jumped off the sofa and rushed to her side.

"Have her back by eleven if you know what's good for you, son!" he yelled as we slipped out the door. Was I glad to get out of there!

We walked down the street. The theater was pretty close, so we decided not to take my uncle's old Ford pickup. The dependable old truck was fine for farm work and trips into town, but not for dates.

Kim looked at me apologetically.

"Sorry about that. Dad thinks he has to question every guy I go out with. I didn't mean to leave you down there that long, but I couldn't get my hair right."

"It looks beautiful, as do you." I wasn't lying. Kim was beautiful. The thing was, her beauty didn't do much for me. I recognized that she was attractive, but I didn't find her attractive, if you know what I mean. She just didn't get me excited. It made me feel very odd, because I knew a girl like Kim was supposed to excite me. I wondered if there was something wrong with me, or maybe if I was just nervous. I'd read that guys could have problems if they were nervous.

Kim smiled. She liked the compliment. I knew I'd said the right thing.

"Next time, though, maybe we should just meet there, or I could pick you up outside?"

"That bad, huh?"

"Yeah, your dad's convinced I have nothing on my mind but sex." I didn't mention the earring deal.

"Hmmmm?" The way she said that made me uncomfortable. I think it was meant as a hint. I was already nervous over what I was expected to do. Should I hold her hand? Should I put my arm around her at the movie? Should I kiss her? What? If I didn't do things right she'd either think I wasn't interested in her, or get mad because I tried to move too fast. As far as I was concerned we could skip the whole thing. I had no interest whatsoever in kissing Kim, or any girl for that matter. I stopped. My face paled. Kim looked at me.

"What is it?"

"Nothing." I started walking again, but I was still stuck on my last thought. I had no interest in any girl. I hadn't really thought much about that before, but now that the words had formed in my mind, I wondered a lot about it. What did it mean? Was there something wrong with me?

I liked girls. I didn't think there was anything wrong with them, but they just didn't do anything for me sexually. That was kind of weird since I was a very physical person. I would've thought that I would have been wild over girls, but I wasn't. Perhaps it was just fear. I had no idea how to act around a girl. It was all so much easier being with guys. I looked at Kim walking beside me. She was attractive by anyone's standards, so why didn't she make my pants dance? Maybe I was just nervous. I was all worked up over whether or not I should kiss her and the thought of anything more terrified me. I felt like I was in over my head.

Kim was talking, but I was so lost in my own thoughts that I barely heard her. When she stopped talking, I didn't know what to say. I ended up mentioning the earring incident.

"I don't think your dad liked my earring, or my chain."

"He wouldn't," she said, rolling her eyes. "But I do. I think they make you look sexy. I love the way the gold accents your pecs."

I knew I was in for a rough ride. She was already telling me she thought I was sexy. Kim was always hinting around about how good I looked. She was always devouring me with her eyes, too. I had the distinct impression that she wanted in my pants. Why hadn't I picked out one of those girls who wouldn't so much as kiss on the first date? I should've gone for one that would probably be a virgin until she got married. Kim wasn't exactly diving into my pants, but I had the feeling she expected some kind of action pretty soon. I didn't have a clue as to what I was supposed to do. Fuck.

When we got to the theater, I made it a point not to sit near the back where most of the heavy necking went on. I sat where I always sat, in the center, about two-thirds of the way down. That's the best place for watching a movie. While the previews were playing, I went out and bought us some popcorn and Cokes. I handed them to Kim and went right back to the lobby. I had to use the restroom. I was so nervous I felt like I had to go every five minutes. I made it back just as the movie was starting.

Kim sat real close to me. That was cool, but I wondered where it would go. I'd never dated a girl before—I'd never dated anyone. I was a total virgin, unless you counted jerking off, then I was about as experienced as you could get. I wasn't sure what I was supposed to be doing. I thought that girls should come with instruction booklets. I guess all guys felt like that. Guys are supposed to know everything about dating, even if it's their first date. Guys are expected to be more experienced than girls in that sort of thing. Where did everyone think they got that experience? Unless they were going with another guy, a date required a girl. I wished I was with a guy, then we could just have watched the movie and not have anything else to worry about. A picture of me sitting there with Jon popped into my head. I had my arm around him. Panic surged through me. What was I thinking? I put my arm around Kim as if to shelter myself from the disturbing image. Kim snuggled up against me. It did kind of feel nice.

I was still nervous and I needed to make another trip to the restroom, but I just held it in. I tried to lose myself in the picture and not think too much about the fact that I was on my first date. It wasn't easy. Kim was pressed up against me and I could smell her perfume. Her presence was impossible to ignore. I kept thinking about that picture of me with my arm around Jon. It really got to me. I couldn't get it out of my head. Why would I be thinking something like that?

After the movie, I took Kim to *The Park's Edge*, located just across the street from the park, hence the name. It had the best food in town, most of it Italian, and it wasn't even all that expensive. It was dimly lit and very romantic. I thought it was just the place that a girl would like. I was rather fond of it myself, but for the food and not the atmosphere.

We were half through eating before I thought again about us being on a date. My nervousness was all but gone. I'd loosened up and was having fun. I guessed dating wasn't so bad after all. I was beginning to understand what my friends saw in it.

Kim looked very sweet as she smiled at me from across the table. She was certainly a pretty girl. I'd noticed a couple of guys looking at her at the theater. They were definitely interested in her. I noticed the look they gave me, too, it was an envious look that made me feel good. I guess having a pretty girl was like having a nice car. There was a certain satisfaction from having something that someone else wanted. I felt a little guilty thinking of Kim as an object. I knew that wasn't right. It still felt good being envied, however.

While we were talking, Kim placed her hand on my wrist. She rubbed up and down my arm a little. I didn't know how to react or what to say, so I just smiled. That seemed to work. Kim smiled back. I wondered what signals I was sending her and where they would take me. I felt like I was conversing in a foreign language. My nervousness returned.

On our walk home, my nervousness was fanned to new heights. The closer we got to Kim's house, the more I worried about what I should do when we got there. I sure as hell wasn't going in, but I knew there would be some awkward moments at the door.

The porch light was on. We stopped just short of its golden glow. Kim turned to face me, then leaned in, just a little. My instincts kicked in again and I pressed my lips to hers and kissed her. It wasn't what I'd expected. I felt no passion, no love; it didn't get me excited at all. It was no more significant or meaningful to me than a handshake would've been, or a pat on the back or something. It was just—nothing. Kim seemed to like it, however. She smiled at me and said "goodnight".

I climbed into the pickup and drove home with a sick feeling in my gut. My lack of attraction to Kim and my thoughts about Jon upset me. I felt lost, like I didn't know where I was going. I knew I was supposed to be dating. I knew I should've liked it. But there was something wrong. It just didn't feel right at all. I didn't know whether I wanted to continue it or not. It would only get more difficult as time went on. The longer we dated, the more I'd be expected to do with Kim, and the truth was I didn't feel anything for her, nothing sexual anyway. I almost felt like I was selling my body or something. The only reason I kissed her was that I felt I had to do it.

By the time I reached home, I decided to stick with dating Kim, at least for a while. Parts of it had been fun and maybe the rest would fall into place. Maybe my nervousness screwed up my feelings. I was still disturbed; my lack of desire bothered me. A very significant thought about that began to form in my head. It wasn't a clear thought, but I knew I didn't want to think about it at all. I pushed it out of my mind, as I did all such thoughts. No, I just wasn't going to think about it.

CHAPTER 4

Awakening Desires

I woke Sunday morning at 9 a.m. The luxury of sleeping in seeped into my tired muscles. I lay in my bed, enjoying the feel of the sheets against my nakedness. I felt rested, despite the arduous day I'd put in with Nathan on Saturday. We'd dug and set so many fence posts I was seeing them in my dreams.

I lay on my back, gazing at the ceiling. My cock was hard and tented the sheets. I reached down and grasped my erection; it sent a shiver of pleasure through my young body. I began stroking, but was interrupted almost immediately by a knock at my door. The door opened and I sat up to hide my hard-on.

"Ethan, you still in bed?" Uncle Jack didn't wait for an answer. "I need you to help me change the rim on the tractor. It'll only take a few minutes, but it's a two man job."

"Yeah, okay," I said sleepily. "I'll take a shower and then be right down."

"Good boy."

Farm work seemed to creep into even my leisure hours. I showered quickly, and then spent the next forty-five minutes struggling with the tractor. Finally, Uncle Jack got the rim and tire replaced and I was free to go my own way. I headed back inside for a bit of breakfast. By the time I was finished, it was nearly 11. Jon was supposed to arrive at 11:30. I went upstairs, changed, and spent several minutes trying to get my hair just right. It was important to me that Jon see me at my best.

Jon drove up not long after and greeted me with his usual wide grin. Just seeing him filled me with contentment. We headed straight for the barn, and the horses.

"Here," I said, pulling a carrot from my pocket. "I want you to meet Wuffa. Feed him this carrot and he'll be your friend for life."

"Sounds easy enough," laughed Jon. He shrank back a bit as Wuffa munched away at the carrot.

"Don't worry, he won't bite you. He knows the difference between a carrot and a finger."

"This," I said, patting one of the other horses, "is Fairfax. He's a little more spirited than Wuffa, but still pretty gentle."

"Hello, Fairfax," said Jon. Fairfax whinnied and snorted, but Jon held his ground.

"Let me show you how to saddle them first." I saddled Fairfax, explaining every step in detail, then led Jon through the entire process as he saddled Wuffa. Jon was a quick learner. After checking to make sure that everything was secure, we led the horses into the small fenced area behind the barn.

"You get on like this," I said, swinging into the saddle. "Just put your foot into the stirrup and push yourself up while throwing your other leg over the saddle."

I jumped down and helped Jon position himself. He didn't swing quite hard enough, so I had to give him a little push on his backside to get him into position. I hoped that my hands hadn't lingered too long on his butt. I held the reins while Jon adjusted to sitting astride the horse.

"Now, you can stay on easier if you keep your feet in the stirrups. You don't have to, but I'd advise it until you learn how to ride. Make sure you don't dig your heels into his flank or he'll take off like a shot out of hell. It's okay to press your heels against him a little to urge him forward, but be easy, or you'll be sorry."

Jon looked a little uneasy, but excited.

"Nervous?"

"A little," he admitted.

"You'll be fine, just remember to take your feet out of the stirrups if you start to fall. And roll when you hit the ground." He looked more ill at ease than ever.

"Here," I said, handing him the reins. "You can guide him by gently pulling the reins to either side. If you want him to stop, just pull back on both at the same time, but don't do it too hard."

"What happens if I do it too hard?"

"He'll rear up and toss you off."

"Oh."

"Don't worry, Wuffa's a gentle horse. You treat him well, and he'll take care of you."

"We'll be buddies, won't we, Wuffa?" said Jon leaning over and patting his neck. Wuffa whinnied his approval.

I climbed on Fairfax and walked him around the enclosure.

"Okay, now, hold the reins up and give him just the slightest nudge with your heels."

Jon followed my instructions and Wuffa moved forward.

"Hey! It works!"

I laughed at the naïve expression on his face. Jon looked like he was having the time of his life. I looked back over my shoulder.

"Try guiding him a little with the reins. Just pull back gently so the reins pull his head in the direction you want to go. That's it. You're not forcing him. It's a partnership. You're just letting him know which direction he should be going."

Jon had a smile on his face a mile wide. We walked the horses around the enclosure for over half an hour, letting Jon get the feel of riding a horse. I enjoyed watching him. It brought back memories of when my father had taught me to ride. It seemed a very long time ago.

I opened the gate and led Fairfax into the large field behind the barn. It was about as long as a football field, and three football fields wide. There was a lot more room to move around, but not too much room. I didn't want to take the chance of Wuffa thundering off with Jon, not that there was much chance of that happening, but I wanted to play it safe.

I showed Jon how to urge his horse into a trot, then a gallop. I could tell Jon was becoming more confident. We rode around for a good half hour and Jon was really getting the hang of it. Once, he turned Wuffa a little too sharp and Jon's inertia sent him sailing off Wuffa's back. He landed right on his ass and Wuffa trotted back to him and stared as if wondering why Jon chose to fly off his back.

"I said to roll when you fell," I laughed. I didn't really mean to laugh at him, but Jon just looked too funny sitting there in the dirt.

"I'll try to remember next time." Jon didn't look too happy.

"What's wrong?"

"I just feel a little stupid."

"Why? Because you fell?" I could tell that was it. "Don't. You stayed on a lot longer that I did my first time. My ass was on the ground more that it was on the horse!"

That made Jon laugh.

"Of course, I was only eight!" I laughed again.

Jon climbed back on and we began riding again. After a few more minutes, we rode back to the barn and gave the horses a chance to get a drink. We left them at the trough and went into the house. I packed us a picnic lunch while Jon sat at the table and talked with me.

I stuffed sandwiches, drinks, cookies, and potato chips into my backpack, everything I could think of that we might want. Jon followed me back out to the barn and we mounted up once again. I took Jon through the gate and we spent a few minutes walking the horses within the fence. When I thought Jon was ready, I opened the gate on the far side of the fence and we rode Wuffa and Fairfax into open country.

The wide fields opened up in front of us, with the forest beyond. We guided the horses down a narrow lane between a cornfield on the right and a soybean field on the left. Jon and I rode side by side as the hot sun beat down upon us.

"I think I'm really getting the hang of this," said Jon. I could tell he was pleased.

"I knew you would. It's not really all that hard, once you know how. Just expect to fall off now and then. I still fall occasionally."

"I'd like to see that!" laughed Jon.

"I bet you would!" I said with my best smart-ass tone.

The sun was baking us. I stopped and pulled off my shirt. It was already becoming damp with sweat. Jon did the same. I noticed how very nice he looked without a shirt. Jon had a real nice build; smooth, firm, and well proportioned. His shoulders were broad and tapered down to a slim waist. His abs were well defined and once more I noted the thin trail of hair that led into his jeans. My breath came a little harder and I felt myself getting the same feeling I did at the theater—when I pictured myself sitting beside Jon with my arm around him. I urged Fairfax forward so that the temptation of Jon's bare torso was out of sight. Still, the image of his well-muscled chest and small, brown nipples was firmly etched in my mind. I screwed my eyes shut for a moment as if I could squeeze out the memory. My hand trembled slightly at my failure.

Jon and I rode all around the farm. I showed him the fencerow that Nathan and I had been putting in. It was taking so long I felt like we were building the Great Wall of China. From there we wandered around the fields. The soybeans were turning brown and soon it would be time for the harvest. The wheat fields were like a sea of gold, blowing in the slight breeze. We rode between cornfields with the tall, green stalks rising above our heads, hiding us from view. In just a few weeks all the land would be cleared of crops, flat as far as the eye could see. But on that day we could see only a few feet through the corn stalks as we wandered through the fields. It was as if we were picking our way through a giant maze.

We rode for nearly two hours, just talking and enjoying each other's company. My eyes kept drifting over Jon's well-formed body. His naked chest seemed to draw my eyes involuntarily. His soft voice and friendly laugh filled me with happiness and contentment. I was at peace when I was with him. I'd never experienced a friendship like I had with Jon. No other friend had meant as much to me, or felt as close.

My stomach growled. It was way past lunchtime.

"Let's go this way. I'm going to take you someplace special," I said.

Jon followed me as we left the fields and headed along a narrow forest path. The trees pulled in close overhead and on either side, making the trail feel almost like a tunnel. Jon and I had wandered all over the farm in days past, but I'd never taken him to my special place. I'd never taken anyone there. I'm not exactly sure why. It wasn't that I considered it secret; it's just that I considered it mine, and mine alone. On that day, however, I felt the desire to share it with Jon.

It was cooler under the great trees, but still warm. I did not miss my shirt in the least. Even in the shade, stray beads of sweat joined together to run down my torso in tiny streams. There was barely any breeze among the trees at all. It felt cooler, but there was a humidity that was not found in the open fields. It was darker in the forest as well, but shafts of light hit the dark earth, penetrating the leaves, making them a translucent green.

The path was a narrow one, probably made long ago by the Native Americans who once trod there. In more recent times it was maintained by deer, traveling from the forest to the fields, to munch on our beans and corn. My own feet often wore the path as well. I liked to escape to my special place when I was feeling thoughtful, or just needed to be alone. I must have walked back and forth on that path a thousand times in the years I'd lived on the farm.

The clearing slowly came to view as we drew nearer, a meadow bright and sunny, it was a dazzling contrast to the shade of the trees. Tiny purple flowers peeked out from the grass and a few yellow ones, too. On a gentle hill stood the ancient cabin, its logs weathered gray by decades of rain and sun.

"Wow!" said Jon, in a voice just above a whisper. "This is so cool."

He slid from Wuffa's back and neared the cabin, reaching out to touch the hand-hewn logs. I felt a certain pride as Jon admired it, almost as if I'd built it myself. I considered it mine, even though it belonged to my uncle. I was the one who took care of it. I was the one who cleaned it out. I was the one who kept it from falling apart from neglect.

"Who built it?"

"Uncle Jack says my great uncle, Franklin Selby, built it. He was a blacksmith. My great grandfather, William Henry Harrison Selby, and a lot of the people who lived around here then helped him. Great Uncle Frank, his wife, and six kids once lived in it."

"All of them, in this?" asked Jon incredulously.

"Hard to believe, huh?" I pushed open the door. It creaked in protest. The interior smelled a bit musty. The cabin hadn't been aired out for a long, long time. We stepped inside, dodging a wasp now and then. The cabin was sparsely furnished. A table and two chairs stood against one wall. There was also a bench and a wood and coal burning cook-stove in one corner. Other than those sparse furnishings, a few candles, and an oil lamp, the interior was empty. There was dirt on the floor and dead bugs. The place was in serious need of house cleaning.

Jon climbed up the ladder and stuck his head into the half-loft.

"That's where all the kids slept. Can you imagine it, all six of them?"

"Wow!" was all Jon said.

We looked around a little more, then walked outside. In contrast to the dim interior of the cabin, the light was blinding and it took our eyes a short time to adjust. Down the hill, just a short distance from the cabin, the sun reflected off a small lake. Its waters sparkled and danced. It was beautiful. I pulled my backpack from the saddle. Jon and I seated ourselves near the cabin, looking toward the lake. Wild flowers surrounded us. The whole scene looked like some painting. It almost seemed too beautiful to be real.

I pulled out the contents of my pack and spread them between us. Jon and I ate sandwiches and munched on potato chips and various treats. We were starving and were far too focused on eating to speak. Words were not necessary. I was completely content, alone in my special place with Jon.

I looked at Jon as he bit into a chocolate chip cookie, smearing his upper lip with chocolate that had melted in the sun. I cared about him, I really cared about him. Somewhere along the line he had become more important to me than I was myself. I felt close to him as I did to no other. He was far more than a friend; he was my best friend and he was dearer to me than I could express.

Jon was always in my thoughts. Sometimes it seemed like I could think of nothing else. Just knowing he was my friend made me happy. Spending time with him was always my favorite thing. It didn't even matter what we were doing. I was happy as long as I was with Jon. We seemed to belong together. We were like Tom Sawyer and Huckleberry Finn. We certainly got into enough mischief to be Tom and Huck. Our horse ride and picnic was the tamest thing I think we'd ever done.

My eyes were drawn once more to Jon's bare chest. The curves and lines of his pecs looked like an artist had designed them. I loved the way his torso slimmed down in a V at his waist. His abdomen was flat and firm and I could make out the lines in his six-pack stomach without difficulty. Jon was beautiful. He was strong and well muscled, the very essence of beauty and grace.

Jon was oblivious to my attention. He was far too absorbed in our meal, our surroundings, and the beautiful day. It was just as well. My open admiration would have embarrassed him—to say nothing of me.

When we had consumed every last morsel, we lie back on the grass and warmed our full bellies in the sun. We were like two little puppies who were too stuffed and too sleepy to move. I slowly drifted off, enveloped by a warm fuzzy feeling and a sense of complete happiness.

I awoke some time later, an hour, perhaps more. Jon was still sleeping beside me with a smile on his face that made him look like a little boy. Wuffa and Fairfax had wandered down to the lake and were drinking and swishing their tails. I was watching them when I heard Jon stir at my side. I playfully punched him in the shoulder.

"About time you woke up, laze-ass."

We both stood, all sweaty and hot. Sleeping in the scorching sunlight was not the best of ideas on a blazing hot day. I felt like I was ready to spontaneously combust. Trickles of sweat ran down Jon's face. He looked at the lake longingly, then turned to me and smiled.

"Let's swim!"

"But we don't have swimsuits," I pointed out.

"What are you, a city boy? Come on." That was a funny thing for him to say, Jon was a city boy.

Jon didn't wait for an answer, he just started running down the hill, tossing off clothing as he ran. I followed at a slower pace, passing Jon's shoes, his socks, and his jeans. I looked up to see him stripping off his boxers near the shore. I caught a glimpse of his little white butt just before he dove into the water. I quickly undressed on the shore, a little self-conscious as I pushed my boxers down over my hips. I'd never skinny dipped before and wasn't accustomed to running around naked, unless I was in the privacy of my own room, or in the showers at school.

Jon dove under and completely disappeared from view, only to pop up a few feet away, water streaming down his firm body. He smiled and laughed, totally free of care. His mood was infectious and I found myself yelling and screaming as we swam and wrestled with one another in the water.

I don't think I'd ever been quite so happy as I was just then. It was one of those simple moments that I wished could last forever. All we were doing was wrestling in a little lake, but it was better than anything I could envision. The day was bright and beautiful, the water clear and cool. We were surrounded by beauty on all sides. And, best of all, I was with Jon.

When we grew tired from our exertions, we set our feet down on the muddy bottom and enjoyed the feel of the cool water surrounding our hot bodies. It was refreshing to be rid of the grime and sweat. I allowed myself to float and Jon did, too. We just floated in the water, feeling the sun upon us. I looked at Jon's face. It was filled with kindness, but was a touch wicked too. He possessed a beauty that was hard to describe. I fought to keep my eyes from going lower than his abdomen, but wasn't entirely successful.

A few minutes later, we waded toward the shore and stood in the water, drinking in the beautiful day. My eyes traveled down Jon's body yet again. I drank in the sight of his magnificent torso, from his muscular chest to tight, flat abdomen. My gaze traveled lower and settled on his long, straight cock and his balls beneath, just above the water. The dark hair that grew around his manhood accentuated it, demanding that I look. My heart beat a little faster in my chest and I felt my own cock twitch and grow. A dull ache began in my nuts and I felt the pressure build. The sensation traveled through my entire body. I devoured Jon's nakedness with my eyes and my cock began to expand even more. I turned quickly away, stepped from the water, and pulled on my clothes before Jon had a chance to notice my erection.

Jon dressed soon after, covering his nakedness, except for his chest. We walked back up the hill, retrieved my backpack, then returned to the lake and mounted the horses once more. We slowly rode back toward home. Jon laughed and joked, but my heart wasn't in it. I was troubled.

New thoughts and feelings flooded my mind. The rest of the day was very pleasant, but somewhat subdued. Jon departed for home just after dark, stopping to tell me that he hadn't had so much fun in a long, long time.

That night I lay in bed, thinking of the events of the day, thinking about how much fun it was with Jon, thinking about how I felt about him—thinking about his body. I could still picture him standing naked in the lake, as if he was before my very eyes.

My body reacted to the picture in my mind, just as it had when I gazed on Jon's smooth, naked skin. A feeling of pleasure tinted with pain began in my groin and spread throughout my body. My cock hardened, and my nuts began to ache. I pushed the sheet down and exposed my stiff penis, standing straight up as if at attention. I wrapped my hand around my pole and slowly moved it up and down. A little whimper of pleasure escaped my lips. I pictured Jon in my mind—Jon smiling, Jon riding shirtless beside me, but mostly Jon standing naked in the lake. My hand stroked harder and faster until I lost control and made a mess all over my chest and abdomen. I cleaned up with a few tissues and fell asleep, wondering about this new direction my life was taking.

CHAPTER 5

Six Words That Changed My Life Forever

During every gym class the next week, I found myself gazing at Jon. I guess I'd always looked at him, but now there was greater purpose in my gaze. I felt drawn to him and to the feelings that looking at his body created. I'd always admired him, even felt a kind of hero worship for him, but those feelings had grown into something more. Those feelings bothered me. Jon was another boy. I knew I shouldn't be having such thoughts about him. I didn't really want to even think about it. The possibilities were far too disturbing, but the feelings were there, and they were *real.*

While we were changing in the locker room, my eyes were drawn to Jon's naked body. I remembered jerking off Sunday night, picturing Jon in my mind. I had that same feeling in my groin in the locker room that I'd had in bed at home. What was happening? Where was this going? Where was it taking me?

I practically devoured Jon with my eyes before I realized where I was and what I was doing. Staring at a naked boy in the locker room was not a wise idea. I didn't want any of the guys to catch me and I sure as hell didn't want Jon to catch me at it. I knew what Jon and the other boys would think if they did. I wasn't so sure about what I thought. My feelings were pretty plain, but they left me confused and disoriented. I felt like my entire world was shifting, tilting at an angle that left me off balance. I was struggling to comprehend just what it was that was going on in my head, and with my body.

Jon was the same boy I'd known for years, but was I? I felt changed, almost as if I was a stranger in my own body. Things weren't going as they should've gone. I had a girlfriend, but it was nothing like I'd expected. I liked Kim. I enjoyed spending time with her, but I wasn't head over heals in love with her. I wasn't even in lust with her. She was attractive to be sure, but she just didn't excite me in the way I expected. I felt like my own body was betraying me. Maybe something was wrong, maybe some part of my body wasn't functioning properly. I wondered if I should see a doctor, but I sure didn't want to tell a stranger about such a personal problem.

I looked around the locker room, wondering if any of the other boys had the same problem. I sure as hell wasn't going to ask. That just wasn't the kind of thing one guy asked another. It was just too personal, too private. I wouldn't even ask Jon about something like that.

Things weren't like they should've been with Jon either. He was my best friend. We were very close. And yet I knew I shouldn't be having the feelings I was having for him. And why couldn't I keep from looking at him? Why did I have such a fascination for his body? After all, it wasn't that different from my own. I pushed my thoughts aside. They were becoming too uncomfortable. It seemed that I'd had to push certain thoughts out of my mind more and more often lately. I didn't want to think about that either.

One thing for sure: I was determined to keep my eyes off Jon. I wasn't all that successful in my efforts, however. My gaze kept drifting back to him. It was if I had no control over my own eyes. I was suddenly very afraid. I quickly finished dressing and rushed out of the locker room. I felt like I couldn't breathe in there. It was like I was being suffocated. What was happening to me? What was I going to do about it?

* * *

After wrestling practice I ran to my locker to pick up a few books I'd forgotten earlier. I almost didn't notice the note that fell at my feet. I picked it up. At first, I thought it was another note from Kim, she was forever sticking little love notes in my locker. This note was not in Kim's neat hand, however, it was typed, and the words upon it made it clear that it was not from my girlfriend.

Six neatly typed words laid waste my life. My hands trembled as I read them, my heart jumped into my throat. There was no signature, no identification of any kind, just the words that forever changed my life.

```
I know you
are a FAG!
```

I looked around, as if whoever had left that note in my locker would be standing there watching me. I was alone, however. I wondered if it wasn't just some kind of joke. Attacking each other's sexuality was one of the favored hobbies of me, my friends, and most teenage boys. Lack of size in the sexual equipment department, alleged perverted acts with mothers and animals, homosexuality, virginity, all these and more were common tactics in the ongoing struggle to score points with put downs. Maybe the note was just an especially devious and nasty attack that one of my buddies would be laughing about the next day. Something made me doubt it, however. I knew in my heart that it wasn't a joke.

I slammed my locker shut, walked to the truck, and drove home. I couldn't stop thinking about the note. I wondered who typed it and more importantly why. What did they want? What kind of sick game were they playing? I was terrified. Someone knew! Before I'd even realized what I'd done, someone else had figured out what was going on. Someone had caught me looking at Jon and assumed that I had the hots for him.

Not knowing who left that note in my locker only made it worse. Someone was fucking with me in the worst way and I had no idea who it was. There was no way to tell. Those notes could have been typed on any typewriter in the school, or even at somebody's home. I had to think. I racked my brain for clues. Sweat broke out on my forehead.

It couldn't have been just anyone. I did have one single clue. It was vague, but it was a start. It had to be someone who had seen me looking at Jon in the locker room. That pretty much narrowed it down to the guys in my gym class. But who among them would do such a thing? Mark? Brandon? Zac? Alex? Nathan? Who? I couldn't think of one person who had any reason to dislike me. Not one of the possible suspects would've done something like that. There just wasn't anyone in my gym class who was cruel enough to fuck with me like that. I had no idea who it was, but that damned note didn't type itself. From that moment on I lived in fear.

❧ ❧ ❧

That note did more than let me know that someone was onto me. It made me face what had been going through my mind. I didn't want to face it, didn't want to think about it, but I no longer had a choice. Could I really be what the note said? Was I really a fag? I thought about the feelings I had for Jon. I thought about the way my heart, and my body, reacted to him. There was no denying the truth: there was no denying the way he made me feel. What I had to decide is just what those feelings meant.

Could I really be a fag? I didn't feel like one, didn't look like one. Then again, I guess I didn't know how one was supposed to feel or look. All I knew was that everything I'd ever heard about those guys didn't seem to fit me at all. Well, not much of it anyway. Hell, I was a jock, how the fuck could I be a fag? Whoever typed that note was just jumping to stupid conclusions. He didn't know what the fuck he was talking about.

I pulled the truck up outside the house, ran in, and changed into my work clothes. My head swam—too much shit was running through my mind. Whoever wrote that note was a fucking liar, but what was I going to do about it? I had looked at Jon in the locker room. I knew what that had to look like to whoever had noticed. And yes, I felt something when I looked at Jon. I didn't know what it was all about, but I sure as hell wasn't a fucking fag!

I walked to the barn, fuming. I fed the chickens, checked to make sure the water troughs were full, did all the stuff I did every day after school. I was so pissed I could have spit bullets. If I found out who left that note in my locker, I'd tear him a new ass-hole for sure. I had more than half a mind to demand that he step forward when I was in the locker room the next day. Then I'd kick the shit out of him until he took it back.

I cooled down a little as I worked. I realized confronting the note writer wasn't a good idea. I didn't want to draw attention to the fact that I'd been looking at Jon while he was naked. I'd done it and I couldn't really deny it. I'm sure some of the guys had noticed. They wouldn't think anything about it, unless I threw a shit-fit about it in the locker room. The more strongly I denied it, the more they'd wonder about me.

I had to keep what I'd done as quiet as I possibly could. I could not face my accuser. If I did, he was sure to label me a fag. It didn't matter if it was true or not, it would stick. I'd be presumed guilty until proven innocent. I knew how such things worked. It made me more fearful than ever. I was screwed.

After I finished my work at the barn, I headed across the pasture to help Nathan with the fencerow. I felt like we'd been working on the damn thing forever. Nathan was struggling with a fence post, trying to get it into place by himself. His slim muscles were straining; it was about more than he could handle. His face was determined, almost angry. I was almost on top of him before he realized I was there. He smiled at me in greeting. I rushed up and together we pushed the post into place. It dropped in with a loud thump.

"Thanks," said Nathan. He grinned at me, clearly glad I'd arrived. His face was streaked with dirt and sweat ran down his slim, tanned torso.

Nathan always seemed to smile when he saw me, it was the smile of an admirer, the smile of someone who looked up to me. It was not a smile that indicated real happiness, however. Nathan was far from a happy boy. I sensed a deep sadness in him that never left him for a moment, even when we were laughing or joking around. It was like his life was so hard and joyless that he could never quite escape it. His sadness was something he pretended didn't exist. I pretended I didn't see it either, and together we ignored it so he could escape it, if only for a little while. It made my heart ache.

We didn't talk much that evening, but Nathan's companionship was a comfort. I felt at ease around him. He was familiar and comfortable. I didn't feel like I had to put up a front with him. I didn't have to act like a jock or whatever, the way I did with so many of my other friends. I could just be me. I couldn't get that note out of my mind, but like Nathan's sadness, I ignored it for the moment so I could have a little peace.

The farm was a tranquil place; peaceful and beautiful. I stood still for a few moments just to feel the wind blowing through my hair. Nathan paused, too, and together we listened to the frogs, insects, and birds. A symphony surrounded us on all sides, easing our pains, calming our minds. Sometimes the old farm seemed almost magical.

We returned to our sweaty task. Nathan and I had been working together for a few weeks. I realized as we strained our backs digging that I'd come to think of him as a good friend. He was always kind, always glad to see me. I looked forward to being with Nathan. I enjoyed his company. I'd never paid much attention to him at school, but working by his side on the farm had broken the ice between us. I thought about telling him about the note, but then I thought better of it. It just wasn't something I felt I could discuss with anyone.

That evening Nathan was exactly what I needed. A friend I could just be with, a friend whose company I could enjoy in relative silence. There was a calmness about Nathan that quelled my fears, slowed my racing thoughts. Even his sadness calmed me. I wondered about its source. I wondered what had so affected that boy. His troubles drew my thoughts away from my own, at least for a while. Nathan helped me by his mere presence, and he didn't even know it.

* * *

The next day at school there wasn't much on my mind except that note. I kept looking around like I could somehow tell who stuffed it in my locker just by looking him in the eyes. I looked over all the guys in gym class, wondering just which one of them sent it. I really did have half a mind to just stand up and say, "Which one of you fuckers called me a fag?" but I knew how foolish that would be.

I'd been real stupid. Hell, I didn't even know why I was looking at Jon. It's not like I had to do it. We were close friends and I loved being around him. Looking at him did make me feel good, but that was it. At least that's what I told myself. I made sure not to look at him too much, especially when he was dressing and undressing in the locker room. Still, I couldn't quite keep my eyes off him. That bothered me a lot, partly because I was afraid the note-writer would see me looking, and partly because I didn't know why I couldn't keep from looking. It reminded me of skinny-dipping near the cabin and what happened that night. I forced the thoughts from my mind.

I was uneasy all day. I felt like I was being watched, like I couldn't do anything without someone knowing about it. If that note was a joke, it wasn't very damn funny. It'd really upset me. If some jerk came up to me laughing about it, I'd kick his ass. And yet, I kept hoping someone would. It would've been such a relief to find out it was all a big joke.

Any doubts I had were erased just after school. I ran to my locker to get rid of as many books as possible. Lying in the bottom of my locker were two folded pieces of paper.

I opened the first one, trembling slightly. The faint scent of perfume eased my nerves. I immediately recognized Kim's delicate hand:

Ethan, call me when you get home okay? I haven't seen you much this week. I miss you. Love, Kim.

I folded the note and stuck it in my pocket. I fearfully opened the second note. On it were just a few typed words, words that made my blood run cold:

```
I know you want Jon's
cock. I should tell
everyone you're a faggot.
You better pray I don't.
Eat shit and die, queer!
```

I refolded the note with trembling hands. A mix of emotions flowed through me. I couldn't tell if I was more angry or afraid. I was enraged that someone was calling me a queer and I was terrified they'd tell someone else, especially Jon. It sure as hell wasn't funny. I was screwed. It didn't matter if the note was true or not. I had been looking at Jon. If the sender of the notes told what he knew, I'd be fucked up. The truth didn't really matter. I knew what everyone would think, and what would probably happen to me.

CHAPTER 6

Wrestling with Doubts

Jon and I met as always just before wrestling practice. For the first time, I felt uncomfortable around him. I knew I was being a coward, but I really didn't want to be seen with him. I was afraid of what someone might think. I was getting paranoid.

"Hey, Ethan, you busy tonight? I thought we could catch that new horror film."

"Uhm, I'm not sure."

"Well, let me know if you can. Mark and Brandon are going. I thought we could all grab a pizza after the movie or something."

"Uh, I'll call you later if I can come. Uh…listen, I need to go to practice."

"We've got almost twenty minutes, what's the hurry?"

"Coach wanted to talk to me about something. I just remembered. Sorry."

I took off, leaving Jon a little flustered. I'd just done something I'd never done before. I'd lied to my best friend. I had no plans at all for that night, even though it was a Friday. Coach didn't need to see me either. I felt like a real rat. I'd seen the look on Jon's face. He was hurt. I wasn't a very good liar and I think he knew I was lying. Hurting him hurt me. I didn't know what to do. Those notes were making me crazy.

I needed a little time to think. I wondered if maybe I should call up Kim when I got home and see if she wanted to go out. I'd avoided doing that because I wasn't so sure I wanted to see her. She'd already roped me into going out on Saturday and I didn't really want to spend Friday night with her too. I wanted to be with her, and then again I didn't. Kim was a lot of fun, but spending time with her was just so difficult for me. I felt like I was being pulled back and forth, unable to decide what I really wanted. It made me want to scream.

I really would've liked to go out with Jon. There was little I liked more. I was being ridiculous. It was just a movie and some pizza after all. Mark and Brandon would be there too, so what was the danger? Would some guy in my gym class accuse me of participating in an all-male orgy? Why was I being so stupid?

I decided to take Jon up on his offer. I felt immediately better when the decision was made. I couldn't let those notes run my life. I couldn't let them keep me away from my friend.

I nearly changed my mind when I climbed in the pickup truck. I felt something crunch under my foot and looked down to see a photo torn out of a muscle magazine. It was of a buff guy wearing skimpy shorts. Typed across the bottom of the photo was a message, "Thought I'd leave you a little gift. I know you'll get off on this, fag boy. Happy 'bating."

"Dammit!" I shouted out loud, then wished I hadn't. A few heads in the parking lot turned in my direction. I crumpled the photo into a ball, tossed it on the floor, and shoved the truck into gear.

I called Jon as soon as I got home. He sounded cautious when he started talking, and kind of sad. I knew then for sure that I'd hurt him. His tone changed completely when I told him I wanted to go. His voice became animated and cheerful. It was if his hurt feelings were erased in an instant. I was gladder than ever that I'd decided to go. Jon was a good friend and I sure didn't want to hurt him. I was thrilled that the damage I'd done was so easily undone.

Jon said he and the boys would pick me up a little before seven. I was excited. I didn't get out all that often and it would be really fun hanging out with the boys. Normally, I'd have wanted it to be just Jon and me, but under the circumstances a small crowd was better.

I showered and changed, then waited until I heard a car horn outside. I ran out and hopped into the back seat with Mark. I looked at Mark as he smiled at me and slapped me on the back. He was looking fine wearing a red shirt and black shorts. Mark was a soccer player. In fact, everyone in the car was a soccer player but me. Mark was really good looking too, with dark eyes and dark hair that never failed to draw my attention. I thought about that for a moment. I did pay a lot of attention to other guys. I never failed to notice when one was good looking, or well built.

All my self-doubts rose to the surface and a wave of depression flowed over me. What was wrong with me? The photo, the notes, and my own thoughts plagued me.

No, I wasn't going to allow that. I wasn't going to let my evening with the boys be ruined. I pushed all those thoughts out of my mind and just tried to enjoy myself. Jon and Brandon were up front. They were talking loud to each other, trying to be heard over the radio. I guess it didn't occur to them to turn it down. We sped off towards town, the car rocking with loud music and crazy boys. It was great. In mere seconds I was having a good time.

We reached the theater and took our seats right before the previews came on. Jon was sitting next to me and he and Mark got into a small popcorn fight. They calmed down as the screen came to life. The first preview was for a great action film with lots of destruction and violence. It was my kind of thing. I wanted to see that one for sure. The next was for some drama that I didn't think looked too interesting. I didn't usually get into that kind of thing. I liked action or comedy, or both. Horror could be pretty good too.

The movie started. I got into it from the very beginning. Two teenaged couples had a car wreck and were forced to take shelter from a wicked thunderstorm in a big old abandoned mansion. I loved the whole idea of a haunted house in a storm. The darkness, the flashes of lightning, all of it was just so cool. Of course it didn't take long for one of the couples to start making out. While exploring the old mansion they had conveniently found a bedroom and just couldn't resist lying down to do a little tongue wrestling. I didn't exactly think it was the right time for such a thing, but hey, it was a movie.

Lightning flashed as the two teenagers undressed each other and really got down to business. The boy had a nice smooth chest. I jumped a little every time there was a bright flash of lightning and peal of thunder. I knew something was going to happen. The music was building too. I sat there in anticipation, almost as if it was I in that room. Sure enough a dark figure stepped out of the shadows and stabbed right through both lovers as they lay naked, pinning them to the bed as they screamed in terror. I jumped a little in my seat. Jon jumped even more. So much for those two. Teenagers never could have sex in horror films. Any time they tried it, they ended up dead.

Soon the murderer was after the other couple, even though they were not having sex. It almost didn't seem fair. The boy bolted out the front door in terror, leaving his girl behind. What a pussy. The girl almost escaped, but naturally she was wearing high heels and tripped at the last second. And of course, it took her forever to get back up. She was slashed to death before she ever got off the floor.

Maybe it wasn't very realistic, but it was a good film anyway. It scared the crap out of me at times. It scared Jon too. He actually grabbed me once. I thought that was funny as hell.

After the movie we all went to a little pizza place and ordered a large pepperoni. Brandon couldn't keep his eyes off a cute little freshman from our school and the rest of us teased him about it. I didn't hang out with Brandon a whole lot, but I knew he was girl crazy. He had eyes for every girl in the place, including our waitress, who was a college girl and way out of his league.

I watched Brandon, wondering why I wasn't more like him. Why wasn't I girl crazy like that? I pushed the thought from my mind before it had a chance to ruin my fun.

We laughed and ate and joked around. I had such a great time. I loved being out with the boys. It was so different from the farm. I thought of Nathan. I wished I'd thought of inviting him along. He'd have really enjoyed himself, too. I made a mental note to include him the next chance I got.

We piled in the car after devouring the entire pizza and Jon drove us around town. He made a couple of circles around the main cruising area near the park. It was getting late, but no one wanted to go home just yet. It was a Friday night and it was meant for fun.

We talked a lot about the horror movie and the foolishness of getting it on in a haunted house. Brandon said he'd be willing to take the risk. No surprise there. I think Brandon would've gone to any length to get it on with a girl. As far as I knew, he'd never done it. Maybe that was why he was so desperate. Then again, with his looks, I had no doubt Brandon could land a girl. Maybe he was just one of those guys who just couldn't get enough.

Jon drove around as we talked, then stopped the car on a nearly abandoned street.

"Why are we stopping here?" asked Mark.

"I just thought of something we can do," said Jon, grinning evilly.

I felt a hint of nervousness descend upon me. Jon had that look in his eye, the look he got when he was thinking of something really crazy. That look often led to some real fun, but more often, it led to something that scared the crap out of me. It was the same look he had when we were both twelve and he wanted to scale some steep cliffs. I got a broken arm out of that adventure. It was also the same look he got when we were fourteen and he wanted to try sledding down the steepest hill in town while it was ice covered. That was a real rush, but I didn't like it so well when I was knocked out cold after hitting my head on a tree. I wondered what was on his adventuresome mind this time.

"Are you guys brave enough to go with me in *there*?" asked Jon, pointing to the old Graymoor Mansion.

Everyone looked out the windows at the huge dilapidated mansion that set back off the street. It had been abandoned for decades and nasty rumors surrounded it. It was Verona's most notorious haunted house and had been the scene of grisly ax murders a hundred or so years before.

"No fucking way!" said Mark. "Not even in the daylight!"

"So, you're scared?" asked Jon.

"Hell yeah, I'm scared." Mark had no trouble admitting his fear.

"I'll do it," said Brandon.

Jon's eyes turned to me. I could see them sparkling in the moonlight. I did not want to go in there. I shared Mark's opinion. I didn't want to look like a coward in front of Jon, however. Jon also had a certain way of getting me to do whatever he wanted. I had a very hard time saying "no" to him. No matter how much I protested, he always won in the end. He gave me a wicked little smirk that said, "Say you'll do it now, because you know you will in the end."

"Okay, I'm in," I said, although personally I didn't even want to step out of the car.

"So, you going to be a pussy, or are you coming with us, Mark?" said Jon.

"I'm going to be a pussy," said Mark, not without some humor. "Just wait, you'll see I was the smart one."

Jon got out of the car, followed closely by Brandon. I wanted more than anything to stay right there with Mark, but I followed as well. We walked up to the big heavy gates and Jon pushed them open. They creaked and groaned and made a horrible noise. It sent a shiver up my spine.

We stepped toward the old mansion. It seemed to grow larger as we neared. It looked sinister and evil. I tried not to think of the horror film we'd just watched. What we were doing was far too much like it for comfort. We drew nearer to each other until our bodies were touching. I felt Brandon's hand on my shoulder and Jon was gripping my arm. They were acting like they weren't afraid, but the way they held onto me made their fear clear. I was holding onto Jon as well, without even realizing it at first. We were so close together it was a wonder we could walk.

"Fred, Velma, do you think this is such a good idea?" I said in my best Shaggy voice, trying to ease the tension. Jon laughed a little, but I could tell his heart wasn't in it.

"Which one of us gets to be Fred?" asked Brandon. "I'm sure not being Velma!"

"I'd rather be Scooby," said Jon.

Our voices died. The silence didn't seem to like being disturbed. I had the oddest feeling that we were being watched, and not by Mark back in the car. Goosebumps crawled up my arms.

Jon was just barely out in front. He put his foot on the lowest step and then we heard it. The most horrible scream I'd ever heard in my life came from somewhere deep inside the house. It sounded like it was at a considerable distance, but it was still quite clear and loud. It sounded for all the world like someone crying out as they were hacked to death with an ax.

All three of us turned and bolted for the car, practically knocking each other down. My heart pounded like I'd run ten miles and the hair on the back of my neck stood on end. We jumped in the car, slammed the doors, and locked them.

"Oh my God!" said Jon, his face filled with excitement.

"What the fuck was that?" said Brandon, practically yelling.

"I almost pissed my pants," I said.

"I think I did," said Jon, laughing.

Mark didn't say anything, but he looked quite pleased with himself. He was kind of smiling. The rest of us talked excitedly about what we'd heard. I must admit, it was rather thrilling. There was no fucking way I'd ever do it again, however. Once was more than enough. I wasn't about to go near Graymoor again, not even in the daylight.

Finally we all turned to Mark, his silence was becoming unbearable.

"Go ahead, say it," said Jon.

"Okay," said Mark, "I told you so."

"You little bitch!" said Jon laughing, "At least we were brave enough to go. We weren't little cowards like you."

"Who's more cowardly," said Mark, "the boy who was too afraid to go, or the one that pissed his pants?" Mark thought that was funny as hell and couldn't stop laughing. It was contagious and soon we were all laughing. It was a welcome relief after our terror.

"Anyone want to go back?" asked Jon.

"Uh, I'll stay here with Mark," said Brandon.

"Me too," I said.

"Hey, it was exciting though, wasn't it?" said Jon.

"I'll give you that," I said.

I felt relieved when Jon started the car and pulled away. I was glad to leave the haunted house behind us. He dropped me off pretty soon after that. It'd been a great night.

* * *

Nathan and I worked most of the next day. I told him all about my haunted house adventure and he seemed pretty impressed. The hours passed quickly with his company. That's one of the things I really like about Nathan—when I was with him, the time just flew by. Digging all those postholes and setting all those posts sure would've been a boring task without him.

The day was bright and clear and hot. I loved the sun pounding down on my naked torso. I loved the feel of sweat dripping off me. It was sure a good day for that. When Nathan and I weren't talking, my mind drifted off into the troubles that plagued me. The notes I'd received in my locker had created some real doubts in my mind. I'd hardly let myself admit it, but deep down I had some doubts about my sexuality. Something just didn't feel quite right. I couldn't bring myself to think about that too much, however. I just couldn't. I told myself that my difficulties were nothing more than a phase, an adolescent adjustment on the way to adulthood. Everything would work out in time. I'd stop being so fascinated with the bodies of other boys and become just as girl crazy as Brandon. But what if I didn't? What then?

As I'd done so often before, I closed off my mind to the possibilities. I simply refused to think about it. Instead, I talked to Nathan. I didn't care what we talked about, so long as we kept talking and I didn't have to think.

CHAPTER 7

Proving My Manhood

Saturday night Kim met me at *The Park's Edge*. I wasn't about to pick her up at her house if it could be avoided. I didn't want to spend one second more with her father than was absolutely necessary. I knew he'd grill me without mercy if he got the chance and I wasn't giving it to him. The first time had been bad enough. I had quite enough problems without dealing with that old geezer.

We ate and talked and Kim gazed at me with that dreamy look in her eyes. Sometimes she made me self-conscious looking at me like that. It was like she was intently interested in my slightest movement. I could tell she was looking at my arms a lot and my chest. I'd caught her checking out my butt a few times, too. It made me feel real good about myself to have her looking at me like that, but it kind of made me feel like a deer caught in the headlights of an oncoming car.

I checked out Kim while we talked. She was very attractive. I wondered why I didn't get excited over her. I mean—most guys would have been drooling over her. They'd have been itching to kiss her. We'd kissed a few times, but it never really did anything for me. Maybe I was just doing it wrong. I wished I could ask someone about it, but whom could I go to? One thing guys don't do is admit to other guys that they are inexperienced with sex. Every guy claims to be an expert in that area. I could just imagine myself in the locker room, asking the other guys how to kiss a girl. Yeah, that would be a riot. I didn't want labeled as a virgin. There wasn't much worse than that, except for...I didn't want to think about it.

I let my eyes drift over Kim's body. Her breasts pushed against her shirt. I'd seen plenty of other guys staring at her chest. I'd heard lots of remarks about it, too, and about her ass. All the guys thought she was hot. Kim's body should've driven me into fits of desire. I should've been lusting after her, the material of my jeans straining with my arousal. Why wasn't it happening?

Kim caught me looking at her chest. She smiled, then laughed when I looked away guiltily. I turned kind of red and she teased me about it. I could tell she liked me looking, however. It probably made her feel good that same way I felt good about her checking me out. It was nice to be admired.

My doubts about my own sexuality flooded my mind. There I was, out with a hot babe. I was having fun. I enjoyed her company. But something wasn't quite right. I wasn't having wild thoughts about getting it on with Kim. I wasn't mentally undressing her. It was like I just didn't care. I felt confused and upset.

After dinner, we ended up at the very movie I'd seen the night before. Verona was a small town and we only had one movie a week. I always teased visitors about the Verona Cinemaplex. We had ten or twelve movies just like the big towns, just not all at the same time.

I pretended I hadn't seen the film before. I didn't really mind seeing it again. When a movie was good, I liked to watch it more than once. It sure wasn't as much fun as it had been with the boys, however. Watching it with Kim was a whole other experience.

Kim screamed and grabbed onto me as the couple having sex on the bed were killed. She held onto my biceps so tight they hurt. During the rest of the movie I had my arm around Kim pretty much the entire time. It was as if I was protecting her. She snuggled up against me and the warmth and closeness felt good. Her perfume smelled nice too.

Maybe I hadn't been feeling anything for her because I was just nervous and confused. Perhaps everything had happened so fast with Kim that my feelings just hadn't caught up with me yet. I'd kind of gotten pushed into the whole dating thing. If the guys hadn't been watching Kim and me the day I'd asked her out, I never would've done it. Then, I didn't know what to do on a date and I didn't want to look like I didn't know. I'd fumbled through everything, feeling like the virgin I was. I was pretty clueless, but I wanted to appear like I knew it all. Maybe I'd just been putting way too much pressure on myself. It was no wonder I couldn't get a hard-on around her. Not being able to get it up around Kim was kind of odd, though, I sure as hell didn't have that problem any other time. Sometimes, I though being hard was my dick's natural state.

I pulled Kim closer to me and faced her. She turned her head and looked into my eyes. I inched closer and our lips met. Her kiss was warm and wet. It did kind of feel good on my lips. It didn't get me all hot and bothered, but it wasn't so bad. I derived more pleasure from it than I had our previous kisses. Maybe it just took getting used to, like beer. At first, beer tasted a lot like I imagined piss would taste, but I'd kind of grown accustomed to it, so it wasn't so bad anymore. I sure liked the way it made me feel. Maybe I just had to kiss Kim a few times before I'd really get excited about it.

I kissed Kim again, wondering when doing so would cause my pants to dance. I slipped my tongue into her mouth for the very first time. There was something kind of sexy about that. Was I becoming aroused? Did I feel a stirring in my jeans? I wasn't quite sure, but our kissing seemed more interesting than before. We pulled away from each other and watched the movie again. I held her close, and wondered if I'd like each kiss a little better than the one before. I wondered about a lot of things.

As I sat there, I played out a little fantasy in my head. I imagined Kim running her hand up the leg of my jeans. I imagined her groping me. That started to excite me, so I delved more deeply into my fantasy. I imagined her unzipping my jeans, leaning over, and blowing me right there in the theater. That did it. I was getting aroused. I was thinking about Kim and I was getting hard. That was more like it. Maybe all I needed to do was stop worrying and just let it happen.

I left my fantasy behind and started watching the film again. I held Kim close, feeling a lot better about things. I was still uncertain about myself, but maybe things would yet fall into place.

After the movie we dropped in on Zac. He was having a party and he'd invited all the wrestling guys over. Most of the guys from the team were there, as well as a lot of others. Zac's parents were out of town and he was having a blast. I sure wouldn't have wanted to be him when they returned. The place was trashed. There was no way he'd be able to clean all that up.

Zac didn't seem to care, however. He was as trashed as the house. I'd seen him buzzed before, but he was falling down drunk. I thought drinking like that was pretty stupid. Some of the guys I knew really liked to get shit-faced, but I didn't see what was so hot about it. I did enjoy a good buzz, however, and I didn't object when Zac pressed a beer into my hands.

I sipped on the beer and talked with the guys while Kim hung on my shoulder. I saw a few of the guys eyeing Kim. That made me kind of proud. It was always nice to have something other guys wanted. It definitely made me look cool in front of them. I leaned over and kissed Kim on the lips. She wasn't shy about kissing me back. Our tongues entwined and all the guys were watching. When we broke off our kiss I had the feeling some of them were breathing a little harder. I bet a lot of them were getting harder, too. I smiled. Showing off my girl was sure fun.

Kim was drinking a little and seemed to be enjoying herself. The music was loud and we were surrounded by friends, so what was not to enjoy? To be honest, what I liked most of all was the envious looks I got from my teammates. I kissed Kim again, running my hands up her sides, nearly touching her breasts. The kiss was long and deep. I knew that would drive the guys crazy. Zac was staring at us, idly rubbing his crotch. His jeans were tented. They looked like they were about to rip from the strain. Zac was drunk, but he was definitely into the little show that Kim and I were putting on. He devoured Kim with his eyes. After a few moments more he stumbled for the bathroom. I had a feeling he was going in there to whack it. I nearly laughed at the thought, but something about it kind of turned me on, too. I pushed that thought right out of my mind and kissed Kim again.

I took a second beer and then a third. I was getting a real good buzz. I stopped there, however. I knew if I drank more I'd get drunk. I couldn't handle all that much beer. I'd only been drunk once and I didn't like it, especially the next morning. Uncle Jack wouldn't give me any shit if I drank too much, but he wouldn't cut me any slack either. If I had a hangover that was just too damned bad. I'd be expected to get up and work just the same. Drinking was a choice and I was expected to deal with the consequences. Uncle Jack was pretty smart. I probably drank a lot less than I would've if he'd just forbidden it.

Kim and I left and took a little walk to clear our heads. It was quiet outside, quite a contrast to Zac's wild party. The music grew fainter as we drew away from the house and soon it was gone altogether. The moon and stars shone bright overhead. Kim walked close beside me and rested her head on my shoulder. There was something comforting in the way she hugged me so close. It was almost like we were one person walking down the sidewalk instead of two. I think that maybe people weren't really meant to be alone. I felt content at that moment, like I had something I'd long been missing.

We found our way to the school and walked out past the football field, all the way to the soccer field where Jon practiced every day. The night air was warm and pleasant. I felt real good from my alcoholic buzz. Kim was looking especially beautiful. I pulled her to me and kissed her. She eagerly returned my kiss and snuggled against me as I held her. She purred like a kitten in my embrace.

Our mouths opened and our tongues entwined. I closed my eyes. I was getting into kissing more and more. Unbidden, an image of me kissing Jon filled my head. I imagined I was kissing him instead of Kim. No! I opened my eyes and kissed Kim more deeply, banishing the phantom of Jon that haunted my mind. Kim's hands wandered onto my chest and felt my muscles through my shirt. She slid her hands around behind me, pulling my lower back toward her. She slipped her hands onto my butt. Her touch felt surprisingly good, but I was uncomfortable.

I thought again about what I'd been thinking about off and on all night. I decided it was time to try it, time to see just how it would make me feel. I was nervous, even scared, but I had to prove to myself that I wasn't what those notes said I was. I had to prove that my feelings toward Jon meant nothing more than friendship. I had to put to rest all the doubts that kept resurfacing, no matter how hard I tried to ignore them.

I took a deep breath to calm myself and kissed Kim again. I ran my hands up over her shirt, feeling her firm breasts. Kim kind of moaned a little as I gently groped her. Kim's hands slipped up under my shirt and ran over my chest. The next thing I knew she was pulling my shirt over my head. Kim certainly wasn't a shy girl. She was forceful—the kind that went after what she wanted.

Kim ran her fingers over my naked skin, tracing my pectoral muscles, and my tight abs. Her hands trailed lower and she groped my crotch. At her touch my manhood came to life and started to grow. It was just like I'd imagined during the movie. I kissed her more passionately, trying to push myself into what I knew was right. I seemed to be edging that way. I wanted to push myself over the edge and feel the way I knew I should be feeling.

Her touch excited me. Her fingers felt good on my naked skin and on the bulge in my jeans. That bulge was growing bigger. Touching her did nothing for me, however. It was as if I were touching cold stone instead of warm flesh. I couldn't make myself get excited over her body. I was so close to what I wanted to achieve, but it seemed just beyond my grasp.

All my arousal was inner directed. It was my body that was turning me on, not hers. I might as well have been alone in my room, experiencing the only form of sex I'd ever known. What was I doing wrong?

I pulled Kim's shirt over her head. I unfastened her bra with difficulty. She stood before me naked from the waist up. I knew she was beautiful, but I just didn't feel it. I groped her breasts once again as she fumbled with my belt and the buttons of my jeans. I kissed her as I worked her own jeans loose. Kim pushed my boxers down and grasped me. She stroked me slowly, making me throb. I pulled away her remaining clothing and we sank to the grass.

I pressed my lips to her breasts, but the sensation did not please me. I felt a sense of revulsion rather than desire. I was living every boy's dream, only to find I didn't want it. No, I had to try and make it work! I was hard after all. I was hard with a girl. That had to mean something.

"Can I…." I hesitated. The words seemed so harsh. I didn't want to say them. I rubbed my hardness against Kim. I didn't have to say the words, she knew what I wanted.

"Yes, Ethan, do it. I want to feel you in me."

I fumbled with my jeans, pulling out the rubber I'd stashed there before I left home. I tore open the package with unsure fingers and unrolled it over my manhood, just like I'd read on the box. That part of me was starting to go soft so I moved quickly. I crawled on top of Kim as she lay on her back on the grass. Somehow I managed to get inside her. My manhood was growing limp. The mere thought of what I was doing gave me a sick feeling in my gut.

Kim moaned and purred and told me what a stud I was. I willed myself to have an erection, but my manhood was deflating. No matter what I did, I couldn't maintain my hard-on. I'd been stiff as steel while Kim was groping me, but when her hand left my manhood, so did the hardness. I was doing it. I was getting it on with a girl. Why wasn't I as hard as rock?

I closed my eyes and gave in to the fantasy that had been pounding at me, trying to break in. I imagined Jon naked beneath me. My penis immediately stiffened. I began to slowly thrust as I pictured Jon's beautiful body in my mind; his arms, his shoulders, his chest, and his cute little butt. I thought about his manhood and immediately a vision of encircling it with my lips came to mind.

I pushed my penis in and out of Kim. I did not make love to her. I fucked her. She was nothing to me. She was less significant to me than my own hand when I was jerking off. She moaned and groaned and told me what a stud I was. I ignored her, thinking of Jon to maintain my erection.

Still my mind fought to deny him. When my thoughts pushed him away in self-preservation, reality slipped in and I felt my erection disappearing. I summoned him back and my hardness returned. Jon aroused me more in his absence than Kim did naked beneath me. I gave in to my fantasy and fucked Kim while I imagined I was making love to Jon. My body was with Kim, but my mind and heart were elsewhere.

I threw my head back and moaned. A feeling of intense pleasure ripped through my body. It was of short duration, however. It hit me in a powerful blast, then was gone. I was no longer a virgin. I felt like I'd lost something, wasted it. I gave myself to Kim, to someone I didn't love, to someone I didn't even really care about.

I lay back disgusted, tears in my eyes. I'd set out to prove I wasn't what those notes said I was. I'd set out to prove that my feelings for Jon were nothing more than friendship. I'd done the opposite.

Kim hugged me close. Only then did I remember she was there. Her body disgusted me and I had to fight to keep from shrinking away. She was purring with happiness and I hated her.

"That was the best I've ever had, Ethan! You're awesome. You're such a stud," she said as she rubbed my chest.

Please! If that was the best she'd ever had then I felt sorry for her. I didn't know what I was doing. I wasn't even hard half the time. The whole thing was over in less than five minutes. I fucked her without love or compassion. It meant nothing and she acted as if it was the most wonderful thing in the world.

I felt like telling her just what I thought, but I held my tongue. This wasn't her fault. I couldn't blame her for my lack of interest. She hadn't forced me into anything. I was the one who wanted it. I was the one who had to prove his manhood. I'd brought this all on myself. Kim was just an innocent bystander. No, I wasn't going to hurt her.

The hatred was still in me, however, and I found it hard to act as I should. I lay there for a while, not wanting to leave before it was appropriate. Kim had allowed me to do what most boys begged their girls for on a regular basis—without getting it. She'd given me herself. She'd given me her body. I had to fight my emotions. Kim was innocent and didn't deserve the wrath I felt within me.

I sat up, then stood. Kim pulled me to her and kissed me. It almost made me retch. I kissed her back, enduring the unwanted intimacy. I was in way over my head. I'd upped the stakes and I had lost big.

We dressed and I walked her home. She talked on and on. I was silent. At last we were at her door. I endured another kiss and she stepped inside, walking on air. I felt like I'd taken advantage of her—used her. I didn't feel very good about myself just then. I wasn't the kind who could just use someone and think nothing of it. I'd done something wrong and I knew it. I knew why I'd done it, but that didn't make it right.

I wondered about Kim's father. I wondered what he'd do if he found out I'd fucked his daughter.

CHAPTER 8

Meeting Myself

I walked away from Kim's doorway, back toward the *Paramount Theatre* where I'd left the truck. The reality of who and what I was dropped on me like a stack of boulders. I'd set out to prove that I was attracted to girls; to prove I wasn't attracted to Jon. Instead, I'd proved that girls did nothing for me and that the only way I could get a hard-on with a female was to fantasize about another boy. True, Kim had made me hard, but I had to admit to myself than anyone touching me like that would've aroused me. I wanted it to mean something, but it just didn't.

I was in such a daze that I was unaware of my surroundings until I found myself standing beside the old Ford. I climbed in and turned the ignition key. The engine fired up and I pulled away from the curb. I just drove around town for a while, aimlessly. I saw all the high school kids sitting on their cars in the park or driving around cruising; cute boys strutting their stuff for cute girls, beautiful females casting their spell on hormone controlled males. For the first time ever, I realized I was really and truly different. I wasn't like everyone else. I was one of those boys that everyone talked about—one of the despised and ridiculed.

I seriously considering ramming the truck into a telephone pole and ending it all right then and there. It would look good in the paper: "Local Wrestler Killed in Accident." It would be a dramatic end.

Everyone would be talking about me. A lot of the kids from school would be crying at my funeral. No one would ever know about me. My tormentor could tell everyone what he knew and they'd just tell him to shut the fuck up because I was dead.

I was thinking crazy. I was being stupid and selfish. I couldn't leave Uncle Jack like that. I couldn't hurt him, or my friends. I couldn't leave Nathan stuck with finishing that fence all by himself. Suicide was never the answer. It brought too much pain to too many. It was the cowardly way out. I was no coward. I knew I had the balls to withstand whatever might come.

When I finally made it home, I didn't go inside. Instead I walked past the barn, to the large fenced in area where I'd taught Jon to ride. His presence still lingered there—like a ghost in the moonlight. Why did he always haunt my thoughts? I walked on, through the fields, following the very route that Jon and I had set less than a week before.

I'd been lying to myself. I'd known that all along. How could I not have known? The one person I couldn't fool was myself. I'd done a fair job of it I guess. My denial, my anger over the notes, all that and more was just smoke and mirrors; an illusion I used to trick myself, at least for a little while. It was an illusion I'd used to hide the unthinkable, to keep myself from discovering my darkest secret—a secret that would change my entire life.

A tear ran down my cheek. I'd failed. I'd ignored reality for as long as I could. I'd held it back, fought it off. I'd tried to alter it, make myself something other than what I was, but I'd failed. I was out of tricks, out of illusions, out of hope. I had to face what I was and deny it no more. I felt like my life was over. Why did this have to happen to me? I hadn't asked for it, didn't want it. Why me?

I slipped under the eaves of the forest. It was dark among the trees, almost too dark to see really. My feet had a memory of their own, however, and guided me. I turned all that had happened over and over in my mind. I was afraid, ill at ease, and yet a kind of calm descended upon me. At least now I knew for sure. I'd tried it with a girl. I'd dated, kissed, and had sex. I knew what waited for me in that direction, and I knew I didn't want it. I no longer had to struggle against what I was. I no longer had to fight myself. The terrible battle within me had ended. I felt like I'd lost.

I found myself at the cabin. It was dark, almost haunted looking. I walked on and sat where Jon and I had eaten our picnic lunch. I could almost feel him beside me. For the very first time ever, I let myself feel for him, without fighting it, without pushing it away, without denying it. I loved him. I loved him more than I loved anyone.

I sat there and explored who I was. I felt like I was getting to know someone I'd just met. I guess I was really. There were so many things I'd never allowed myself to feel, so many thoughts I'd never allowed myself to think. Yes, such feelings and thoughts tried to force their way to the surface and break through, but I'd battled them, beat them into submission. I'd wrestled them the way I wrestled my opponents during matches. I'd ignored the real me as best I could. I'd hidden myself from myself. At last I could get to know me and feel the emotions that flowed through me naturally. I found that I liked me.

A smile crossed my lips. I loved Jon. It felt good to love someone. I hadn't really, not since my parents died. I loved Jon so much it hurt. I loved him with all my heart. I loved him as a friend, yes, but there was so much more. I wanted to be with him, be at his side every moment. I wanted to do everything with him, share his life. I wanted to sleep with him, make love with him.

I thought of Jon's body, of its smoothness and firmness. I thought of his full, red lips. I yearned to kiss him, to touch him. I yearned to make love to him. I didn't want just sex with Jon—I wanted love. My desire for him was intensified a hundred fold because of the way I felt about him.

I thought of the other boys that surrounded me every day. I thought of how I'd looked at them, noticed them. Yes, there was no doubt about what I was. Of all those beautiful boys, Jon was the most beautiful of all, at least to me. There were many just as attractive as Jon, several more attractive I guessed. To me, however, none of them were the equal of Jon. I saw him not only with my eyes, but also with my heart. I loved him. I was in love with him.

I wondered how long I'd been in love with him. When had it happened? When had the love of friendship crossed the line and become something far greater? How had I hidden it from myself? How could I not have known? How was I going to bear the pain of the knowledge I so suddenly possessed?

I looked out at the lake. The moonlight reflected off the water, making it look like a million shimmering diamonds. It was a beautiful sight. Trees surrounded the lake on all sides but one; giant oaks, smooth maples, and gnarly sassafras. Their leaves were a deep, dark green, nearly blue in the moonlight. The little clearing and lake was a place of such beauty that I felt as if I were sitting in some long forgotten kingdom of the elves. I found myself wishing that Jon was at my side, sharing the beauty of it all. I wanted to share everything with Jon. I wanted to share my life with him.

I guess that was just another fantasy. There was just no way he could possibly share my feelings. One in ten is what they say, right? There was only a ten percent chance he was into guys like me. Even if he was one of the minority, that didn't mean he'd love me. I knew it was a vain hope. He couldn't possibly feel the same way about me that I did about him. We were good, close friends, but I was sure that was as far as it went for Jon. I think he loved me, but as a friend only. When he looked at me, the same feelings were not inspired that were aroused in me when I gazed upon him.

A deep sadness descended upon me. I felt isolated—alone. I was in love with Jon, but all that I wanted with him could not be. I could never tell him how I felt. To do so would have been to risk losing him. I couldn't bear the thought of that. I couldn't live without Jon in my life, even if he was only a friend and nothing more. Our friendship was dear to me, a thing precious beyond calculation. Jon could never love me as I loved him and I'd never tell him. I'd never share my feelings. I felt so alone.

My heart ached. A sob welled in my chest and forced its way up. I bowed my head and cried. I cried for what I was and for the life I'd never have. I cried for the one I loved, who could not love me back. I felt cursed. What had I done to deserve this? What kind of cruelty made me love someone I could never have? I felt that I must have done something horrible beyond thinking to deserve my fate. I cried until I was exhausted, my mind numb with sorrow and grief.

I arose and walked back the way I'd come, seeing nothing, feeling only sadness. If I could've willed myself dead I would have done so, just to escape. At that moment I felt completely isolated, as if I were outside, looking in on the rest of the world sharing life and love. I was the only gay boy in a straight world. My life was over.

It was late when I returned to the farmhouse. Uncle Jack was already in bed. I pulled off my clothes, fell onto my mattress and cried myself to sleep. My only hope was that I'd never wake up.

•

CHAPTER 9

My First Day as Me

When I awoke the next morning, I felt like a different boy. It was as if the Ethan of all those years was gone and replaced by another. I walked across the room and looked in the mirror. I looked the same, but I knew I wasn't. Everything had changed.

"I'm gay," I said to myself, trying it on for size. It made me uncomfortable. I stared into my own eyes, seeing the bottomless pit of sadness and despair. "I'm gay," I said out loud, "and no one else is ever going to know about it."

As soon as the words were out of my mouth, I thought once again about the notes. Those notes rarely left my thoughts. Just knowing that someone else knew about me made me uncomfortable. It wouldn't have been as bad if they'd just come up to me and said it to my face. Doing it secretly, anonymously, instilled me with fear. I couldn't help but wonder who it was and what they wanted.

It was worse now. Before, I'd told myself it was just bullshit. I'd told myself that I wasn't what those notes said I was. Now, I knew I was exactly what those notes accused me of being. I was a homosexual. I was a fag.

It was Sunday, so I showered and ate breakfast before beginning my morning chores. After those there was quite a bit of farm work waiting on me. The morning was like all the rest, except now I did it as a gay boy. I knew that I'd been gay all my life, but for a long time I didn't realize it, and after that I lied to myself about it, so it really was like I was a whole new person. It was like someone who found out one day that he was a prince. He'd been one all along, but he didn't know it, so suddenly he was something quite different from what he was before. The analogy was a pretty bad one, I couldn't think of anything similar between being gay and being a prince, but it helped me clarify my thoughts.

As I gathered the eggs from the hen's nests, I thought about something Uncle Jack had said to me once, about the importance of having a son. That's the one thing Jack felt was missing from his life. He'd been married, but there were no kids. I was the closest thing he had to a son. I guessed that was one of the reasons he'd taken me in when my parents died.

"When I'm gone, I'll leave all this to you," he said. "I know it ain't all that much, but it'll be a good place to raise a family. I imagine you'll find a wife without any trouble, and father lots of strong sons."

I guessed that wouldn't be happening. I'd always assumed it would. A wife and children always seemed pretty far in the future, but that's where I'd always thought my destiny lie. Now I had to think about a whole new future. I guessed I'd be more like my Uncle Jack; farming alone, without a son. I'd be childless for other reasons, but still the parallel was pretty clear. Maybe that shouldn't have mattered so much to a seventeen-year-old boy, but it mattered to me. I'd never have a son. Just knowing that left me feeling empty and incomplete. I felt like I'd lost someone close to me. My heart ached for the son I'd never know, that would never be. I felt like I'd cheated him out of his life.

New thoughts like that kept coming into my head unbidden. My whole world felt like it had been shaken up, and all the pieces fell somewhere they weren't before. My mind shifted from one thought to another. It was all so confusing and disorienting. Nothing was as it had been before.

I felt as if I couldn't go on, but I knew I had to. I either had to go on with my life, or just lay down in the dirt and die. It wouldn't be easy to go on. Nothing would ever be easy again.

I finished my chores and walked across the pasture to join Nathan, already hard at work on the eternal fencerow. Actually, we were nearly finished setting the fence posts. I figured we'd be done with that part of the task sometime the next week. I was glad about that. I was heartily sick of digging holes for fence posts. Of course, even that wasn't the end of it. We still had to attach hundreds of yards of the actual fencing. No farm job was ever done.

"Yo, Nathan!"

Nathan looked up as I called to him. Even at a distance I could tell he'd been crying. His eyes were all red and his face a little puffy. I pretended not to notice out of politeness and he didn't say anything. Nathan was unusually quiet. He had become a bit of a talker since we came to know one another fairly well. The cloud of sadness that hung about him seemed thicker today. He didn't even smile at me the way he usually did. I wanted to ask him what was wrong, but I wasn't sure that was such a good idea.

Nathan's mood was a reminder that everyone had troubles. Sometimes I forgot that things weren't perfect for everyone else. I felt pretty overwhelmed by everything happening in my own life and yet, I had the feeling that Nathan had bigger problems than me, if that were possible. I'd never seen such an unhappy boy. Even when he laughed, there was an edge to him, like he was afraid someone would come along and snatch that little bit of happiness away. Today, he wasn't laughing at all.

Nathan struck a root with the post-hole digger. He slammed the digger into the hole with all his might, over and over. I could see the anger in his eyes and the turmoil, and I knew it had nothing to do with striking a root. Nathan pounded the digger into the earth a few more times, then threw it down, walked a short distance away, and sat on the grass.

He had his back turned to me, but I could tell by the movement of his shoulders that he was sobbing. My heart ached for him. I almost started crying myself. My own problems were driving me into the ground and seeing him in such pain just made me more certain that the world was a wicked, evil place.

I wanted to help, but I didn't know how. I just stared at his back as the seconds ticked away. I took a deep breath, then walked over to him and sat down on the grass at his side. He didn't look at me, but he was still crying.

"Nathan…" I started, but I didn't know how to go on. I thought for a few moments. "Sometimes it helps to talk when something's wrong," I said. He was quiet for a while, then he looked at me with watery eyes.

"Why do you care?" He practically shouted at me. I let his anger wash over me, knowing it was the result of his pain.

"Because I'm your friend," I said. That seemed to give him pause. He wiped his eyes on the sleeve of his shirt.

"Nathan, what's wrong?"

He looked at me again. I could tell he really, really needed someone to talk to, but he was afraid, afraid to trust. I sat there waiting patiently. I knew better than to push him. I just sat there, letting him know I was there for him.

"I'm just tired of everything. I'm tired of not having any friends. I'm tired of not having anything. I'm tired of the other kids making fun of the way I look."

"Well," I said, struggling to find the right words. "Like I said, I'm your friend, so you have at least one. And…Well, I don't see anything wrong with the way you look. You look pretty good to me."

"How'd you like to wear the same clothes to school everyday! Everyone laughs at me. I can't help it because we're poor!" He started crying all over again. I put my hand on his shoulder.

"No, you sure can't," I said.

"I'm so sick of this damn shirt!" said Nathan. "I can't even remember wearing another one. It wasn't even new when I got it. It was my dad's. I'd just like to burn it so I don't have to see it anymore." He was bawling. I felt so very bad for him. I wished that I could make all his pain go away.

"Then let's do it," I said, almost without thinking. I thought it was a stupid thing to say for a moment, but once I thought about it, it didn't seem like such a bad idea.

"Huh?"

"If you hate it so much, let's burn it."

Nathan looked at me like I was out of my mind, or like I was some kind of freak.

"My parents would kill me. Besides, what would I wear then, huh?"

"I've got shirts you can have."

Nathan looked at me like he couldn't believe what I was saying. I could tell the idea of someone giving him something had never occurred to him. I think it really got to him. He looked really touched, like he realized for the first time that someone cared about him. Seeing him so affected by something so simple made me want to cry.

"Nah, I couldn't take nothing from you. It wouldn't be right."

"Why not?" I said. "We're friends. Besides, I want to. It would be rude not to accept."

"Would it?" he asked naively.

"Yes," I said. "It's always rude to turn down a gift. Come on." I got up.

"Where we going?"

"To the house, it's time for a break anyway."

I started walking and Nathan followed. He wasn't crying anymore. He seemed kind of bewildered. I led him inside and up to my room. He'd never been there before.

"It's big," he said.

"What?"

"Your room."

"Oh well, not really."

"It's way bigger than my room and it's all yours. I have to share with my little brother." Nathan looked around like he was in a museum or something.

"Take off your shirt," I said and disappeared into my closet.

Nathan stripped his shirt off his slim body and sat on the edge of my bed.

"Here, try this on," I said, tossing him a shirt. While he was putting that one on, I pulled others from the closet. I also pulled out a couple of pairs of jeans. I came back out with quite a big stack. Nathan's eyes got big.

"Hey, you look good in that," I said. I guided him to the full-length mirror. "See, you look better in it than I ever did."

"No way I could look better than you," he said. There was more than a touch of admiration in his voice. It made me smile.

Nathan looked at the stack of clothes on the bed, then back at me.

"I can't take all your clothes!" he said.

"Come here," I said, guiding him to the closet, showing him hanger after hanger of shirts, pants, jeans, jackets, and more.

"All that is yours?" he asked incredulously.

"Yeah." It really struck me that he thought my wardrobe was so unbelievable.

"But, I still can't take your stuff."

"Hey," I said, "I want you to have it."

Nathan still didn't look too comfortable with the idea. I pulled off my shirt and walked to the bed.

"Here," I said, pulling on a shirt. "You really think I can wear this?" I intentionally chose a shirt that was way too small for me. My biceps strained against the sleeves and the shirt ended just above my navel. Nathan laughed.

"Or how about this?" I said. I quickly slipped out of my jeans and chose a pair from the stack. I couldn't even get them past my thighs.

"Just imagine me wearing this to school!" Nathan started laughing at how ridiculous I looked. It was good to hear him laugh. I changed back into my normal clothes.

"I can't wear any of this stuff," I said, "but you can. Here, try these on." I handed Nathan a pair of jeans. He slipped out of his. I noticed his briefs looked like they were a hundred years old. I opened up my dresser and pulled out a few pairs of boxers, and some socks.

"Here," I said, "take these, too. I never have enough room in my dresser for all my crap."

Nathan looked like a little kid who'd awakened on Christmas morning to find the whole house filled with toys. I experienced vicarious happiness as I watched him. Nathan pulled on the jeans and looked at himself in the mirror. He smiled.

"Hey, you look sharp!" I said. "The girls are gonna be after you!" Nathan turned a little red and looked away from me.

I looked through the pile and picked out a worn shirt and pair of jeans.

"How about these for work clothes? Here, put them on."

Nathan dressed and we gathered up all the clothes and put them in a big bag. When he wasn't looking I slipped in a pair of my old sneakers. I knew they'd be a little big for him, but he could use them.

We walked back outside and I stopped by the trash burner. I gathered a few handfuls of pine needles from under the pine trees nearby and threw them in. I handed Nathan a book of matches.

"Now's your chance," I said.

Nathan looked from me to the trash burner and back again. He struck a match, ignited the pine needles, and tossed his old shirt and jeans on top. We stood there and watched as the flames consumed his tattered clothes.

"I sure won't be wearing those anymore!" said Nathan laughing. He looked me in the eyes. "Thanks, Ethan, I really mean it."

"Hey, I needed to clean out my closet anyway. Now I'll be able to find stuff when I want it." Nathan smiled at me for a moment, then he rushed over to me and hugged me tight. I held him in my arms, feeling his heart beat quickly in his chest.

"Thank you," he whispered. I ruffled his hair, then we separated and headed back across the pasture to the familiar old fencerow.

❧ ❧ ❧

Late that afternoon, after Nathan and I were done working, I borrowed the truck from Jack and headed for Koontz Lake. I needed to get my mind off things and I couldn't do that moping around the farm. It was a warm day and I was sure some of the guys would be at the beach. I could lose myself in a few hours of fun. It was hot in the truck cab and I rolled down the window. The rush of air felt cool on my sweat-dampened shirt. I thought about pulling it off, but that wasn't a bright thing to try while driving. Jack's truck was an *old* green Ford from the 1950's, but I'd be up to my ass in trouble if I wrecked it. I liked the truck myself; there was something comfortable and familiar about it. I liked the way it smelled. That might sound kinda odd, but the cab had this distinctive scent to it that I found enjoyable. I can't even describe the scent very well, as it didn't smell like anything—except maybe a cornfield during Indian summer or the hayloft on a hot day. If Jack ever wanted to get rid of the old Ford, which I knew he never would, I wanted to buy it.

I parked the truck in the asphalt parking lot at Koontz Lake and got out. I pulled off my shirt and tossed it on the seat. The sun felt warm and soothing on my bare chest; kinda like a massage. The beach was crowded, probably because everyone knew we didn't have many warm days left. It was September, after all, and most often it was too cool to swim at this time of year. We'd had a recent heat wave, however, that made it feel like July or August.

I was relieved when I looked around and didn't spot Jon. I'd almost not come for fear he'd be there. I just wasn't ready to see him yet. I spread my towel out on the hot sand and sat down to pull off my shoes and socks. The sand burned my bare feet a little as I made my way to the water's edge. The lake was surprisingly warm, but still created a cooling sensation as I waded in deeper and deeper. When I was up to my navel, I dove under the water. Right as I began my dive, I saw something that grabbed my attention so completely that I actually gasped as I was going under—which was a very bad idea indeed. I came up sputtering and choking, hoping no one noticed me make a fool of myself.

I jerked my head this way and that until I spotted him—the boy that'd caught my eye and nearly caused me to drown myself in three feet of water. He was the same boy I'd talked to briefly at a school dance just the Thursday before, but now he wasn't wearing a shirt. I spotted him, snapped a mental picture, and looked away. All I could think was *WOW!*

His name was Taylor and he was incredibly cute. In fact, he was without doubt the best looking boy I'd ever seen in my entire life. He had long blond hair, greenish-blue eyes, and a face so handsome it was downright angelic. He was slim and graceful, in a word—beautiful. If I hadn't been so head over heals in love with Jon, I'd have fallen for Taylor in a flash. I felt like I was falling for him anyway. I'd thought about him a lot since the dance. I tried to turn my mind from such thoughts; I had enough problems already without getting all starry eyed over another boy. Dealing with my obsession for Jon was task enough.

I couldn't keep from looking at the hot blond kid now and then. He was so beautiful he was like a work of art or something. I wished I had a picture of him to just tack up on my wall or somethin'. If Michelangelo or Leonardo or one of those artist dudes were alive, I'm sure they'd have fallen all over themselves to paint him or sculpt him or something.

I had to keep my waist under water because looking at Taylor was getting to me. My swimsuit was tented to the breaking point. I felt like my dick was gonna rip right through it. I intentionally ignored the hottie for a while and swam around to cool my passion. It took a good long time to get myself under control.

A bit later, I saw the blond angel talking with some guys I knew, so I joined them, just to get a closer look at him and hear his voice once more. It wasn't long before my eyes met his. He smiled at me and I just about melted.

"Hey, Taylor, right?" I asked.

"Yep, and you're…Ethan?"

"I forgot to ask you where you were from the other night."

"We just moved from Ohio. I'm startin' school tomorrow."

"I feel for you, dude."

"Why?" Taylor looked just a touch fearful.

"I feel for anyone who has to go to our school," I said laughing.

Taylor grinned. Damn he was cute!

We talked some more. I loved the sound of his voice. It had a certain softness to it, but it was still manly. I had the feeling that Taylor would make one hell of a singer.

"Brandon! Dude!" I said as he appeared and joined our little circle.

"What up, Ethan?"

"Just messin' around."

"You seen Jon?"

"No."

The mere mention of Jon's name was enough to make me uncomfortable. I looked around, half-expecting some boy to be staring at me with cold, hard eyes.

"Hey, we still on for Thursday evening?" asked Brandon.

"Sure," I said, "Mark'll be there and so will Jon." A part of me wished Jon wasn't coming, but I'd asked him a day or two before I'd admitted to myself that I was gay and that I was in love with him.

"Cool."

In just a couple of minutes, Mark joined us as well. The sight of Mark and Brandon's bare chests drew my attention away from Taylor a bit. That was probably a good thing, because I was likely paying too much attention to him. I really had to watch it.

I became aware of something as I stood there. Something was up between Mark and Taylor. I could just tell. It wasn't anything they said, but there was something about the way they looked at each other. Their eyes kept meeting and I felt like they were communicating something without talking. I'd seen them at the dance, too. I'd seen them talking and I'd seen Mark run like a scared rabbit. It was weird.

After a bit, Mark just kinda drifted away. There was definitely something on his mind. A minute or two later, Taylor left too, heading in the same direction that Mark had taken. I watched him as I chatted with Brandon and the guys. He disappeared into the bathhouse down the beach, just as Mark had not long before.

It wasn't long at all before Taylor strolled back in my direction. He didn't rejoin our little group, but stood looking out over the lake. I didn't know what had gone on in the bathhouse, but he was positively glowing. He'd smiled a lot when we were talking, but he was grinning from ear to ear now. He looked like he almost couldn't contain himself; as if he were about to float right up into the air.

When he turned he caught me watching him. He smiled and even blushed a little. He ran to me laughing and joined our little group once again. As we were all talking, Mark returned. He didn't join us immediately, but rather swam in the lake for a while, then came back and started talking while rivulets of water streamed down his muscular chest. I didn't fail to notice that his eyes met Taylor's time and again. Mark's face had its own glow and he looked happier at that moment than I'd ever seen him in my entire life.

I wondered what had passed between those two. I didn't exactly think they'd hooked up in the bathhouse for a quickie, but something had gone on. I almost laughed out loud when I thought about Mark and

Taylor going at it. It was just too funny. Mark was so straight he could've been the Straight Jock Poster Boy. I let my imagination wander for a few moments, fantasizing about what could've gone on if they were doing it. I had to knock that off real fast because it was getting me excited. It was ridiculous anyway. Mark, gay? There was just no way. Taylor sure wasn't a likely candidate either. Still, there was somethin' goin' on.

I took another swim to cool myself off; I needed it in more ways that one. Taylor had disappeared by the time I came back, so I hung out with Mark and Brandon. Mark kinda looked like he was off in lala land. His mind was clearly elsewhere. He had this big, dopey grin on his face that made him look particularly cute. I was dying to ask him what it was all about, but I knew better and kept my curiosity to myself.

CHAPTER 10

Uncertain Friendships

Nathan didn't go home right after work on Thursday evening the way he usually did. I invited him to stay. Jon, Brandon, and Mark were all coming over for a big barbecue and campfire. We had a huge pile of brush that needed to be burned and I thought it would be cool to just hang out, eat, and watch the flames. Of course, the plans had been made before everything had happened with Kim and I'd come to the realization that I was queer. To be honest, I was no longer looking forward to it, but I couldn't very well cancel it when I'd already invited everyone over. Besides, it might distract me from my problems.

Taylor, the totally cute boy I'd been drooling over out at Koontz Lake, was coming, too. I'd been seriously contemplating inviting him when Mark asked if he could bring him along. Mark and Taylor were tight; where one was, so was the other. Taylor only started school on Monday, but he and Mark were already the best of friends; at least it looked that way to me. I wondered a lot about those two, especially after what I'd witnessed at the beach.

I really didn't want to be near Jon at all. I'd been a little uncomfortable around him ever since I'd started having sexual thoughts about him. Now that I was certain of how I felt, I knew I'd be more uncomfortable around him than ever. Part of me just didn't want to see him ever again. Of course, part of me couldn't have lived with that. I loved Jon; he was my best friend, and I couldn't even imagine life without him. That night, however, I was hoping that he just wouldn't show up.

Nathan and I got the fire going before anyone arrived. I did love the sight of a big fire blazing away. The heat from it was fierce and we had to keep our distance. I loved the smell of the wood smoke. It reminded me of camping.

We moved a grill out near the fire and I lit the charcoal to get it ready for later. There was nothing better that food cooked outside. The very smell of the charcoal was making me hungry.

Nathan was in very good spirits, quite a contrast to a few days before. That sack of old clothes seemed to make him feel better about everything. I just wished I could help him more. I know it had to be tough to be poor.

My concern over Nathan had actually helped me quite a bit. I was so worried over him that I forgot to worry about myself quite so much. If I'd been alone, I'd have sunk into a pit of despair, but I didn't have time for that. I had to take care of him.

My troubles were still with me. They sure weren't going to disappear in a day, nor in a hundred days. I was reminded, however, that everyone had problems. It made me feel a little silly for wallowing in self-pity. Then again, my problems were a whole lot worse than those that most people faced. I knew there were those even worse off than me, but that didn't mean that my life wasn't a total, fucked up mess. I'd been slapped in the face with the realization that I was gay. I was the kind of boy that everyone made fun of, that everyone called names, that everyone hated. I knew I had to hide what I was, or face the consequences.

On top of all that someone knew. While I'd been hiding my homosexual thoughts from myself, someone else had seen right through me. They didn't have layers of carefully built up denial clouding their vision. They'd noted the look in my eyes as I gazed at Jon and had identified it in a flash.

The whole situation terrified me. Someone knew my most tightly held secret and they were holding it over my head. I felt so controlled and powerless. I lived in fear of what they might want from me and what I might have to do to keep them quiet. The truth was, I was willing to do just about anything to keep my secret. I wasn't naïve. I knew what happened to boys when they were outed. It didn't matter how popular I was, or how much people liked me, if I was outed it would all be over. I just couldn't stand the idea of being ostracized. I was popular and I just didn't think I could handle losing that. If my classmates found out about me, it would be a hard, fast fall. I'd go from popular to outcast over night.

The boys all showed up in Brandon's car. Mark and I went into the house to gather up some junk food and other supplies while the rest joined Nathan by the fire. I saw Mark through my new eyes, the eyes of a gay boy. He was very attractive. I'd noticed that before, of course, but I looked at him without denial clouding my vision. For the first time I could see him and admit to myself that I found him sexually attractive. Mark was sizzling hot!

Mark's dark hair and eyes made me breathe just a little faster. His well-formed torso made my breath come faster still. His hard muscles tensed and flexed with his slightest movement. Mark was toned to perfection. He was wearing a pair of sexy soccer shorts that just about drove me crazy. I was definitely in lust.

I took a deep breath and tried not to let such thoughts consume me. I was trying to take in too much, too quickly. I was like a dehydrated runner than was trying to drink too fast after a race. I had to fight my impulse to gulp. I had to take in my new world just a little at a time.

Mark and I took a couple of big trays filled with potato chips, dip, brownies, cookies, and just about everything else one could imagine out to the bonfire. I went back in for some chicken while the guys moved a big picnic table out by the grill. By the time I returned everything was set out and everyone was having a great time. I tossed the chicken on the grill and starting brushing it with barbecue sauce. I wasn't a great cook, but I was a master with grilling. My barbecued chicken was much admired, and quickly devoured on most occasions.

Everyone sat around the, fire, talking and laughing, while gulping sodas and munching on junk food. It'd grown dark, but the boys kept throwing brush on the fire and it lit up the whole area like it was day. The golden light lit our young faces, making us look like we belonged to some lost tribe. I loved the feel of companionship that was in the air. There was just something special about being with friends.

Nathan was laughing along with everyone else and was having a great time. He'd expressed some concerns about fitting in, but the guys acted like he'd been one of us all along. Nathan was a very likable boy with a great personality. I was glad he was doing so well. I wanted to draw him into my circle of friends. Nathan needed friends. He was too isolated and alone.

Taylor seemed to fit in well too. He'd only been going to our school for a few days, but he'd already joined the soccer team. That was no doubt one reason that he and Mark had become friends so quickly. Everyone seemed to like him and I could see why. He was friendly, kind, funny, and he was always smiling.

I kept watch over the chicken, dowsing flames when they got too high and brushing on just the right amount of barbecue sauce. My duties as cook didn't keep me from joining the fun, however. It was great to have a night with the boys.

Being in a crowd helped me deal with Jon. If we'd been alone together I know I'd have been very quiet and withdrawn. I just didn't know how to act around him. The realization that I was in lust and love with him fell on me like a ton of bricks. Our relationship had totally changed overnight. Jon knew nothing of that, of course, but I had a whole new world of things to deal with where he was concerned. Things could never be the same again.

In the crowd I could more or less avoid direct contact with Jon. He was just one of the group and nothing had to get too personal between us. I think he sensed something was up. I had trouble looking him in the eyes and I wouldn't even get too near him. I was so bewildered by my own thoughts about him that I just didn't know how to interact with him anymore. It was almost as if he were a different person and no longer the boy who'd been my friend for so many years.

Jon was one of the very first friends I'd made when I came to live with my Uncle Jack. It was a rough time for me. I'd just lost my parents and was starting at a new school. I don't know what I'd have done without Jon. He just kind of latched onto me and became my friend. In no time at all we were hanging out together all the time. He was the best friend I'd ever had; we were Tom and Huck.

I wondered what Huck would think of Tom if he found out what was going through his mind. How would Jon react if he found out I was in love with him? What would he do if he knew I dreamed of kissing him? What would he do if he learned of the other wild things I wanted to do with him? I shuddered to think about it. I pictured him shrinking from me in revulsion. Jon was my best friend, but I knew that friendships could end in a heartbeat over such things. Most guys just couldn't deal with it. More likely than not, Jon would retch if he knew the things that went through my mind.

I looked at all my friends laughing and joking around. Would they be my friends if they knew? What would they think if they found out I was gay? Would they suddenly make sure they never took their shirts off around me? Would they be uncomfortable if I touched them? Would they refuse to wrestle with me? Would they even want to be around me?

I had a sick feeling in the pit of my stomach that I'd be banished from my circle of friends if they ever found out about me. They were great guys, but that didn't mean anything. Gay boys were hated with a vengeance at our school. There was no worse insult than being called a fag, no greater put down. Being gay would cast me down to the very bottom of the social hierarchy. I'd be worse than nothing. I'd be *one of those.*

The smile faded from my lips. I felt like such a fake, hiding what I was from my friends. I wished that I was still hiding it from myself. That way I wouldn't have to know I was an outsider. I wouldn't have to know that those boys were only my friends because they didn't know the truth about me. I was friends with boys who could well hate me if they knew what I was. I suddenly felt like I had no friends at all.

I looked at Nathan. He was smiling and happy. It warmed my heart to see him that way. He looked up to me, admired me, but what would happen to that if he found out? Everything in my life was so uncertain. Were any of my friends really my friends, or would they become my enemies if my true self was revealed? I felt like I no longer knew any of them, or even myself. I felt like I'd lost touch with the whole world.

The more I thought about it, the more apprehensive I became. The notes in my locker filled me with terror. Whoever knew about me could expose me at will, and quite likely would. When that happened, it was all over. Someone had it within their power to destroy my life. Knowing that gave me greater anguish than I could possibly express.

I looked at my friends and wondered if the boy who knew my secret was one of them. Everyone was suspect. Would one of them suddenly turn to the others and say, "Guess what? Ethan's a fag." The very thought made me shudder.

I felt a little foolish for being so paranoid, for suspecting even my friends, but were my fears really so unreasonable? I didn't know how any of them would react if they found out I was gay. If one of them had discovered my secret, he might well not be my friend any longer. Such a person would be in a very good position to torment me. He could send me anonymous notes and sit back and watch me squirm. What better way to enjoy the full effects of my torment than to play my friend and enemy at the same time?

The suspicions in my mind took the joy out of the evening. How could I have fun with my friends if I suspected that they might turn on me? How could I laugh and joke with them when I knew that one of them could be the very person that was tormenting me?

I walked away from the circle of light and the laughter of my friends. I was overwhelmed by sadness and consumed by despair. A sob welled up in my throat and tears flowed from my eyes. I walked across a field of soybeans in the darkness, feeling as if my world was at an end.

In the dark, I could cry without anyone seeing me. In the dark, I could hide my feelings from my friends. In a way, I felt like I'd always be in darkness, always hiding my feelings, always concealing the real me. I was living with a secret that no one could know. It made me feel more isolated and alone than I thought was possible.

"Ethan, are you all right?" asked a voice in the darkness behind me. It made me jump. I didn't know anyone was near. It was Jon. He'd followed me.

I wiped my eyes on my shirtsleeve before I turned around. I tried to steady my voice before I spoke. I was not successful; it trembled, betraying me.

"I'm okay," I lied. What could I do but lie? I couldn't share my pain with him. He was my pain, at least to a large extent. I couldn't let him know what tormented me.

Jon put his hand on my shoulder and peered into my eyes. I turned away from him so he could not read the pain there.

"Ethan, something's wrong, something's very wrong. I'm your friend. Let me help you."

Those words just about made me bawl. How long would he remain my friend if he knew? How long would he care about me then? I wanted to die.

"Just leave me alone!" I snapped at him. Jon jerked back like I'd struck him. I was immediately sorry for yelling at him. It was anger he didn't deserve. I looked at him, sorry for hurting him. "Look, Jon. I appreciate you wanting to help, but you can't. Just give me a few minutes alone and I'll come back, okay? I just need some space right now."

I could tell he didn't want to leave me alone. He wanted to help. I could see the hesitation. I know that he nearly refused to leave. Then he thought better of it.

"Okay," he said quietly and walked back across the field.

I watched him disappear into the darkness, hating myself for hurting him, hating him because I loved him. I fought to rein in my emotions. I pulled myself together, slapped a fake smile on my face, and returned to the bonfire.

CHAPTER 11

Awkward Encounters

I spent the next week avoiding Jon. It had simply become too difficult to be near him. I loved him so much it hurt. The intensity of my attraction to him was almost unbearable. What I'd experienced before coming out to myself was nothing compared to what I had to endure after I'd acknowledged that I was gay. Admitting what I was opened the floodgates. It released emotions and feelings that had been pent up inside me for so long that they threatened to overwhelm me. The love I felt for Jon was so intense and powerful that it hurt. Feeling that love and knowing that what I wanted could never be was more painful than I can describe.

The physical anguish was nearly as agonizing. My longing glances at Jon were what had brought my homosexuality into the light of day, but I'd still been denying to myself that I was hot for him. The denial was gone and my desire for him was at a fever pitch. My lust was out of control. The mere sight of Jon flooded my mind with wild, erotic fantasies. The thoughts kept coming whether I wanted them or not. It was as if years of suppressed images were forcing their way in my consciousness. I must admit, many of them were enjoyable, to say the least, but I'd rather not have been so overwhelmed with them. It was just too much, too fast.

My body was in a continual state of sexual arousal. It was a state that I much enjoyed, but it was far too much of a good thing. I felt like my entire body was on fire. I couldn't even imagine the sheer mass of hormones that must have been surging through my system. I was jerking off three, four, sometimes five times a day just to relieve the tension and pressure and even that wasn't cutting it. My hyper aroused state was something I just couldn't shut off. The only time my boxers weren't tented was when I wasn't wearing them. I took the phrase "horny teenage boy" to new heights.

All this might not sound like a problem, but believe me, it was. My intense sexual needs were driving me out of my mind. They added to my other problems until I felt completely overwhelmed.

I couldn't avoid Jon entirely of course. We had gym together and usually sat together at lunch. I started showing up as late as possible for second period gym so that Jon would already be dressed and out of the locker room by the time I got there. I couldn't trust myself not to look at him and doing so was suicide. Whoever knew about my attraction to Jon had enough on me already. I wasn't going to give him more ammunition with which to destroy me.

At the end of second period, I showered and dressed in record time and then disappeared, or I waited as long as I could before entering the locker room. I did everything I could to avoid being in there with Jon, especially when he was naked. In my over aroused state I couldn't risk the least exposure to his beautiful, naked body. If I glimpsed so much as his bare chest, my manhood grew as stiff as steel. The last thing I wanted in the locker room or showers was a hard-on.

It was even more difficult to keep my distance from Jon at lunch. I tried to avoid sitting right next to him. I made sure there was at least one person between us, then I'd busy myself talking to other guys so I didn't have to talk to Jon. Some days I just skipped out on lunch all together. I couldn't converse with Jon in anything but the most generic way. A simple, "How's it going?" or "How you doing?", was about all I could manage. Even then I had trouble looking him in the eye. The thought of anything more meaningful terrified me.

I ducked our before practice conversations, too, by pretending I had to be at wrestling practice early. The last thing I wanted was to sit alone with Jon for a few minutes. At one time, that was my favorite part of the day, but not anymore. My homosexuality had stolen that pleasure from me. I felt like it had taken away my best friend.

As hard as it all was on me, I knew it was equally hard on Jon. He knew I was avoiding him and he didn't have a clue as to why I was doing it. I know it hurt his feelings and that made me feel worse than ever. I wished that I could make him understand, but I just couldn't tell him why I felt I had to avoid him. I was hurting our friendship, but I was powerless to stop what was going on. I no longer had control over my own life.

I found a letter addressed to me as I walked away from the mail box. That was unusual in itself. I normally received only junk mail and every now and then one of the wrestling or fitness magazines that I subscribed to. A knot of fear rose in my throat as I looked at the letter. The address was typed and there was no return address. It was postmarked "Verona" and was thick.

I opened the letter with unsteady hands and a small stack of Polaroid's fell out. They were all pictures of Jon. They looked like they'd been taken at Koontz Lake. Jon was shirtless in all of them, but they'd been taken from some distance away, so they weren't as clear as they could've been. There was one that was closer, taken in the bathhouse, obviously while Jon was changing. He was bent over and it showed his bare butt, as well as scrotum hanging between his legs. I stared at the photo and my cock throbbed in my jeans.

I shook my head to clear my thoughts and pulled out the letter. It was neatly typed, just like all the notes I'd received. As I read it, there was no doubt it was from the very same person.

> Hey faggot,
>
> I thought you'd enjoy these pictures. I bet the one showing Jon's ass made you hard, didn't it? I'm sure you'll be jerking over it like the little fag you are.
>
> Scared, big boy? I guess those muscles of yours aren't helping you now, are they? You think you're such a bad-ass, but you're nothing, but a fucking queer. Just keep waiting, fucker, the ax is gonna fall.

❖ ❖ ❖

I swallowed hard. First he left notes in my locker, now he was sending them to my home. What was next? The last part scared me the most. "The ax is gonna fall," filled me with dread. I almost wished he'd just get it over with. The waiting was driving me out of my mind. Even more, I wished there was some way I could stop him. If I could only find out who was sending the notes, then maybe I could convince him to keep his mouth shut. I would've been relieved if he sent a note demanding cash or somethin'. Then, I'd at least have something to work with—a place to start. As it was, I didn't know what the fuck was up. I didn't like to admit it to myself, but I was terrified right down to my toes.

I felt a little awkward around Nathan, but I think I was more at ease in his presence than I was with anyone else. His open admiration for me gave me a little boost when I needed it the most. He made me feel good about myself despite all my self-doubt. Of all my friends, he seemed the least likely to turn on me if he found out I was gay. I had no way of knowing for sure, of course, but he seemed an accepting boy. That gave me some piece of mind. If I was outed, maybe I'd have at least one friend.

Nathan had sure enjoyed the bonfire. He talked about it a lot. He really liked my friends, too. I think that was the first time that he really got to hang out with a group of guys. It was very sad. I was glad that I was able to bring something into his life. Sometimes I felt so bad for him I was ready to cry.

I wanted to include him more often, but I was a little afraid for him. I was bringing him into the group as my friend. If I was outed, the others might turn on him just as they did me. I knew that I could be setting him up for a fall that he certainly didn't need. Then again, the others could hardly dump on him for being my friend, since they were my friends, too. I just hoped that if I was found out, I wouldn't drag Nathan down with me. I hoped he wouldn't be considered guilty by association.

It was a problem I gave a lot of thought. If things did go bad, there was one thing that could save Nathan, one thing that would allow him to still be a part of my circle of friends, even if I was not. If it came to it, I'd tell him to denounce me himself. If he called me a fag in front of the others, that would distance him from me enough to save him. He wouldn't have to go down with me.

❧ ❧ ❧

"Are you mad at me?" asked Jon. I could hear the strain in his voice over the phone. I'd just come in from the fields when he called on Saturday night. It had been days since the barbecue and I'd barely spoken to him in all that time.

"No, I'm not mad."

Silence. There was awkwardness between us that hadn't been there before.

"Um, you want to do something tomorrow?" asked Jon.

"Uh, I can't. Uncle Jack needs me to help him tomorrow." I hated lying to Jon, but I just didn't want to see him. I just couldn't, not alone, not yet.

"You sure you aren't mad? You sound mad."

"No. I'm not, really. What would I have to be mad about?"

"I dunno."

"Well there, see, there's nothing for me to be mad about, so I can't be mad. I'm just busy. Uh, we can do something next weekend, okay?"

"Okay. Well, I gotta go. Bye."

"Bye, Jon."

I felt empty as I put down the receiver. Jon's voice sounded dead. I had half a mind to call him back up and say we could do something the next day after all, but I thought better of it. I had to sort a few things out before I saw Jon again. There was so much going through my head that I didn't know how to act around him anymore. I just needed time to think. I'd had a few days already, but it just wasn't enough. I needed more time.

Kim was another one that I wanted to avoid. Talk about not knowing how to act around someone. The last time we'd been alone together, we'd had sex; sex that she thought was awesome, sex that utterly repulsed me. I didn't want to touch her again. The mere thought of kissing her made me gag. Now that I'd had her, I knew she was not what I wanted, not at all. I didn't want her, or any other girl. Sex with a girl disgusted me. I couldn't help but think that the whole world was turned upside down. Most people seemed to think that sex between two guys was disgusting. I thought that sex between a guy and a girl was gross. Each to his own I guess. At least I knew what was right for me. If only it weren't such a long, hard road.

At school on Monday, I endured Kim's kiss on my cheek yet again. Ever since our night together, she'd kissed me whenever our paths crossed. I had to fight to keep from shrinking away in disgust. It wasn't so bad on the cheek, but when she slipped her tongue in my mouth it almost made me retch. At least I was safe from that at school.

I concentrated on being kind and attentive. Despite how I felt about it, we'd slept together and that came with certain obligations. I knew I couldn't keep going out with her, but it was not the time to break up with her. It just wasn't right to have sex with her, and then dump her. It was only with supreme effort that I was able to pretend I even liked her. I knew none of what had happened was really her fault, but I still felt anger toward her. I hid it as best I could.

I'd gone out with her the night before. It was unavoidable. I made sure that there wasn't the slightest opportunity for sex. We went to a movie, we ate out, and then I took her home. Kim had suggested a nice, quiet walk, but I knew that walk would end up with us naked on the grass. I didn't want any part of it, so I lied about having to be home. I'd been doing a lot of lying since I found out I was gay. My whole life had become a lie.

I think Kim sensed that there was something wrong. She created opportunities for me to kiss her that I ignored. She set up situations that would have allowed us to be alone and I sabotaged them. I was doing the exact opposite of what most boys my age would've been doing. If any of my friends had such a willing girl, they'd have been falling all over themselves to be alone with her.

The pressure was building and I was ready to snap. There was just too much going on for me to bear. Something had to give. The whole thing with Kim, and with Jon, was enough to make me crazy. Even if I didn't have those notes hanging over my head, my life would've been difficult. With them, it was almost unbearable.

❧ ❧ ❧

For the first time in more than a week, I arrived for gym at my normal time. Jon looked at me in the locker room like he was gazing at someone he didn't know. My recent behavior toward him had him baffled. I didn't have to fake anything with Jon the way I did with Kim, but it was still awkward. Admitting to myself that I loved him made me look at him in a whole new way. I just didn't know how to act around him. When we talked, it just wasn't quite the same.

I was done with avoiding him, however. I just couldn't keep it up. I'd just have to get through it all somehow. It was hard—very hard. Jon pulled off his shirt and I felt my manhood begin to throb. I seemed to have no control over my own body. I looked at Jon with love and desire in my eyes. Watching him undress made my heart race and made me feel funny all over. That had happened many times before, but now that I knew just what it meant, it was a hundred times more intense. My eyes were glued to Jon as he slipped out of his jeans and boxers. I was practically drooling.

I tore my eyes away from him. What was I doing? Was I crazy? I was doing exactly what I'd been trying not to do. All those days of avoiding

Jon were to keep me from ogling him and there I was back at it the very first thing. I was out of control. I looked around the locker room, paranoid, but no one seemed to notice. Was my tormentor even there? The fear descended upon me again. Who had sent me those notes, and why?

I was edgy. I half expected someone to jump up and point an accusing finger at me. It wasn't something I just felt in the locker room, either. I felt it everywhere. I felt like I was waiting to be struck by lightning. It wasn't a feeling I needed. I had plenty to deal with without the worry of someone accusing me of being a fag. Someone was watching, and I was terrified.

I opened my gym locker and immediately slammed it shut again. I glanced around, but no one seemed to notice. Jon was nearly dressed and so were the others. I snapped the combination lock shut and went to the restroom. I lingered until I was sure everyone was gone, then I returned to the locker room. It was empty.

I worked the combination with shaky fingers. I opened the door. Inside, the small locker was plastered with pictures torn from magazines—pictures of naked guys. They looked like they'd been ripped from a *Penthouse* or some such magazine. They'd been girls in some of the photos, but they'd been carefully ripped out to leave only the men. I quickly tore all the photos off the inside of my locker, waded them up, and buried them in the trash.

I looked for a note and, sure enough, I found one.

```
It gets worse, faggot, much
worse. My fun hasn't even
begun. Die fucker!
```

I tore the note into tiny pieces and tossed them in the trash. I dressed out for gym and tried to pretend that nothing had happened as I joined the others. I wondered which one of them had done it. Whoever it was, I wished he'd die.

❧ ❧ ❧

I set down at lunch that day with a great cloud of worry hanging over my head. Jon sat across from me. It was the first time I'd sat so near him in days. In a crowd, I felt more at ease with him and things were more like they were before. Mark sat by us, as did Taylor. Those two were *always* together. There were reasons for that: they were both sophomores and both played the same position on the soccer team. Mark had been pretty tight with Brad, the other center forward, before he moved, so I guess it wasn't unusual that he be so tight with Taylor.

There seemed to be something more there, however, at least it seemed that way to me. I almost felt that they looked at each other the way I looked at Jon, but that was crazy. Still, there was something between them. Maybe it was just friendship. I suspected more, but I also suspected I was seeing more than was there. Just because I looked at other guys like that, didn't mean that every guy was doing it. The whole world was definitely not gay.

One thing was for sure, if those two were gay, I could certainly understand the attraction. Owning up to what I was allowed me to really look around and admire the young males about me. Both Mark and Taylor were hot! Mark was a jock; all firm muscle, and he was handsome as hell. Taylor had a softer, more sensual look. He was way cute. He was almost too pretty to be a boy. His hair was blond and longer than I'd ever seen on a guy. It must have gone half way down his back. If I hadn't been so in love with Jon, I'd have fallen for Taylor in a minute; Mark too for that matter. Jon was the one I loved, however, and that made him more attractive to me than any other guy.

I looked at Jon across the table. He was chewing on some macaroni and cheese. His lips were full, his mouth beautifully shaped. I almost got lost in his face, noting all the little details that I'd forced myself to ignore before. I was so in love with him. How was it possible that I'd been able to lie to myself about that for so very long? I felt like my heart would burst. My feelings for him were that strong. I yearned to reach across the table, take his hands, and tell him how much I loved him in front of everyone. I felt a sob forming in my throat. I knew that was a dream that would never come true. I looked at Mark and Taylor again. If they were more than friends...if they were in love, I hoped they were able to express it, for I was not.

CHAPTER 12

Wrestling with Opponents and Problems

I checked my locker after school as I did everyday, and breathed a sigh of relief when no note was there. After my slip up in the locker room, I was sure I'd receive a note taunting me about it, but maybe my tormentor thought one note was enough for a day. The lack of a note hadn't removed my problem, though—someone still knew. One of the boys around me had it within his power to ruin my life. I couldn't stand anyone having that much control over me, but what could I do?

I met Jon after school for the first time since I'd started avoiding him. He was as easy going as ever and his familiar ways helped put me at ease. It felt like old times. I knew that things would never be as they used to be, but maybe I could handle being in love with Jon. Still, it was hard on me. I dreamed of holding hands, walks in the moonlight, soft kisses, and so much more. It was hard being so near Jon when what I really wanted was to hold him in my arms. He was kind of like some precious treasure in a museum, I could look, but not touch.

Oh how I wanted to touch. I ached to just hold him close. I yearned to nuzzle my nose against his neck and feel his warm breath upon me. If only Jon could love me as I loved him. Part of me wanted to throw caution to the wind and just tell him how I felt. My mind crushed that idea as soon as it formed, however. Such a risk was stupid. Not only would it not get me what I wanted, it would destroy the friendship I had with him. Better to be friends and enjoy his company, than to have nothing at all. I couldn't bear the thought of being without Jon. I grew sad and it darkened my features. Before I slipped too low, I forced my thoughts in other directions.

"You going to watch me wrestle this afternoon?"

"Sure, if I can. I'm not sure when soccer practice gets out."

"We don't start our meet until 4:30 and my match won't be up right away."

"Cool, I'll be there then."

"Uh, you want to do something this weekend, on Sunday?" I asked. It was time to stop putting my life on hold and to quit avoiding my best friend. I had no idea how I'd handle our time alone together, but I couldn't hide from Jon forever. Trying to do that would just hurt us both.

"Sure. Hey, I know what. There's something I've been wanting to do for a long time. My grandfather showed me this cave not far from here. I think I can find it again. You wanna go check it out?"

"A cave? Really?"

"Yeah."

"You're not messing with me are you?" I'd never heard of a cave in northern Indiana. I didn't even know it was possible.

"I'm serious, it's real. You'll see. So you want to go?"

"You bet I do!"

"Awesome. It's a date then."

I paused at his choice of words. Oh how I wished it was a date.

We smiled and laughed, and made fun of our teachers. It seemed that at least a little of my world was back to normal. I still felt the sting of unrequited love as I sat there with Jon. I still experienced the overwhelming sexual arousal. But we were talking once again like close friends. That meant more to me than I'd ever guessed.

* * *

I looked around the gym as I waited for my match. The notes I'd found in my locker were still hanging over my head. I was getting paranoid. Did one of the guys on my wrestling team write those notes? Was he watching me even now, just waiting to see who I was looking at? More than half the guys on my team were also in my gym class. Whoever sent me those notes could well have been right there. I tried to erase all those thoughts from my mind, but I wasn't entirely successful. Knowing it could be anyone really got to me.

I walked out to the mat for my match. Kim was in the stands yelling my name and waving. I thought about our night together, then pushed it from my mind. Jon was there too, cheering me on. I gazed at his handsome face and sighed. Nathan was also there, with his little brother, Dave. I smiled at them. I was surprised to see Nathan. I thought he would be working at the farm. I found out later that he'd made a deal with Uncle Jack to work more hours on Saturday if he could have some time off to watch me wrestle.

I shook hands with my opponent. I recognized him from the finals last year. He hadn't won, but he was tough. I didn't let that shake me, but I had an uneasy feeling, like I was being watched. I wondered again if my tormentor was keeping an eye on me even then. I tried to force such thoughts from my mind. I had to concentrate on my match. At the moment, nothing else mattered.

I'd done very well in the few matches I'd wrestled during the season so far. I'd managed to win every one of them, most with pins, but a few on points. All my hard work had really paid off. Each match and each opponent was different, however. I knew that my past victories meant nothing in my current bout.

My opponent and I took our positions for the first period of our match. Wrestling matches were always divided into three periods of two minutes each. The first period always started in the upright stance, with the wrestlers facing each other. The other two started in the referee's position, with one wrestler on his hands and knees in the defensive position and the other with his arm encircling his opponent in the offensive position. Of course, there weren't always three periods. If one wrestler successfully pinned the other the match was over.

The match started and my opponent and I circled each other. He lunged in as fast as lightning, going for a hold, but I evaded him with ease. I think that shook him up a bit. He realized that he was up against someone pretty good. I rushed at him and got a pretty fair hold on him, but couldn't take him down. It was like trying to subdue a lion. If there's one thing I loved, however, it was a challenge. I was beginning to wonder if I didn't have more of a challenge than I could handle. The blond muscle-boy I was wrestling caught me off guard and took me down. That gave him two points. Before I knew what was going on, I was on my back and the referee was on the mat to see if my shoulders were touching. I had to use all my strength to keep blondie from pinning me.

My opponent was really well built. He was pretty good looking too. That kind of threw me. His body distracted me. His biceps bulged, his pecs flexed. I felt myself getting excited. That's not what I needed. I focused the unwanted sexual energy into battling my opponent. He was tough as nails. After what seemed an eternity, I managed to twist around with my face to the mat. Despite my opponent's efforts to keep me down, I pushed myself up off the mat. Actually I pushed us both up as blondie was forcing his entire weight down upon me.

The first period ended and I was behind 0-2. I knew I had to do better if I was going to win. I didn't let blondie's lead get to me. I knew I could take him. I could still beat him on points, or by pinning him.

I started the second period in the defensive position. I waited on my hands and knees as blondie encircled my abdomen with one arm and positioned himself with one knee to the mat. I knew he'd try to force me onto my back as soon as possible. That was always the goal of course, but blondie seemed to like quick moves. His strategy was to strike lightning fast then bring his strength to bear.

The referee started us and blondie did just what I thought. I was ready for him. Instead of resisting him with every ounce of my strength like he expected, I shoved my body in the very direction he wanted me to go. He was concentrating so much force into getting me on my back he found himself overshooting the mark. He couldn't stop his own inertia. I used his strength against him to break his hold.

My opponent was on his back. I'd managed a reverse. That was good for two points so we were tied. The look on my opponent's face was one of pure disbelief. His concentration was broken. He fought me with everything he had, but I'd rattled him. In just a few moments I pinned him. His firm young body felt good trapped beneath me. What felt even better was winning. Seconds later the referee proclaimed me the victor.

I watched my teammates from the bench. They all did well with their matches. Our entire varsity team was tough. It was hard to decide who was the best among us. Steve was an awesome wrestler, with some really slick moves. Zac was fast as lightning and powerful beyond belief. Brett, Tyler, Graham, Alex, Marty, and Scott all had their own strengths. The others were really good, too. I knew I had a real talent for wrestling, but a few others on my team were every bit as good in my opinion. I think out of the entire team that Steve, Zac, Marty, and myself were probably the best. I knew my own strengths and weaknesses and I could recognize wrestling talent when I saw it. Steve, Zac, and Marty had it. The others had it, too, but those three and I had a little something extra. Still, not one of the guys on our team would've been an easy target for me. Like I said, our team was tough.

We won the meet with ease. The guy I wrestled seemed to be about the only really good wrestler on the other team. Every single one of us took his match. That was pretty rare, at least it had been on the junior varsity team. I couldn't remember any meet when we'd all won. I was pumped. We really kicked ass!

Kim ran over to me right after the meet. She brushed my sweaty hair out of my eyes and kissed me on the lips. I concentrated on not recoiling. My teammates didn't miss seeing her kiss me.

"See you in the locker room, stud-boy!" yelled Zac as he ran past. That kind of embarrassed me, especially when the other guys all yelled, "Bye, stud-muffin. Bye, hot lips," as they made their way to the lockers.

"You were awesome!" said Kim.

"Thanks." I don't mean to sound conceited, but I was pretty awesome at that meet. My opponent was tough. He probably should have whipped my ass. I was pretty proud that I'd been able to take him.

Kim's admiration made me feel like a rat. She was all excited over me and I was only waiting for the right opportunity to dump her. I felt like a traitor. She'd given herself to me and I didn't want her. My elation over my win dissipated and a cloud of doom formed over my head once again.

Nathan walked up with his little brother and congratulated me.

"Dave, this is someone I want you to meet," said Nathan. "This is my friend, Ethan."

I shook Dave's hand. He looked so much like his brother and yet, there was a pronounced difference, too. At first I couldn't figure out what it was, but then I noticed Dave's eyes. They sparkled with a happiness that I rarely noticed in Nathan's. Dave seemed a little shy, but after all, we'd just met, and he was nine years old.

"You're strong," he said, looking at my arms. I laughed.

"Hey, Nathan, I need to change, but you guys want to come home with me? I have a lot of chores to do, but we could show Dave around while I do them."

"That would be great," said Nathan. "Would you like that, Davy?"

"I sure would!" I loved Dave's enthusiasm.

"And I guess I'll see you Friday night, or before," I said to Kim.

"Call me tonight," she said.

"I will."

I didn't really want to call her at all. I didn't want to have anything to do with her. I was glad I'd be spending time with Nathan and Dave instead of her. For once I was glad I had farm work to do. It spared me from yet more uncomfortable moments with my "girlfriend".

I had to find some way to get Kim out of my life. I couldn't keep avoiding her and making up excuses. A thought crossed my mind. Even as it entered my head I felt wicked, but it might bring an end to things without me having to tell Kim I didn't like her. Before I lost the courage to act on my plan, I kissed Kim so my remaining teammates could see and ran into the locker room.

"I'll be out in a few minutes guys," I shouted to Nathan and Dave over my shoulder.

"Hey stud," said Steve as I entered. "Kim looked like she was ready to undress you out there. Is there something you haven't been sharing with your buddies?"

"Maybe," I said, then began undressing for a shower. My answer was calculated to bring on the questions I wanted my teammates to ask.

"You and Kim been doing a little wrestling of your own?" asked Marty. I smiled in such a way that the answer was clear.

"How was she? Come on, tell us."

I looked around the locker room like I didn't want to tell, but was being badgered into it.

"Nah, I can't tell."

"You'll tell. We're not letting you out of here until you talk, right guys?"

My teammates gathered around in a tight circle. I knew if I got mad they'd give it up, but I wanted them to pressure me. Everything was working out just like I hoped it would.

"Come on," said Steve, "spill it. You fucked her didn't you?"

I looked around the circle like I was embarrassed to talk about it.

"Yes."

The locker room went crazy with guys hooting and howling.

"How was she?"

"I've had better," I lied. It had to be a lie; before Kim I was a virgin.

That caused more yelling.

"I bet you banged the fuck out of her. No wonder she's so happy."

It went on from there, with crude comments and claims of prowess on the part of every guy in the room. It was typical locker room bullshit. Of course not all of it was bullshit. I really had fucked Kim.

I showered, then dressed, listening to my teammates still going on about Kim and me, and their own sex lives. I hoped the seed I'm planted would take root. With any luck at least one of those guys wouldn't be able to keep his mouth shut. When what I'd said got back to Kim, my troubles would be over, at least as far as she was concerned. I didn't feel very good about what I was doing, but I couldn't stand another minute with her. Besides, if my plan worked, it would allow her to dump me. It would be better for her to be angry than hurt.

CHAPTER 13

Nathan's Little Brother

I met Nathan and Dave outside the locker room and we all piled into Uncle Jack's old Ford. Dave was a little on the shy side, but I talked to him just like he was my age and he liked it. It wasn't long before he was talking more than his brother. Nathan smiled at me and I could tell he appreciated the attention I was giving Dave.

I could tell Nathan cared a lot for his little brother—it was something in his eyes as he looked at him and something in the way he gripped little Dave's shoulder that made it evident. I had a feeling that Nathan was more of a father to him than their real dad. It was just as obvious that Dave looked up to Nathan. The admiration he had for his older brother was plain to see in his animated features.

Dave's eyes were glued to the windows as we drove up to the farm. He was interested in everything. His excitement caused a pang of sadness in my heart. I knew Nathan's family didn't have much, and I knew that little Dave probably didn't get to go anywhere outside of school, or do anything fun. From the look on his face, you'd have thought he was visiting Disney World instead of an old farm.

We hopped out of the truck and went inside.

"I'm starving," I announced. "Let's eat something before I get to work."

I pulled out a big plate of cold fried chicken, some slaw, cooked apples, and most of a blackberry pie. There was always plenty to eat at Uncle Jack's house. I set three plates on the table and we attacked supper. Whenever Nathan or Dave slowed down I made sure to insist they eat more.

"You guys have got to help me get rid of this chicken or I'll be eating it all week!" I said.

I wasn't lying, but it was also a good way to make sure they got plenty. I was always worried about Nathan not having enough to eat. From the look of Dave, he didn't get enough either. I was always sending something home with Nathan from the over-packed backpack I took to the fields each day. I had no doubt that Nathan gave most of it to his little brother. I made a mental note to pack even more in that backpack in the future.

By the time we left the table, I knew no one was hungry. We'd gorged ourselves. Before I started to get sleepy, I ran upstairs and changed. Nathan insisted that he and Dave do the dishes. By the time I came back down, they were already done.

My main task for that evening was restacking the bales of straw and hay in the loft. It wouldn't be long before Uncle Jack would begin baling both straw and hay, so the old bales needed to be moved to the side and stacked high to make room for the new. Luckily, the evening wasn't too hot. The main reason I was stacking bales near sunset is that the loft could turn into an oven during the day.

"So how can we help?" asked Nathan as we walked toward the barn.

"You'll be sorry you asked," I said.

We entered the barn and climbed up the worn wooden ladder into the loft. It was filled with the sweet smell of hay. I loved it up there. It was like a whole other world.

It was considerably warmer in the loft than it was outside. The tin roof of the barn seemed to just suck in the heat and hold it there. It wasn't too bad, however. None of us would suffocate.

"We need to move all the bales over to the south side of the loft. Make sure to keep the straw separate from the hay.

"Sure thing," said Nathan. "Hey, Dave, give me a hand with this."

The two brothers started stacking bales together. I knew Nathan could handle the bales by himself, but it was nice the way he made his brother feel useful. Of course, he really was useful. Two guys on one bale made it a lot easier on boys their size. I started stacking bales right along beside them. I appreciated their assistance. The job would only take half as long with them helping.

"After this I need to let the cattle into the pasture, so we can take a look around there. Then, I've got a few things to do here in the barn, so we can do some exploring."

We talked all the time we were working. Dave grew at ease around me a lot faster than his brother had. He had a more outgoing personality. He seemed a lot more sheltered from the harshness of life, too. I didn't sense the same pain in him that I did in Nathan. I had no doubt that Nathan protected his little brother from a lot of things.

Stacking bales of straw and hay wasn't exactly exciting, but I enjoyed myself with the guys helping me. It made me happy to be around them. It also helped me to turn my thoughts from my troubles, and I sure had plenty of those to spare.

By the time we were finished, both Nathan and Dave were red faced. I could understand why—my arms were aching. Lifting one bale isn't too tough, but lifting several dozen can be tiring.

We walked outside and I showed Dave all the points of interest, not that there were all that many. He was excited about everything. He was fascinated by the tall stalks of corn and seemed equally interested in the wheat and soybeans. I had a feeling the only corn that boy saw came out of a can. From the way he acted, I really don't think he'd ever seen corn growing before. That seemed a bit odd. After all, we were in Indiana.

We walked to the far end of the closest pasture. I opened the gate and allowed the cattle to move into the next meadow. Dave watched them go by, fascinated. They were just cattle, but little Dave gazed on them like they were a herd of elephants. I couldn't help but smile.

There was something very special in the way that boy derived such enjoyment from simple things. It seemed like a gift God had given him. His family didn't have much, so he was given the gift of truly appreciating things that most others took for granted. I had that gift myself, although to a lesser degree. Sometimes I just came to the loft, lay back, and smelled the hay. At other times, I lay outside at night, watching the moon and stars. Sometimes all it took to make me happy was a warm sunny day. Then again, I liked rainy days too. At times I seemed to be able to find pleasure in just about anything. That had been a very valuable thing in my recent past. It may have been the only thing that kept me sane.

As the last of the cattle passed by us I closed and locked the gate. Dave looked at me and smiled. I could understand how Nathan cared for him so. He wasn't even my little brother and I felt like protecting and taking care of him. He made me wish I had a brother just like him.

I took the boys to the corn silo and we stepped inside. It was empty, but soon it would be filled to the top, more than fifty feet overhead. I'd always liked playing around inside the round structure when I was younger. There was still something rather interesting about it. Dave paced around the walls, going in an endless circle. He started running and Nathan chased him until two or three circles later he caught him and wrapped his arms around him in a hug. Those boys didn't have much, but they did have each other. Perhaps they were richer than I thought.

By the time we made our way back to the barn, it was getting dark. I turned on the lights and took care of all the small tasks I performed each evening. Dave was interested in anything and everything. He seemed the most fascinated by the chickens, however, especially a little brown and white hen. He picked her up without fear and petted her, although I'm sure it was the first live chicken he'd ever seen in his life.

"I wish we could have one of these at home," said Dave. "She would make a good pet."

It was love at first sight. I could tell that little hen meant a lot to Dave. It seemed almost silly, but he had some special attachment to it. It would've been easier to understand if it was a puppy or a kitten, but it was a cute little thing. I'd never thought of a chicken as a pet, but I guessed it wasn't such an odd idea after all. I mean, why not? Holding her sure made Dave happy and that was what was important.

"Why don't you take her home?" I said.

"You mean it?"

"Of course I mean it, she's yours."

Dave lit up, but almost immediately a sadness covered his face.

"No, I couldn't do that. It wouldn't be right to take her."

"And there's no way we'd be allowed to have a chicken for a pet," said Nathan. "Our parents would freak." That gave me a moment of pause. It was just a casual reference to his parents, but I think it was the first time I ever heard him saying anything about them.

"Well, how about I give you the chicken and you keep it here," I said. "How would you like that?"

"I can't," said Dave. "I couldn't let you just give her to me."

I could tell Dave really wanted that chicken, but couldn't bring himself to accept her as a gift.

"Well, Nathan and I could use some help tomorrow. We've got a lot of stuff to do to make up for all the time I was at the wrestling match. If you'd be willing to help out, I could pay you in chicken!"

"Would it be all right?" said Dave, looking up to this brother. His face was so animated and he was so excited over such a little thing that it made my heart melt. It had the same effect on his brother too.

"I guess that would be okay," said Nathan as he mussed his brother's hair. Dave looked at the little hen and petted her. I don't think I'd ever seen anyone so happy in all my life. I don't think I'd have been that excited over a new car.

"I guess you can have your brother bring home whatever eggs she lays," I said.

"Huh? Eggs?" said Dave.

"When you own a chicken, you also own the eggs."

"Coooooool," said Dave. You'd have thought his hen could lay golden eggs from the expression on his face.

"Thanks, Ethan", said Nathan smiling. "We'd better be getting home."

"Want me to drive you?"

"No," said Nathan quickly, there was something almost fearful in his voice. "We'll just walk. See you tomorrow."

"See you tomorrow, Nathan. You too, Dave."

"Bye, Ethan." Dave stooped and set his hen down, petting her once more. "Bye, Henrietta." It seemed his chicken already had a name.

I followed them out of the barn and watched them walk down the road. Dave was only a few years younger than me, but he made me think once more of having a son, or more precisely of not having one. Spending just a little time with him made me regret that I'd never be a father. I'd never thought that much about it before, but once I knew I'd never have a son, I started to want one. Watching Nathan look out for his little brother made me feel that something was missing from my life. I needed someone to care for. I knew Nathan's life was hard, but in a way he was very lucky. He had a great little brother. Someone to love and someone that loved him back. If I could've had a son, I wondered if he would've been like Dave. I guess I'd never know. It was just one of the things I had to deal with—it was just another part of being different.

CHAPTER 14

The Boys on the Farm

I met Kim the next day in the halls at school. I expected that she might be angry. I thought some of the guys might've been talking about what I'd said in the locker room. Either they hadn't, or it just hadn't gotten back to Kim yet. She was all smiles when her eyes met mine. Her happiness wounded me like a blow to the head. I knew it was a false happiness and that it couldn't last. I knew she was happy about something that wasn't real. I didn't love her—didn't even really like her. I was just waiting until our relationship would end. I felt like the worst kind of rat.

The day was uneventful, but something happened during lunch that brought me pain. It wasn't even anything all that big and I shouldn't have let it get to me, but I just couldn't help it.

I was sitting at the table with Nathan, Jon, Brandon, Mark, Taylor, Steve, Jeremy, Marty, and a few others. This little freshman walked by and I noticed that Marty was eyeing him with a very clear expression of distaste on his face. I wasn't the only one that noticed it.

"What's the matter with you?" said Brandon.

"That boy," said Marty. "I think he's a faggot."

"And why do you think *that* Marty?" asked Brandon in a tone that seemed to indicate he thought Marty was just a little dumb for even thinking about it.

"Ewww, a fairy," said Jeremy, before Marty had a chance to answer.

"Look at the way he walks," said Marty. "And look at how he holds his wrists."

"You're stupid, Marty," said Brandon.

"Hey, blondie, come over here," said Jeremy to the boy.

The boy looked confused, but realized Jeremy meant him. I think he was kind of intimidated by a table full of sophomores and juniors. He walked toward us cautiously, then stood there looking nervous and uncomfortable.

"What's your name, blondie?" asked Jeremy.

"Shannon."

Marty snickered at both the name and boy's soft voice. His voice was kind of feminine.

"Okay, just wanted to know," said Jeremy with a fake lisp. "Now fly on out of here."

Marty and Jeremy started laughing and so did some of the other guys. I didn't think it was one damn bit funny. Shannon's face paled as he turned away and he looked like he was ready to cry. He hadn't failed to notice Jeremy mocking him.

I was pissed. I wanted to tell both Marty and Jeremy what a couple of losers I thought they were. I wanted to go over to Shannon and tell him to just ignore them. I couldn't do it, however. I couldn't stand up for a boy that had just been accused of being gay. I was afraid that doing so would reveal what I was. I felt like I was in a wrestling match where I couldn't defend myself. All I could do is lay on the mat and let my opponent pin me. I felt impotent and weak. I was both angry and hurt at the same time.

Jeremy was still talking with a lisp and Marty had joined him.

"Come on, Marty," said Jeremy. "Let's go spend some time alone together behind the bleachers."

Both of them busted up laughing as they walked away. A lot of the guys at the table thought it was pretty funny, too. I didn't find it humorous in the least. I knew they weren't making fun of me, but it felt like it. It didn't matter that their actions weren't directed at me. The feelings I was hiding inside were exactly the same. I felt sick.

In a way, they were making fun of me. Since I'd admitted to myself that I was gay, I felt very protective of all the other gay boys in the world. I knew the pain they suffered. I knew the horrible torment that was hurled upon them by their friends and even family. None of my friends knew my secret, and yet many of them hurt me daily. Every little gay put-down cut into me, let me know that I was different, and that they considered boys like me freaks.

I shuddered to think of those that had it even worse. I'd heard about this one gay boy who thought that he had a good day if no one called him "faggot." That was pretty sad. And that wasn't as bad as it could get either—not by a long shot. I knew there were boys out there who thought they were lucky if they made it home without getting beat up. There were even a lot of boys who got kicked out by their parents when it was discovered that they liked boys. How could parents do that to their own son? How could they turn their backs on their own child just because he was gay? The problems that other gay boys faced made my own pale by comparison, and yet sometimes I didn't know if I could make it through the day. Life shouldn't have been that way for anyone.

That evening I rushed home and, as always, Nathan was already at work. I could see him in the far distance working on the fencerow. I could make out a smaller figure, too; Nathan's little brother was with him. After changing, I went straight out to them. Dave was trying to help Nathan set a post, but it was just more than he could handle. Both boys looked at me and smiled when they saw me coming.

"Hey, Dave. I have some stuff I need you to do in the barn."

He listened as I explained the tasks he needed to perform. They were the chores I did every morning and evening, more time consuming than difficult. I knew Dave could handle them all and I was sure he'd like feeding the chickens.

"And before you leave today, don't forget to get your eggs out of the refrigerator. I put them in a little bag for you. There were two today. Maybe she's even laid another one," I said. "And say 'hi' to Henrietta for me."

Dave smiled and took off for the barn. Nathan and I watched him go. There was sort of a bond between Nathan and I at that moment. I almost felt like Dave was my little brother, too. To be honest, I felt like he was my son. Something about him tugged at my heart. I found myself wanting to look out for him the way Nathan did.

Nathan and I dug out a couple more postholes before Dave returned. He was smiling from ear to ear.

"I fed the chickens and Henrietta came right up and ate out of my hand!"

Nathan and I both smiled as Dave talked on about what he'd done in the barn. That boy sure did get excited about everything.

There really wasn't much for Dave to do, but we assigned him the task of shoveling the dirt back in the hole and tamping it down once we'd set the pole in place. He seemed pleased with himself that he was earning his chicken. He really was a help too. Things went a little faster with him there. The chores he did in the barn sure saved me some time.

I was happy that evening. I let the scene with Shannon flow from my mind and just enjoyed the beautiful weather and the companionship of Nathan and his little brother. When I was with them, I felt a closeness that I hadn't felt before. A loneliness left me that I hadn't even realized was there. Nathan and Dave almost felt like my family. I hadn't felt anything like that since losing my mom and dad.

Nathan seemed a little happier too. He still had a pall of sadness hanging over him, but seeing his brother happy made him happy. I could tell he loved him more than anything.

After we'd worked a good long while and the shadows were lengthening, I told the boys I had something to do and left them to themselves for a bit. I walked to the house and made three big submarine sandwiches for us. I wrapped them up and put them in the backpack. I also stuffed in a bag of chips, half a dozen soft drinks, some brownies, and those little pies with the filling wrapped in a glazed pastry shell. I picked blueberry because I especially liked those. I threw in some chocolate bars, too. I knew it was more than we could eat, but I intended for the boys to take whatever was left home.

I walked back out to the fencerow and declared it break time. The boys had been hard at it and were glad to sit down and rest. The stars were coming out overhead as we arranged ourselves on the grass and began devouring supper. Nathan had remarked days before that he felt guilty for eating with me all the time. I explained that it was part of his pay, that he'd earned it. It wasn't exactly true, but it wasn't a lie either. It made him feel better anyway. I was sure glad to have him around for a few meals. Eating by myself all the time got pretty boring.

Dave talked up a storm while we ate. He was one excited little boy. I could tell he loved the farm and I told him he could come and visit any time he wanted. I was pretty sure I'd be seeing quite a lot of him and that was fine by me.

It didn't take me long to get full. I finished my sandwich, had a few chips, and ate a brownie, but that was as much as I could manage. The thought of a chocolate bar didn't even appeal to me, so I knew I'd eaten plenty. Any time I turned down chocolate, it was a sure sign I was stuffed.

I lay back and Dave starting pointing out constellations in the sky. He was much younger than I, but he sure knew a lot more about astronomy than I did. I could pick out the big and little dippers, and sometimes the seven sisters, but that was about as far as I could get. Dave pointed out constellations I'd never even heard of before. He was a sharp little guy.

By the time we finished eating, it was too dark to work. It was past quitting time anyway. We'd made some really good progress setting posts. The work seemed to go even faster with Dave around.

I pulled a grocery bag out of my pack and filled it with all that was left. I insisted Nathan take it with him as I was too lazy to put everything back up. Nathan and Dave sure wouldn't be hungry for quite a while with all that stuff. I walked them out to the road, then said goodbye before heading for the farmhouse. It had been a wonderful evening and night.

It was Friday night, date night. I dreaded it. I'd been hoping the shit would hit the fan and that Kim would dump me, but my little plan hadn't worked out yet. Perhaps it never would. I wondered if I should start coming up with a new one. Or perhaps I should just be a real dick so she wouldn't like me anymore. I didn't like the idea of mistreating Kim, however. I felt I'd already done enough to her without piling on more pain. Of course, she wasn't experiencing any pain yet; that was to come. She was as happy as could be, but she was living in an illusion.

I made up a lie about having to be home early again. That would save me from any suggested walk in the darkness, a walk that would surely lead to sex. I wanted to avoid that at all costs.

We went to a movie. I made sure we were positioned near some guys on the wrestling team and some girls that knew Kim. That way I wouldn't be expected to try much of anything. I did kiss her a couple of times, because I knew that's what she expected. I hated it. I felt like I was being a traitor to myself. I found it repulsive as well. For most of the movie, I just sat there with my arm around her and tried to pretend she wasn't there.

A few hours later the date was over. I was relieved. It really sucked that I had to waste my Friday night on a girl. Hell, I'd rather have been home doing farm work than spending time with Kim. I couldn't wait until our relationship was over.

CHAPTER 15

An Expedition Under The Earth

On Sunday, just before noon, Nathan stuck his head in my bedroom doorway.

"I'm not late, am I?"

"Nah, come in, I was just changing."

Nathan sat on my bed as I stripped down to my boxers, then pulled on some old and sturdy clothes suitable for exploring a cave. I'd invited Nathan along, after okaying it with Jon. Nathan never seemed to get to go anywhere or do anything. He was such a sad boy. I was taking it upon myself to add a little excitement and happiness to his life.

Nathan's words were awkward as he sat swinging his legs. I think my near nudity must have made him uncomfortable. As soon as I pulled on my jeans he found his tongue again and began excitedly talking about our expedition. It was good to see him so animate and happy. To hear him talking you'd have thought we were going to the moon or something.

"Hey, that was cool the way you beat that blond guy in your wrestling match the other day."

"Yeah, that's six matches I've won now. Undefeated! Yeah!" I raised my arms over my shoulders and flexed like one of those bodybuilders.

"Of course," said Nathan with a wicked gleam in his eye. "I heard he wasn't very tough. Must be true if a wimp like you could take him." Nathan was smiling from ear to ear. It was the first time he took a shot at me like that. He'd never before teased me the way most boys tease each other. He was really getting at ease around me.

I stepped quickly over to him and raised my arm like I was going to backhand him. I was instantly sorry I'd done it. Nathan flinched like I was really going to hit him. His face turned white and he actually cowered before me. He quickly recovered and nervously laughed, but the image of him shrinking from my hand in fear was burned into my mind.

We both chose to pretend we didn't notice his reaction and I wrestled him down and tickled him, demanding he recognize my prowess on the wrestling mat. He was laughing so hard he couldn't breathe before he succumbed to my demand.

"Let's go," I said.

* * *

Just a few minutes later, we'd picked up Jon and were following his directions. I expected to be driving miles out into in the country, but Jon directed me to turn off on a gravel road that was just beyond the town cemetery.

The road we were on looked like it hadn't been used in a decade. I'd been on it myself once before, but I didn't go far; there just wasn't anything there. The road was narrow and the trees grew close on either side and met overhead. It was dim in there, like a tunnel, even in the bright light of day. I imagined it was pitch black in there at night.

"Park here," said Jon, indicating a small drive that led to nothing, but must once have been a road or drive to a house. "The road turns into mud a little further on. We have to walk from here."

We were at the far edge of the graveyard, right where it met the forest. I glanced at the forlorn graves as we gathered up water bottles and extra clothing. Jon pulled out his flashlight and double-checked it. I felt like a real idiot for not remembering to bring one myself. We'd all have to rely on Jon's. I could just picture his light going out, leaving us all in utter darkness who knew how far under the earth.

I looked at the cemetery and its moss covered stones. The graveyard was ill tended at this far edge. It was the earliest section of the old burial ground. I wondered if maybe the graves were so old that even the mourners and all their descendants were dead. It gave me an odd feeling, knowing that every single person from that time was gone. It was if a whole world had disappeared into the mist. Something about the sight of those weathered tombstones made me feel lonely and desolate.

The feeling soon passed. I was with Jon and that always meant fun. Nathan seemed to be as excited as he could possibly be. Seeing him enjoy himself gave me a sense of vicarious happiness—it was fun to see him having a good time. I was glad we'd asked him along.

Jon pulled off his shirt and stuffed it into a backpack he'd pulled from the back of the truck. He pulled the straps over his shoulders. My eyes ran over his muscular chest with deep admiration—and desire. The way the straps of the backpack hugged his pecs made him look hotter than ever. Jon seemed so powerful—so sexual. I felt myself getting a little too excited. I averted my gaze when Nathan caught me ogling him. That was the only bad thing about Nathan being there, it made it harder for me to check out Jon.

We set off down the road and, sure enough, just a little further on, the road turned to dirt. It had rained the night before and the road was so muddy we chose to walk on one of the high banks on the sides. We passed the remains of old drives that led to long gone homes. Here and there were the rusted hulks of old farm machinery and abandoned appliances. I could make out foundations and scattered concrete blocks, all mostly hidden by vines and tall grass. Once I caught site of an old farm building, leaning heavily to the side, but still standing. The whole place seemed haunted. It was like an abandoned world. The silence was ominous and gave the impression it didn't want to be disturbed. I felt like we didn't belong there.

I pulled my mind from dark thoughts and enjoyed the beautiful day and the companionship of my friends. Jon spotted a strong dangling vine, ran at it, and sailed across the old road yelling like Tarzan. He looked a little like Tarzan, too, with the muscles in his arms and chest bulging as they supported the weight of his body. He tossed the vine back across and I was surprised when Nathan grabbed it and swung across as well. I was seeing a wild streak in Nathan I'd never noticed before. He was really beginning to come to life.

I nearly lost my footing as I landed and Jon and Nathan thought that was hilarious. They would have really lost it if I'd fallen on my ass in the mud. We pushed on, the road beside us growing more and more overgrown. Soon it was hard to tell it was a road at all. Once it may have been well trod, but now it was all but forgotten.

I walked behind Jon, noticing how very good he looked from that angle. He sure had a cute little butt. Jon never failed to get me excited, but on that day the mere sight of him was making me pant. I tried to control myself, but it was a losing battle. There was just something about Jon that drove me out of my head with lust.

Nathan caught me looking at Jon once again. I could read something in his eyes. I couldn't quite put my finger on what it was, but it most resembled anger, or perhaps disgust. Nathan didn't say anything, but I could tell he didn't like what he was seeing. I tried harder than ever to keep my eyes off Jon, but it seemed a task that was beyond me. We walked a short distance further, then left the remnants of the road, turning to the north. We hadn't gone very far when Jon stopped.

"We're here," he announced.

"Are you sure about that?" I asked. "I don't see anything."

We hadn't come that far away from where we'd parked. I was sure we weren't more than half a mile from the edge of the graveyard. If there was a cave there, I was sure everyone would have known about it. I'd never heard of a cave anywhere around, until Jon mentioned it.

"I'm sure," said Jon confidently. "I bet you can't find the entrance, even though it's right here."

Nathan and I looked around. All we could see was a short, rocky hillside. There was no evidence of a cave opening.

"I don't see it," said Nathan.

"Me either," I said. "Is there really a cave out here or is this some kind of gullibility test?"

"Oh, you're plenty gullible, Ethan, but there's a cave," said Jon, grinning. "Come over here."

We followed him a short distance to what looked like a just another part of the rocky hillside. Jon leaned down and moved a wide, but none too thick slab of irregular stone to the side. There was nothing but blackness beneath. It was just a small hole, like a yawning mouth, leading in, and down.

Jon took off his backpack and slipped his shirt back on. He pulled a flannel shirt and jacket out of his pack and put them on too. Nathan and I pulled out the warmer clothing we'd brought along as well. It was very uncomfortable putting on a sweatshirt in such sweltering heat. It was September, but the weather was much warmer than normal. It felt more like August.

"I'm burning up!" said Nathan.

"You won't be once we get inside," said Jon.

We edged to the side of the hole. I couldn't see anything but blackness within. It looked like it just dropped straight down, but Jon lowered himself into the hole and slowly disappeared. Nathan followed and I brought up the rear.

It was pitch black in front of me until Jon snapped on his flashlight. I saw in its light that the cave grew wider and deeper up ahead. The entrance was so small that I could barely squeeze through, but what I saw before us was roomy enough. The passage was like a narrow hallway carved out of stone.

"How'd you find this place?" asked Nathan.

"My grandfather showed it to me before he died. We didn't come in, but he showed me the entrance and told me there was a big cave inside. I remember he shined a flashlight through the entrance and I could tell it was true. He said the Indians had used it for shelter hundreds of years ago. He also said something about smugglers or robbers using it as some kind of hideout. I don't know if he was serious or not."

"How far does it go back?" I asked.

"I don't know. I've only been here a couple of times. I was by myself, so I didn't explore very far. It's kind of scary in here alone."

I could see what Jon meant. It was kind of scary with the three of us, especially after what Jon had said about smugglers and robbers, not that I thought any of them lingered after all that time.

"You're the first guys I've ever brought here. I don't think my grandfather even showed it to my dad. I don't know if anyone else knows about this place." Jon paused for a few moments. "It would be a good place for a murder." Jon laughed evilly as if he'd lured us into a trap, then smiled. Even his smile looked eerie in the dim light. Sometimes Jon had a dark sense of humor. His voice alone could scare the crap out of me at times.

We walked slowly on. The cave was fairly dry, but I could hear a faint "drip, drip" now and then and the walls were damp in places. The passage turned and I figured we were more or less headed back towards where we'd parked the truck.

"Here, this is as far as I've been," said Jon.

There were two passages before us. We debated, then decided to take the one that led more or less straight ahead. Before proceeding, Jon took off his backpack again and pulled out a huge spool of nylon fishing line. He tied one end securely to a large rock and handed me the spool.

"Here, keep unrolling this as we go. We don't want to get lost in here."

The spool of line comforted me. I was wondering how we'd find our way back if there were many passages, or even if we just got turned around in the cave. I could picture us wandering around until the batteries died in Jon's flashlight. Then we'd be stumbling in darkness until we fell into some dark hole or died from lack of food and water.

Jon led us on. The passage had been like a featureless tunnel up to that point, but soon I noted stalactites hanging down from above and stalagmites growing up toward the ceiling. The passage was looking more and more like a cave as I understood it. It also grew damper as we went on, and down. The floor continually sloped and I knew we were walking deeper and deeper under the earth.

"Look at that," said Jon as he shined his flashlight to the roof. There, about fifteen feet above our heads was a little bat hanging upside down. It seemed unaware of our presence, but it moved enough that we could tell it was alive.

"Wicked!" said Nathan and his voice echoed in the darkness.

I could see Nathan's face in the dim light. He seemed enchanted by the cave. I could understand his awe. It was the coolest place I'd ever been, and to think it was right there, so close by, all the time. It was right under my nose, so to speak, and I never knew it existed.

Speaking of cool, the temperature was far lower in the cave than it was outside. It had to be eighty up above, but I'd say the temperature was about fifty or sixty in the cave. I was glad I had my sweatshirt on. After the heat of the day outside, the cave felt downright cold.

"Watch this," said Jon and snapped off his flashlight. "Have you ever seen anything as dark as this?"

It was the first time I'd experienced real darkness. At night, there was always the light of the moon and stars. Even if clouds obscured them, they still cast light. There was also the light of the farm, from the house and barn and outside lights. Even the darkness at the entrance to the cave couldn't compare to it. At the entrance, light filtered in from above. Deep in the cave, there was no light at all. I tried flapping my hand right in front of my eyes and could see nothing. I'd never experienced anything like it before.

"It's just like I said," Jon whispered quietly in my ear "this would be a great place for a murder. I could be pulling out a knife right now and you'd never know it, you'd never see it coming." He laughed evilly once again. He was so close I could feel his hot breath on my neck. I knew he was just kidding around. Well, I was pretty sure. He did frighten me, however. I thought about the notes. What if Jon was the one sending them? What if he knew I was desperate for his body? What if he'd lured me to the cave to kill me?

Jon yelled and jabbed my back with his hand. I screamed, thinking for a second that he'd stabbed me, that he really was going to murder me. Jon turned his flashlight back on and the light rushed in. I looked down at my chest as if expecting to see my clothing soaked with blood. My heart was beating so fast I thought it would burst. Jon laughed his head off, so did Nathan.

"I got you that time," he said when he could stop laughing long enough to get the words out.

"You little bitch!" I said with a smile. "Don't do that! You scared the shit out of me."

That just made him laugh more of course. I couldn't help but laugh myself. I had to admit, it was pretty clever. My heart rate slowly returned to normal. I should've known Jon would pull something like that. He was always up to something.

When Jon and Nathan were done laughing at my expense, we slowly continued on. We were in no hurry. There was too much to look at to be in a hurry. Everywhere our eyes turned there was something new to discover. Each rock formation was different, having grown over the centuries. It was hard to believe that the slow drip of water had created all that was before us. It was almost beyond imagining that such wondrous stalactites and stalagmites had formed over hundreds and hundreds of years. I wondered just how old the caves were, and who had been there in the past. I thought of the Native Americans that Jon had mentioned. I didn't doubt that they would have made use of the cave had they known of its existence. I kind of doubted that robbers and smugglers had been there, but who knew?

I looked at Jon's face in the dim light as we walked. He was beautiful, so beautiful it made me heart ache. For a moment I was lost in a fantasy. I pictured myself pulling Jon to me and kissing him right there in the cave. I could taste his sweet lips, feel them pressing against my own. It was wonderful.

I had to snap myself out of my daydream. Nathan was looking at me again and I know he'd noticed I was gazing at Jon. I knew how stupid and reckless I was being, but I still couldn't seem to stop myself. Where Jon was concerned, I had no self-control.

Jon screamed loudly and jumped back, colliding with Nathan and me, nearly knocking me on my ass. I was so startled and frightened that I practically pissed my pants. My heart was pounding in my chest, just as it had when I thought Jon had stabbed me. I was sure I'd turned as white as a sheet, not that anyone could see. Jon's scream echoed throughout the cave, adding to my fear.

Nathan and I edged forward to see what had so terrified Jon. He was standing just before us, looking just a little off to the right.

"Holy shit!" said Nathan.

Nathan and I drew a little closer and the three of us huddled together looking at Jon's discovery. There, not five feet away, was a human corpse. It was old, but it wasn't just a skeleton. Flesh still covered the bones and the remnants of clothing were still draped over the body. It looked a lot like the pictures I'd seen of Egyptian mummies, but better preserved.

Jon ran his light slowly over the corpse. It was lying partially on its side, halfway out of a broken coffin. The lid lay in pieces, but the rest of the coffin was easy enough to make out. It was a plain wooden coffin like they used a hundred and more years before. Our eyes moved upward as Jon shined his light on the roof of the cave. There was a section where the ceiling had given way and the earth had fallen through. There wasn't much to see, but it was obvious how the corpse and its coffin had come to rest in the cave. I was just glad it had fallen long ago and hadn't dropped down near us as we walked past. I think I'd have died of terror if that had happened. I was still pretty scared as it was.

I guess I'd been right about the cave leading back in the direction of the graveyard. We must have been right under it. It was creepy thinking about all the graves that must be overhead, hundreds of them. I just hoped no one else would be dropping in while we were there.

Jon turned the light back on the corpse. The face looked back at us with only hollows where there should've been eyes. The light brown hair was still there, however, looking dried out, but otherwise like the dead man had just been buried. It was obvious that the corpse was that of a male. It was well enough preserved for us to tell that even without the suit he was buried in.

"I wonder who he was?" said Jon.

I was half afraid the corpse would rise and tell us.

"Let's get out of here," said Nathan. His voice was high pitched and shaky. He was clearly very frightened. I didn't blame him, my heart was still thudding wildly.

"Ah, come on, Nathan, let's go on and see what else we can find," said Jon. "This guy isn't going to hurt us. Of course, if you really want to turn back..."

Nathan looked at me. I'm sure he could read a little fear on my face, but also curiosity. I wanted to find out what other secrets that old cave might harbor.

"Okay, let's go on," he said. I could tell Nathan was scared out of his wits and I could tell he wanted to act brave in front of me. Nathan seemed so young. It was hard to believe he was almost the same age as me.

We walked on and on, deeper into the cave. I was amazed that all this was right under the town and no one seemed to know about it. I didn't even think there were supposed to be caves in northern Indiana. I'd been to the Marengo and Wyandotte Caves in the southern part of the state, but I'd never even heard of one this far north.

After a good long while Jon stopped at the edge of a wide shallow pool. It was only about half a foot deep but it was about fifteen feet wide and twenty long. The surface was perfectly still and reflected the roof above like a mirror. I drew close to Jon and we leaned over, looking at our own reflections. I put my arm around Jon's shoulders without even thinking about it. I didn't even realize I'd done it until I noticed it in the reflection of the pool. Jon didn't seem to notice it either.

Jon and I drew closer and closer as we peered into the pool. Our faces were practically touching. I turned to Jon and he looked at me. I wanted more than anything to press my lips to his. I was so consumed with desire for him that I nearly did just that. I caught Nathan's reflection in the water. He was looking at me, at my arm around Jon, and at my lips that were mere inches from Jon's. He had a queer look on his face that I could not read. I could tell, however, that he didn't like what he was seeing. I slowly pulled away from Jon, trying to make it look like I hadn't been thinking about kissing him.

Nathan probably saved me just then. If he hadn't been there, I think I would've kissed Jon. I didn't want to reveal myself for what I was, but the desire to kiss him was overpowering. For a few fleeting moments I was willing to throw away everything for a single kiss. Those moments had passed and I was glad that Nathan had stopped me. I just wondered what I should say to him about it. I decided to say nothing, unless he cornered me on it.

"I think my batteries are getting weak. Maybe we'd better start back," said Jon.

Nathan and I agreed. Neither of us cared much for the idea of being in those caves with no light.

We headed back the way we came. I slowly wound in the fishing line I'd been letting out, but I don't think we would've had any trouble finding our way back even without it. After the first branch, the cave had been one long twisting and turning passage. Of course, we hadn't explored it all the way back. Who knew what lie in the far reaches of the cavern? I hoped that I'd get a chance to find out someday.

I caught glimpses of Nathan looking at Jon now and then. He didn't look at him in the same way I did. Nathan had something quite different on his mind. He looked for all the world like he disliked Jon, but I couldn't think of a single reason why he wouldn't like him. Jon had never been anything but kind to Nathan. They barely knew each other and nothing bad had ever passed between them. Nathan's feelings seemed as mysterious as the furthest reaches of the cave.

When we passed the corpse again, we stopped to examine it more closely. I think all of us had a morbid curiosity about it. There was just something fascinating about the long dead man and his broken coffin. It was kind of eerie too, and spooky, but that just made it more interesting. We gazed at him for a few long moments, then went on. It wasn't long before we were back at the entrance. It only seemed to take half as long going back as it had coming in.

As we climbed out of the tiny opening, the heat hit us like a wave. It was unbearably hot after the coolness of the cave. We wasted no time in stripping off our jackets, sweat shirts, and shirts. Once again I admired the beauty of Jon's torso and once again Nathan noticed me looking at Jon. He didn't like me looking at him—not at all. He didn't say a word about it, but I got the message as surely as if he'd shouted it to me. I averted my eyes and tried to control myself.

Jon and I laughed and talked on the short walk back. I was more at ease around him than I had been. It was hard dealing with the feelings I had for him, but I didn't want to let those emotions interfere with our friendship. At first I'd avoided him, because I just didn't know how to act around him. Doing so only served to hurt me, however, and Jon. I'd never do that again.

I was slowly finding out that I could act as I always had with Jon. After all, he didn't know I was in love with him. He didn't know the mere sight of him filled me with overpowering desire. There was no reason for things to be any different between us. I just had to keep my feelings hidden from Jon, as I'd kept them hidden from myself.

Nathan was a bit out of sorts, but Jon and I drew him out by joking with him. He seemed to resist Jon's humor, like he didn't want to be cheered up by him, but it wasn't long before he brightened up again. I tried my best to keep Nathan from feeling like he was a third wheel. I know my attentions naturally flowed to Jon when he was around, but I made a real effort to make Nathan a part of things. I wanted him to be happy, he deserved it.

CHAPTER 16

Hell to Pay

On Monday, Kim was giving me the cold shoulder. She didn't talk to me in the halls between classes the way she always did. When my eyes met hers she seemed hurt and angry. I had the feeling my plan for ridding myself of her was working, but I didn't feel very good about it. I was glad it seemed to be succeeding, but I wasn't too proud of myself for the method I was using. I should've taken my time and come up with something better, something that wouldn't have started the whole school whispering about Kim and me. I should've thought more about her than myself. Instead, I'd latched on to the first idea that popped into my head.

I'd acted rashly in my desperation to get rid of her. The mere thought of what I'd done with her made me sick to my stomach. I had to fight to keep from being angry with her over the whole thing. She didn't deserve my anger. All she was guilty of was letting me do what I wanted. It was my fault, not hers. I still had trouble controlling my emotions. I felt like she'd stolen my virginity. I felt like I'd been raped. I knew neither of those things were true, but that didn't stop me from feeling that way.

Kim didn't speak to me the entire day. The few times I saw her, she looked too angry to talk to me. I wasn't looking forward to dealing with her. I half wished that she'd go ahead and lay into me and get it over with. I knew what was coming and I knew it would not be pleasant. Kim didn't confront me, however, she just avoided me. I could feel her anger, like a wave of white heat, whenever she was near.

The boys made lots of crude comments in the locker room before and after wrestling practice. Everyone seemed to have the need to comment on me banging Kim. It'd been that way since I'd admitted I'd fucked her. I actually didn't mind that. I'd moved up a notch in everyone's eyes. I'd laid a girl so that made me cool, at least in the eyes of my teammates. I enjoyed the attention.

Kim was waiting for me in the gym as I walked out of the locker room after practice. The moment I'd been dreading had come. It was time to pay for my popularity with the boys. It was evident that Kim was not happy at all. The others guys noticed as quickly as I did.

"I don't think I'd want to be in your shoes just now," Steve said quietly as he and the rest of my teammates abandoned me to my fate. I knew they'd all be watching whatever was about to happen.

I walked toward Kim, afraid. It's not that I thought she was going to hurt me, although a swift kick in the nuts wouldn't have surprised me too much. I was afraid of the whole confrontation, mainly because I was at fault.

"You're just like all of them, aren't you?" she asked.

"What?" I said, kind of confused.

"You just can't keep from bragging. You had to go and tell all your buddies about what you did with me, didn't you?"

"Hey, I just said..."

"You just told them everything! Didn't you?"

"Kim, listen, you didn't exactly say I couldn't tell anyone."

"Did I have to say that? I thought you'd be smart enough to know I didn't want my sex life announced over the school loudspeakers. Or are you such a big, dumb jock that you can't figure that out?" She emphasized each word by poking me hard in the chest.

I had an instinct to placate her, to say things that would calm her down, to tell her I was sorry. That would defeat my purpose, however. If I followed my instincts, all the trouble I'd caused Kim, and myself, would be for nothing. I ignored my instincts and did my best to be a real ass.

"Listen babe, you know you liked it. You know you want it again. So what if I told a few of the guys. Hell, everyone knows you fuck around, so what's the big deal? It's not like half the guys on the team haven't fucked you anyway. Come on, Kim, I'll take you for a little drive and we can have some more fun."

I felt like a total creep saying all that. I wasn't the kind of guy who said that kind of bullshit. I needed Kim to think I was, however, and she did.

"You are the only guy on the wrestling team I've ever dated and you know it! And as for what we did, you weren't that great, Ethan. Don't flatter yourself."

"You said I was the best you'd ever had," I shot back.

"What did you think I was going to say? That was nice, but Bobby's a lot better?" She rolled her eyes. "You want the truth, Ethan? Do you? The truth is you're lousy in bed! And I'll tell you something else! I've always heard that muscular guys like you build themselves up to compensate for a small dick—and after seeing yours, I know it's true!"

I was silent for a moment. I knew some of my buddies could overhear and Kim was embarrassing me. I forced myself to go on with it.

"Come on Kim. You're just angry. You *know* I'm not small. Let's go somewhere private and I'll make it up to you. I'll give you what you need, baby."

"I don't need you, your ego, or your big mouth, Ethan! I can replace you with any guy in this gym," said Kim.

"And I bet you will."

"Bastard."

"Slut."

"Fuck you, Ethan!"

With that she was gone and out of my life. I looked around embarrassed and it wasn't an act. A lot of my teammates had witnessed the whole thing. I could tell they were kind of shocked because not one of them said anything to me about it. I think I might have felt better if they had cut me down over losing my girlfriend and over her comments about my sexual performance. Their silence cut into me more than any taunt they could have hurled at me.

I wasn't happy at all about Kim saying I had a small dick. Things like that could get around. The guys who'd seen me in the showers knew it wasn't true, however. I was bigger than most of them. The girls had no way of knowing how I was hung, but I guess that didn't matter since I wasn't interested in them anyway. Still, if word started going around that I had a small cock, it wouldn't be fun. I might even get a nasty nickname out of it. I sure as hell didn't want to go through life being called "little dick" or something like that.

I left the gym and drove home. What an embarrassing experience. Damn, she'd really let me have it. At least Kim was no longer a problem. I felt like a real ass over the whole thing, but at least I didn't have to touch her again.

CHAPTER 17

Trouble for Nathan

Having Kim out of my life was a relief. The anxiety I felt every time we went out, or even when I just met her in the halls at school, was almost overpowering. I can't say that I didn't enjoy myself with her now and then; parts of our relationship had been fun, but I was glad it was over. The bad had always outweighed the good.

I wished I could rid myself of the mysterious note writer with as much ease. He didn't strike very often, but he didn't need to. I knew he was out there—watching me, waiting. Not knowing who he was, or what kind of game he was playing, preyed on my mind. Receiving anonymous notes was far more frightening than having someone come up and accuse me to my face. I was constantly wondering just how much he knew, or guessed. I felt like I was fighting an invisible foe. He could be standing right next to me and I'd never know. Someone was watching and I didn't like it one bit. When I arrived at school the morning after Kim had dumped me, there was another note waiting on me in my locker.

```
Your girl dumped you, huh? No
surprise there. Your camouflage
is gone now.

Wear a wife-beater to school
tomorrow, or I'll start to spread
rumors. You wouldn't want anyone
to know you like cock, would you,
faggot?
```

I slammed my fist into the locker, making those around me jump. I crumpled the note into a tight ball and stuffed it in my pocket. The fucker was actually telling me what to wear to school now. I wanted to tear him limb from limb, but how could I fight someone I couldn't even see? Even if I knew his identity, he held all the cards. I was screwed.

Still, I had to find out who was doing this to me. I couldn't stand not knowing. As I sat in classes that day, I made up a list of suspects. Unfortunately, that list was merely a roster of the boys in my PE class. I couldn't eliminate a single suspect. It could've been any of them. There were certainly some that I felt like crossing off. There were guys in there that I was sure wouldn't have sent me those notes. Then again, I couldn't think of a single one of the boys who would have sent them, so I left all the names on the list. I think I would've felt better if I could have narrowed down my list of suspects even a little. Every name I could cross off would take me one step closer to identifying my tormentor, but I was unable to take a single step in that direction. I was no Sherlock Holmes.

I was thinking yet again about my suspects as I performed my chores in the barn after wrestling practice. I was so focused on the problem that I couldn't even remember having cleaned out the stalls. They were clean, however, so I must have done it. I hated that I let my tormentor get to me that much. That's probably just what he wanted, to keep me guessing and worrying. I tried to push the whole thing out of my mind, but it wasn't easy. I succeeded for a while now and then, but my paranoid thoughts always came back.

I walked out to the fencerow to find Nathan hard at it. The posts were all set, but there was still the task of putting up the actual fence. We'd barely started on that task. Nathan was struggling with a large roll of fencing, trying to unroll it to the next post so he could attach it. It was really a job for two people, but Nathan was straining his guts out to do it all by himself. I noted that the fencing was attached to four more posts than it had been the day before. Nathan hadn't done bad all by himself.

I grabbed the fencing and helped Nathan to unroll it. I stopped almost before I started, however. Nathan was doing his best to keep his face turned from me, but I still got a glimpse of what he was hiding.

"What happened to you?" I asked, taking him by the chin and pulling him in my direction. His eyes darted about nervously.

"Oh this," he said, like he didn't realize at first I was talking about his black eye. "I hit my face against that pole down there a little while ago. I slipped." He swallowed hard.

Nathan wasn't a good actor and he wasn't a very good liar. His face wouldn't have shown a bruise like that after such a short time. He hadn't smacked his face against a pole either. Someone had hit him.

"Did one of the boys at school hit you?" I asked.

"No." I could tell Nathan was getting edgy.

"Then who hit you?"

"Let's just drop it, okay? I told you I hit my face."

Nathan was frightened. He almost looked like he was ready to cry. I hesitated. I thought it best that I find out who'd done it to him, but it was clear he wasn't going to tell me anything. If I badgered him, he'd just get angry. I'd just bring him more pain. I decided not to press him. Doing so would not do any good.

"Just be careful around that pole," I said.

"I will."

"Maybe this is something you shouldn't handle alone. When you're ready, I hope you'll let me help you, Nathan."

Nathan bit his lower lip and nodded his head. I hoped he understood what I meant. I hoped he knew I wasn't talking about putting up fencing. I hoped he'd come to me for help when he forced himself to talk about it.

We both put our backs into it and unrolled the fencing to the next pole. I held it in place while Nathan hammered in the pointed hooks. It wasn't an easy job. I don't know how Nathan had handled it himself. I had a feeling, however, that Nathan was accustomed to handling quite a lot all by himself.

Nathan seemed more at ease when we left the topic of his black eye behind. He asked me about wrestling practice, as he always did, and I talked about it at length, as I usually did. Nathan seemed full of questions and was so genuinely interested in what I had to say that I found myself talking on and on. I told him about pretty much everything going on in my life (except the notes in my locker and my love for Jon, of course). Nathan was so easy to talk to that I felt I could really open up to him. I even discussed things with him I never would've with another guy, nothing monumental, but things about my feelings and beliefs. I'd grown comfortable around Nathan. He'd become a good friend.

Nathan talked about little and did not share as much of himself as I did. I think he was embarrassed about his life at home. He'd only talked once about being poor, that day we burned his old clothes and I gave him new ones, but I knew it bothered him. I'd learned what not to talk about and what not to ask him. Sometimes I felt I was stepping around Nathan on tiptoes. I did my best to respect his privacy. After all, I had things I didn't want to share either. He was a good friend in any case and I enjoyed his company.

I did worry about Nathan getting enough to eat, and his little brother, too. I know he would have died before admitting he was hungry, but I could read it in his eyes. His underweight body and slightly hollowed cheeks spoke volumes. Nathan didn't have an ounce of fat on him. I always made sure I brought plenty of stuff to eat when I came out to work with him. I also made sure there was plenty for him to take when he went home, plenty for both him and his brother. I couldn't bear the thought of either one of them being hungry.

CHAPTER 18

Cute Boys at the Water Park

I walked into school wearing a white tank top. I absolutely loathed having to wear it. I'm come real close to just saying, "fuck it," but in the end I couldn't do that. If I'd suspected my tormentor was bluffing, I'd have called him on it and refused, but I knew in my heart he was dead serious. I couldn't afford rumors. I was in enough danger as it was. It pissed me off to be controlled. It was nearly unbearable. Only one person knew how I was being dominated, but that was humiliating enough. I felt like my shirt had "I'm a pathetic loser" written on it.

I feared what was to come. I was knuckling under to my blackmailer. It was a sure sign of weakness. If he didn't already, he'd know he had me by the balls as soon as he saw me wearing the shirt. I wanted to just rip it off, but I knew I couldn't do that. I was so frustrated I could've screamed.

Word had spread throughout the school that Kim had dumped me. A few people knew about it the day after it happened, but pretty much everyone knew now. I was rather embarrassed about being dumped, even though I was the one who had engineered it. I was glad that I had the balls to chose that path and endure the rejection. I could've taken the easy way out and dumped Kim instead, but I'd caused her enough pain. I wasn't about to add to it by hurting her feelings as well. I'm sure the way I acted did hurt her feelings, but she'd have been even more hurt if I'd have dumped her. The break up was pretty messy, but it was the best I could do. It was better that Kim think I was jerk. Ending things with a jerk was surely a lot easier on her than ending things with a nice guy. She wouldn't be missing me; she'd be glad she was rid of me. Getting dumped did have one advantage. It preserved the illusion that I was interested in girls.

Jon was worried about the break up. He thought it would get me down. I could tell he was making a special effort to keep my spirits up. I did need cheering up, but it didn't have anything to do with Kim. I had my regrets, but that was over. The notes were dragging me down. Being controlled like a trained animal was depressing and frustrating me. I couldn't stand the fact that someone could tell me what to do. It was even worse than that—my tormentor had it within his power to ruin my life at will. I felt like I was constantly waiting for the ax to fall.

Jon joked and laughed as we sat together at lunch. He acted crazier than ever and I know most of it was for my benefit. Everyone seemed in a pretty good mood. The whole usual crowd was there.

"Hey, Ethan, want to go to the water park on Sunday?" asked Jon. "It might be our last chance."

Jon was right about it being our last chance. September had turned to October and cold weather was on the way. A recent heat wave had made for a very warm fall so far, but it couldn't possibly hold much longer. Soon it would be way too cool to swim.

"Sure," I said. I loved swimming and Jon knew it. I especially loved the big water park that was about an hours drive to the west. It had some kick-ass slides. I especially loved the one called *The Cyclone* that was enclosed and looped around like crazy. That one always made me feel like I was going about a hundred miles an hour. My mind was suddenly filled with thoughts of all the different slides. I loved that place. I could have lived there! Jon knew just how to cheer me up.

Before the end of the day, Jon had invited Brandon, Mark, and Taylor as well. The whole gang would be going. Jon had managed to completely change my mood.

❧ ❧ ❧

That evening I walked out to join Nathan, carrying my pack as usual. This time I had something extra in it.

"Hey, you want to come to a water park with me and the guys on Sunday?" I asked him as we worked. "Dave can come, too."

Nathan hesitated. I could tell he wanted to go, but I could also tell that something held him back. I knew just what it was and I'd taken care of it in advance.

"Here," I said, pulling a package out of my pack, "I got you something after practice."

Nathan looked at the package, then at me.

"Call it an early birthday present," I said. "I'll pay for you guys to get in, too. I *really* want you to go with me."

Nathan opened it up and took out a pair of dark blue swim trunks. He smiled at me.

"I'd love to go!" he said.

I pulled another pair of swim trunks out of the pack, a pair that were red and somewhat smaller.

"Here, these are for Dave."

"Thanks," said Nathan. "He'll love these."

Nathan seemed to grow a little sad, despite his excitement over our planned outing.

"You can't keep giving us stuff," he said. "It's too much and I don't have anything to give you."

"It's not too much," I said. "And you give me something every day. You're always nice to me. You listen to me. You make me laugh. You're a good friend. That's worth a whole lot more than a pair of swim trunks."

Nathan smiled. I loved to see him smile. I just wished he could do it more often.

"Um, what's at this water park anyway? I've never been to one."

I started in on an hour-long description of the park while we worked. Nathan probably got a lot more information than he wanted, but he didn't seem to mind.

* * *

Nathan and Dave showed up at the house about mid-morning on Sunday. I was already in my swimsuit, a bright blue pair that looked pretty good with my white shirt. The boys went up to my room to change into theirs while I fixed us some sandwiches for lunch. Uncle Jack came in from the fields and he joined us when we all sat down to eat.

I was every so slightly nervous about Jack, his manner could be brusque. I soon learned I had nothing to worry about. He was as nice as could be. I could tell he really liked Nathan, and Dave, too. Before we were done eating he'd promised Dave he could ride in the combine during harvesting in the fall. That surprised me. I'd never really thought Jack was the kind that would take to kids. He'd always been kind to me, however. I guess I'd never seen him around a kid to really know if he liked them or not. I was glad he got on so well with Dave.

Little Dave sure liked Uncle Jack. I think he kind of thought of him like a grandfather. He asked him lots of questions about farming and listened intently while his bright little eyes sparkled.

"Want to see my chicken?" asked Dave.

"I sure do," said Jack.

"Just remember, we have to leave soon, Dave," I told him. Jon was soon due to pick us up.

"I'll be back in just a sec!"

Dave grabbed Uncle Jack's hand and led him out the door. There was a smile on the old man's face. I could tell he had some of the same paternal feelings for little Dave as I did. That boy was just so likable.

Just a few minutes later all three of us piled into Jon's car. It was pretty crowded as there were seven of us all together. In addition to Jon, Nathan, Dave, and myself, Mark, Taylor, and Brandon were along for the ride, too. Dave ended up riding on Nathan's lap. No one minded that it was a bit of a squeeze. It was a blast.

When we got to the water park, both Nathan and Dave looked totally overwhelmed. I was sure they'd never been to anything like it before. I'd been pretty impressed my first time too. There were water slides there over four stories tall, a huge wave pool, food booths, games, and all kinds of stuff. It was a water-theme amusement park that just seemed to go on and on forever.

We all hung out in one big group for a while, going from slide to slide. Dave's favorite was one called *The Abyss*. It was a really tall enclosed slide that dropped almost straight down until it looped up at the end shooting us all flying through the air until we splashed to a stop in the pool below. I went down it with Dave in a little raft and got tossed off at the end. It was fantastic.

The day was fine and warm, but not hot. One really cool thing was that the park wasn't crowded at all. In the summer it could be packed, but on that day there was practically no wait at any of the slides.

I was having an awesome time; all of us were. I couldn't even remember having so much fun. There was some pretty good scenery at the park. Cute, shirtless guys surrounded me. That was kind of a dream come true in itself. My eyes were always spotting some new boy with a nice chest. It was my kind of park!

After a while we split up into little groups and went our separate ways. Mark and Taylor took off together, Brandon and Jon did, too. I stuck with Nathan and Dave most of the time, but switched off to join the others now and then. We all kept meeting up over and over, so it didn't really matter who was with who.

I went off to myself for quite a while, as well. I kept riding on *The Hurricane* over and over. It was a really intense slide, but what I liked about it most was the boy working there. Each slide had an attendant that told everyone when they could go, so there wouldn't be any collisions on the slide. The boy doing that for *The Hurricane* was way cute. He had a gorgeous chest, well-defined abs, and beautiful blond hair. I couldn't keep from looking at him. I didn't really try all that much. Almost no one knew me at the water park, so I could be a little freer checking out other guys. I definitely enjoyed boy-watching, especially the young hunk at *The Hurricane.*

He noticed me looking at him and that I kept appearing over and over. The way he smiled at me, and the way he looked at me, made me feel like he just might be checking me out too. I wasn't sure of course, but I had a feeling that he was into boys just like I was. That possibility made my heart race. I had to readjust my swimsuit because it was getting a little confining. The cute blond boy didn't fail to notice that. I caught him looking at my bulge and he grinned at me.

I almost worked up the courage to approach him and talk, but I couldn't quite do it. I was drawn to him, but going up to him was just more than I could handle. We flirted with each other as I rode his slide over and over, but that's as far as it went. I didn't have the courage for more. Even after I left the water park, I thought about him for days and days. I regretted not having talked to him. It was a rare chance to talk to another gay boy, and a real cute one at that. I kept thinking about him, wondering what might have been.

❧ ❧ ❧

The entire gang met at the picnic area at about two. I was supplying the food and I'd brought along quite a stash. There were bags of chips, all kinds of junk-food, snacks, cookies, soft drinks, sandwiches and just about anything else one could imagine. We all pigged out and then lay around sunning.

After a short rest we started wrestling and goofing around. I must admit that watching my friends wrestling shirtless on the grass was more than a little exciting for me. Seeing their muscles bulge as they grappled with one another was quite an erotic sight. I was already aroused by the hot boy on *The Hurricane* and watching my friends wrestle turned up the heat.

Mark started getting cocky after pinning Jon and then Brandon. It was funny to watch him jumping around holding his hands over his head acting like he was the master of the universe. He looked pretty damned hot too.

"Yeah! I can take anyone!" he yelled.

"You think so?" I said.

"Yeah, punk! I can even take you!"

"You're full of shit, Mark. You and Taylor together couldn't pin me."

"Oh, I smell a challenge," said Jon.

Mark and I stood there eyeing each other. It was all friendly, but we were calling each other out.

"Okay, tough boy," said Mark. "If you think you're man enough, it's you against Tay and me."

"All right," I said. "You guys have five minutes to pin me."

"We'll only need two, won't we, Taylor?"

Taylor just smiled and nodded.

Brandon set the timer on his watch.

"All right, go!" he said.

Mark and Taylor faced off against me. We circled. I was a far better wrestler for sure. They weren't even wrestlers, they were soccer players. There were two of them, however. Two on one was never easy, in anything. Mark was pretty strong too, and Taylor was no weakling. I knew it would be a tough contest, but that was fine by me.

Mark rushed in. I prevented him from getting the hold he wanted, but he did latch onto my arm. Taylor was on my other arm in a flash. Before they could get me down I lifted Taylor up in the air and broke his hold. I think he was kind of surprised I could lift him with one arm. It wasn't easy.

I turned on Mark and took him down. I had him on his back pretty fast. Taylor used that opportunity to attach himself and pull me off balance. Wrestling two guys at once sure made things interesting. They did their best to get me down, but they couldn't quite manage it. I broke free once more.

The guys were all yelling and cheering. They seemed to be cheering for whoever was at a disadvantage at the moment. I heard Jon shouting my name and then moments later he was urging Mark and Taylor on. I was having an awesome time and, I must admit, I was showing off for my friends. I was in my element—I was wrestling.

Taylor came in for me and it was a mistake. I wrapped my arms around his slim torso and pulled him down. I wrestled him onto his back even though Mark was trying to pull me off. I held Taylor down. In a match it would have been a pin. I didn't hold him long, however. Mark pulled me to the side and had me face down in a flash. He and Tay struggled to get me on my back, but they couldn't quite do it. All of us were laughing a little as we wrestled and that didn't help us. I for one tended to get a little weak when I laughed.

"Two minutes left!" announced Brandon.

"I knew you little weaklings couldn't handle me," I taunted.

"Oh, that's it!" said Taylor smiling.

Mark and Taylor were all over me. I tried to get up off the ground, but one or the other of them always managed to get a good hold on me. I never could quite get free. I nearly had Mark pinned, and then Taylor again, but just before I could manage it, they broke away.

Those boys were both pretty strong. If they'd known a little more about wrestling, I would've been doomed from the start. They were wearing me out as it was.

Taylor tackled me and took me down onto my back. He pounced right on my abdomen and leaned over with his hands on my shoulders. His long, blond hair fell down in my face. I must admit that he was a bit distracting. It's not easy to ignore a beautiful, well-built, blond boy when he's on top of you! He was so cute.

Mark pressed his hands down on my shoulders. At the same time Taylor dropped on me, pressing his body full length against mine. His firm body felt so fine. I could feel his bulge pressing into me and, if I wasn't mistaken, Taylor was rather excited, if you know what I mean. Talk about distracting! My shoulders went down on the grass. There was just too much force and weight being exerted against me. Brandon got down to our level and pounded out the count on the grass.

"He's pinned!" he announced.

We got up and Mark and Taylor ran around with their arms in the air yelling "Yeah!" like they'd just won an Olympic Gold Medal. I couldn't help but smile.

"In your face, loser!" said Taylor to me laughing. He slapped my back and then gave me a quick hug.

Pretty soon we all returned to the slides. I, of course, got back to the well-built boy on *The Hurricane*. We ran around like crazy until it was about eight. I gave the cute boy one last longing glance, then departed with my friends. We all piled in Jon's car once more and headed home. It was one great day.

❦ ❦ ❦

The day at the water park had taught me that I could still have fun with Jon. It didn't solve my problems, however. I was still in love with him, and it still brought me pain. When I was alone, I spent a lot of time thinking about Jon. I can't even count the times I walked back to the cabin and the lake. I thought best when I walked. It was like I needed my body to move forward so my thoughts could do the same.

It felt good to be in love with Jon and yet, if I could've wished that love away, I think I would have done so. It hurt to love him. It hurt to know that I could never have what I really wanted. I almost wished I was still lying to myself about being gay. When I was living in denial, I was able to hide most of that love from myself. I didn't think about not being able to have the life I wanted with Jon, because I wouldn't admit I wanted it. I couldn't go back, however. There was no going back. I'd never be able to fool myself again.

I'd been watching Jon—wondering. He didn't have a girlfriend, and never had as far as I knew. He talked to girls, flirted with them sometimes, but hell, so did I. He never seemed to go beyond flirting. I'd never seen him on a date. On most Friday nights he just hung out with me, when I hadn't been going out with Kim that is.

I wondered a lot about Jon's lack of a girlfriend. Jon was very good looking. He was cute, and built, and fun to be around. Surely he could've found a girl if he wanted one. Surely girls had asked him out, even if he was too shy to ask them. I could well see why girls would want Jon. I sure did. So why didn't he date?

I looked for clues that Jon might be gay. He did look around some in the locker room. I'd seen him check out other guys. Then again, that didn't necessarily mean anything. Most guys checked out other guys in the locker room, especially their equipment. Most were just seeing if they measured up. A lot of guys had kind of a hero worship for other boys, too. I'd almost convinced myself that's what I had for Jon before I admitted the truth.

And then there was the way we joked around; the sexual innuendo, the way we kidded each other about our desires. It wasn't uncommon for one of us to tell the other "You want me, don't you?" or "Bend over, baby." or "Blow me." I was pretty sure it was all just a joke to Jon. With me it was different, sometimes when I said those things I wasn't kidding. Sometimes when Jon said them, I wanted to comply.

I wished I could flirt with Jon the way I had with that boy at the water park. Then I could find out if he was interested. I couldn't do it, however. It was just too much. That cute boy at the water park was a stranger—Jon was my best friend. I just couldn't take the chance.

Maybe Jon was gay, but I just didn't have enough proof. He was a very nice guy, however, and my friend. I was beginning to think of taking a risk with him. I wasn't planning on telling him I was in love with him, but maybe I could tell him I was gay. Maybe it would be safe to admit that much. Of course, that was quite a lot to admit. Maybe, if Jon was gay, then he'd admit it too and something could happen between us. It was something I was beginning to give a lot of thought. I had no intention of opening up to Jon anytime soon, but maybe, sometime in future, I would. The truth is, I was terrified of telling Jon the truth, even part of it. He could easily react in a very bad way, friend or no friend. I might even lose my friendship with him and that I could not stand. I just didn't know what to do.

The weekend after our trip to the water park, Jon invited me to a graveyard party. It was really a soccer team thing, but he said no one would care if I showed up. He picked me up and we drove out near the cemetery on the edge of town, parking on the same old deserted lane that we had when we explored the cave, only not as far back.

It was after dark and the cemetery was one spooky place. I'm not all that superstitious, but I do believe in ghosts and I had the feeling some were around. I tried not to hang on Jon like some chickenshit, but I felt a compulsion to grab his arm. Of course, I always wanted to hang on Jon and it had nothing to do with being afraid.

Only a couple of other guys were there when we showed up, but more and more came in and things really got going. Someone brought a radio and played some sweet tunes. One of the guys pushed a beer in my hand and I downed it real fast. Personally, I thought beer tasted like piss (what I imagined piss would taste like anyway), but I liked the way it made me feel and I was getting used to it. I took a couple of swigs from a whiskey bottle that was being passed around and I was feeling fine. I toned down my drinking after that. I didn't want to get wasted. I knew I'd be sick as a dog if I did. I got really drunk once and spent most of the next day puking my guts out. It was not an experience I wanted to repeat, especially since Uncle Jack would have no mercy on me.

I leaned back against a gravestone and looked at the other boys in the light of a lantern. There were some really good-looking guys on the soccer team. As a group, they weren't quite as well built as the wrestlers, but they were way hot. Mark showed up with Taylor about an hour after Jon and I arrived. Talk about a fine body. Mark made me drool. Taylor was so beautiful he made my heart ache. I'd fantasized about making out with him more than a few times. I'd fantasized about Mark a lot, too, and we did way more than just kiss in my fantasies.

Jon pulled my thoughts away from cute guys when he started telling ghost stories. I'm not a coward, but he kind of freaked me out. I guess it had something to do with the fact we were sitting in the middle of a graveyard! Jon could make his voice real eerie and frightening when he wanted and this was one of those times.

I was sitting near Jon and I had to resist the urge the lean up against him. I wanted to be as close as I possible could, but I didn't want the guys to see me hanging on him. I didn't know what he'd think about it either.

I kind of zoned out for a while. I might have even fallen asleep. I was kind of dreaming about this murderer with a hook instead of a hand, but I think that was Jon's story. I'm not sure. Anyway, I came to when I heard Devon talking real loud.

"What are you fags doing?" he yelled.

That got my attention real fast, everyone else's too. Devon was staring down at Mark and Taylor, just glaring at them. I wondered what the fuck was up.

"What is all the noise about?" asked Jon.

"Mark and Taylor were all over each other, they're fags dude!"

Neither Mark nor Taylor said a word. I wished I hadn't zoned out. I think I might have missed something good. The whole thing kind of scared me, however. It hit way too close to home.

"You're drunk," said Jon to Devon, clearly dismissing him.

Devon was a little unsteady on his feet. He was drunk. He had the distinct look of someone who was about to barf. He just stood there, staring down at Mark and Taylor.

"I still think they're fags."

"In the condition you're in, you wouldn't know a fag if he bit you!" yelled Brandon. He laughed so hard at his own joke he fell right off the tombstone he'd been sitting on.

"Bite me and we'll see!" said Devon. Now all the guys were laughing.

I laughed, too, but I didn't think it was very funny. I noticed Mark and Taylor weren't laughing either. I wondered once more if maybe there wasn't something going on between them. I'd never have suspected Mark of being a homosexual in a million years, but he had been sitting real close to Taylor and those two were practically inseparable. It seemed like there was something there, at least to me. You know what they say, it takes one to know one.

No, I was being stupid, and I was a little out of things myself. Both Mark and Taylor had girlfriends—pretty ones too. They hadn't been dating them too long, but they were dating. There was nothing to Devon's accusation. He was drunk and I was seeing things that weren't there. Still, the incident frightened me. What if I'd been sitting real close to Jon or somethin' and Devon came over and went off on me for it?

The mere thought of anyone calling me a fag in front of others chilled me to the bone.

Mark and Taylor left pretty soon after that. Taylor was practically bombed and Mark swayed a little. They both looked a little shaken up. Jon took me home about an hour later. I was pretty unsteady myself. I was out like a light as soon as I hit the bed.

CHAPTER 19

Mark and Taylor Exposed

Only a few days after I began to seriously consider telling Jon that I was gay, something happened that made up my mind for me fast. There was no more debate. The answer was a definite *No.* There was no way I was going to risk being outed.

I heard the first whispers about it before school. At lunch, I got the whole story. Mark and Taylor were both queer. What's more, they'd been caught getting it on together by Mark's father. That must have been the ultimate nightmare. Mark's dad had called his soccer coach and Coach McFadden had outed them both right in front of the entire soccer team. What a bastard.

Everyone was talking about it. No one seemed able to believe that Mark or Taylor could possibly be gay. They were both popular jocks and just didn't fit anyone's ideas of what gay guys were supposed to be like. There was no doubt about it, however, they were gay. They'd been caught getting it on and they weren't bothering to deny it. I wasn't as surprised as most of my classmates, but even I was kind of taken back by the whole thing. I'd seen the way they looked at each other. I'd felt there was a special closeness between them. Still, I didn't really believe either one of them could be gay. I'd written the whole idea off. I was sure I'd only been seeing what I wanted to see. I was wrong—I'd seen what was really there.

In a way, it made me feel a lot better about myself to know that those two were gay. Both Mark and Taylor were incredible athletes. College scouts had already been looking them over and they were only sophomores! It was unheard of. Both of them were smart as could be and way more popular than I was. They were both hot as hell too, not that their looks came from being gay, but I still noticed.

Watching what happened that first day taught me a lesson. Verona, Indiana was no place for gays. I watched as Mark's and Taylor's friends turned on them left and right. Mark came into the cafeteria as I was sitting there with a bunch of guys. No one talked to him. He ended up sitting alone. I felt so sorry for him. I wanted to go over and sit with him, but I just didn't have the balls to do it. I had troubles of my own. The notes in my locker were never far from my mind.

It became obvious that I couldn't go sit with him when the guys from my table started in on him. I don't know how much of it Mark could hear, but they were saying the most disgusting things about Mark and Taylor that I'd ever heard said about anyone. It made me sick to my stomach just listening to them. I didn't want to be a part of it, but I was afraid to get up and leave too fast, so I sat there for a while, feeling like a coward for not taking up for Mark.

One thing really struck me hard. Jon usually sat with Mark at lunch, but he avoided him. I saw Jon with his tray. I saw him spot Mark, and I saw him quietly disappear into the crowd and act like he hadn't seen him. I had my answer about what Jon thought of homosexuals. And to think I'd almost admitted to him that I was one.

* * *

Nathan mentioned Mark and Taylor while we were working on the fencerow that evening. He seemed really shocked by the whole thing. To

Nathan's credit, he wasn't down on Mark and Taylor. He never said one disparaging thing about them. He was just amazed. I could tell it was really on his mind because he didn't stop talking about it.

"How can either of them be *gay*?" he asked.

"What do you mean?"

"I mean...well, Mark's a jock. He's built as well as you, well, almost. He's a soccer star. He's popular. He's, I dunno..."

It was clear that the same thoughts were going through Nathan's head that had been playing through mine. It was rather hard to believe. Mark and Taylor upset all the stereotypes. I knew from personal experience that the stereotypes didn't always hold true, but still the revelation that those two were queer was still hard for me to believe.

"I just don't believe it!" Nathan kept saying over and over.

The next few days were all about Mark and Taylor. It seemed there was nothing else anyone could talk about. They were like one of those news stories that the press keeps covering over and over. There was just no getting away from it.

Something significant did happen the day after the news of Mark and Taylor's "outing" hit. I walked into the lunchroom and saw Mark and Tay sitting together. A lot of guys were talking shit under their breath, but those two were trying their best to ignore it. Jon came out of the line with his tray, but this time he didn't act like he didn't notice Mark. Instead, he went right over and sat down by him. Brandon joined them, too.

I got into line and grabbed my tray. I headed over to Mark's table and sat down right beside Taylor. It took a lot of courage to do it. I could feel eyes staring at me. I was extremely uncomfortable, but I did it anyway. Jordan and Matt had been talking to me in line and they followed me and sat down, too. Even Steve, one of the toughest guys on our wrestling team, sat with us. That was kind of a surprise because I knew Mark and Steve had been into it not too many days before. They'd kicked the crap out of each other at the beach. At least that's what I'd heard and there were black eyes and bruises to prove it.

I felt good sitting there. I felt like I was doing something positive. A lot of guys didn't like us sitting with Mark and Taylor, but I didn't care. I wasn't going to treat them like crap when I didn't want to. I sure as hell wasn't going to be down on them for being gay.

I cautiously looked both of them over as I sat there. Boy were they cute! Mark was one of the sexiest boys in school. He was good-looking and very nicely built. Taylor was a dream come true. I'd never seen a boy that good looking before in my entire life. He was almost too pretty to be a boy. Okay, I know I've said all this stuff before, but it's true! Maybe the stereotype about all the cute guys being gay was true, too. I doubted that, but I liked to believe it.

Mental pictures of what they'd probably done with each other kept popping into my mind. Wow! They'd been living the life I wanted. The sexual images flooded my mind. I had to stop thinking about it before it aroused me too much. Just thinking about them kissing each other was enough to send me into orbit. Not all my thoughts were about sex, however. There was something even more important here. Mark and Taylor obviously loved each other. I wondered what it felt like to love someone and be loved in return.

Things got kind of nasty when Devon came up and started talking shit. It made me want to crawl under the table. He gave me a really nasty look, me and most of the others there. Brandon and Jon stood up and Brandon really went off on Devon. He scared the crap out of him. I thought for a few moments that there was going to be a big fight, but Devon backed down real fast when he found out no one was with him. I couldn't help but smile as he stalked off. A victory for us gay boys!

Jon was clearly standing up for his friends. That changed everything again. I wondered once more if Jon was gay or not. He didn't seem to be, and yet, neither did Mark or Taylor, or me for that matter. I sure as hell wasn't going to tell him I was gay without really thinking it over, however. I'd seen first hand how nasty things could get. Jon seemed pretty accepting of Mark and Taylor, but he might not be so accepting of me. It was a totally unpredictable situation. If I went so far as to tell him I loved him, anything could happen.

The danger of my own predicament was brought home to me that very afternoon. Just before heading for wrestling practice, I found another note in my locker. I read the neatly typed words:

> Enjoy having lunch with your faggot friends? You three have plans for later? You sick bastards. I hope you burn in hell. Your time is coming, fag-just you wait.

I swallowed a knot of fear in my throat. That last part was the most frightening: *Your time is coming, fag—just you wait.* What was that supposed to mean? I was afraid I knew.

I thought hard about who was in the cafeteria that day, but hell, I think every boy in my gym class was there. The note scared me. I couldn't do anything without my tormentor knowing about it. I had to find out who he was!

I'd been making at least a little progress in that direction. I could definitely cross Mark and Taylor off my list. They sure as hell wouldn't be sending those notes. Talk about lack of motive! I also crossed Brandon and Jon off. After the way they'd been sticking up for Mark and Taylor, there was no way they were still suspects. I was especially relieved to cross Jon's name off my list. Sure, he wasn't a very likely candidate, but who knew? Jon being my tormentor would have been the ultimate nightmare.

I also marked Steve off my list. He'd sat at Mark's table. He hadn't taken up for him the way Jon and Brandon had, but when Devon looked to him for support he blew him off. No, Steve wasn't my man.

That was five down, but there were way too many to go. I wondered if I'd ever get to the bottom of it. Of course, maybe I should've been hoping I wouldn't. The one sure way I'd find out what I wanted to know was if my tormentor went public. I didn't want to find myself in the same spot that Mark and Taylor were in. I didn't want to find out who was tormenting me that way.

CHAPTER 20

Coming Out to a Friend

My life seemed like it was turned upside down, or at least on edge, but things weren't so bad. Wrestling was going really well. I'd had eight different matches and I won every single one of them. Most of them weren't even all that close. All my hard work was really paying off. The whole team was doing well. We didn't have another meet where every single one of us was victorious, but more of us won than lost.

Four of the varsity wrestlers were tied for first place on the team and I was one of them. I hadn't thought much about the possibility when I joined varsity, but I realized now that I had a good shot at having the best record of the year. Hell, I had a shot at having the best record *ever.* No one had ever gone through an entire season undefeated at our school. A guy named Dave Ward had ended the season with only one loss several years before. His name was on a trophy in the school trophy case. It excited me to know I had a chance of knocking old Dave out of his place.

I was deadly serious about wrestling. I wouldn't have missed a practice or workout if I was dying. One defeat would ruin my perfect record and destroy my chances of outdoing my teammates. If I lost just one match, I'd have to hope and pray that the others would lose at least once as well. I didn't want to operate like that—wishing for my teammates to lose wasn't what I was about. I wanted to be the best so bad I could taste it, but how I got there was every bit as important as actually getting there.

I couldn't afford to slip up. I *had* to win. When I was wrestling, I tried not to think about that too much. The pressure was distracting and that's a very bad thing in wrestling. I didn't want to lose my shot at being number one by thinking about it too much.

I guess I shouldn't have made such a big deal about it, but for some reason, it meant a whole lot to me. Hell, it meant a lot to most of the guys. Whoever had the best record each year had his name added to a big banner in the gym. It might not sound like it, but that was a really big deal at our school. It was the equivalent to being inducted into the Hall of Fame. If I could keep things up, it would be my name up there. Years and years later I could come back and there it would be.

I was careful not to let my farm work slip up either. Nothing could stop Uncle Jack from pulling me off the team if he wanted. I didn't think he'd do that, but I wasn't taking any chances. I knew Uncle Jack needed me on the farm real bad. The workload was almost more than we could handle, even with Nathan pitching in.

I was beginning to worry about Nathan. He'd always been a sad boy, but he seemed more withdrawn for some reason. For a few weeks he seemed to be doing better. I'd been including him in my plans whenever I could and took him out just for fun now and then. He seemed almost a different boy when we went to the water park, but right after that he slipped back into his old ways. He seemed even worse off than he had been before. It was all pretty subtle, but I could tell something had changed. Of course, he wouldn't talk about it. Any time I asked him anything the least bit personal he clamed up. He just didn't want to discuss what was bothering him.

I even considered asking Dave if he knew what could be wrong with Nathan, but I decided that wasn't a wise idea. Things might be going on that Dave didn't know anything about. If he started asking questions, it could just make things harder. Asking Dave might've made Nathan angry with me as well. It really wasn't any of my business, but Nathan was my friend and I wanted to help him.

I found myself wanting to talk to Nathan about my own problems. I *desperately* needed to talk to someone about what was happening in my life. I needed to talk about Jon, and about the notes. Not having anyone to share things with made dealing with everything that much harder.

In the past, Nathan and I hadn't talked about anything very meaningful. At least not often. He refused to discuss his personal life and I was afraid to discuss mine. I did share my thoughts and feelings with him to a great degree, but not the things that were really eating at me. I just couldn't. We mainly spent a lot of time talking about wrestling. I couldn't stop talking about it and Nathan seemed to like hearing about all my matches and even the practices. Perhaps we talked so much about wrestling because there were so many other things we couldn't discuss.

I'd grown to trust Nathan and I considered him a friend. The problem was; there were still things that were difficult to discuss even with friends. There were certain topics that could end a friendship pretty fast. Despite that, I'd given the idea of telling Nathan a few things some real thought, just like I'd thought a great deal about opening up to Jon. Nathan was a little different, however, not so much was riding on him. I cared about Nathan, but I wasn't head over heels in love with him.

As we continued our work with attaching the fencing to the poles, I found myself drifting ever closer to sharing secrets with Nathan that I never thought I'd share with anyone.

"What do you think of Mark and Taylor?" I asked. "About them being gay?"

Nathan kind of shrugged his shoulders.

"I dunno, Um, well..." He seemed a bit uncomfortable with the topic, but I pressed on anyway. After all, I wasn't asking him about his personal life.

"Does it bother you? Creep you out? Or is it cool with you?"

"Why should it bother me? What they do is their business, not mine," he said.

"It's kind of weird finding out they're queer, though, isn't it?"

"Yeah. I'd have never thought they were gay. The news sure surprised me."

"Life's full of surprises," I said, leveling my gaze at Nathan. He looked at me with a question in his eyes. I think he picked up something from the tone of my voice and my expression. I think he knew I was heading somewhere. I swallowed hard.

"What would you say if I told you I was gay?" I asked him. My voice trembled slightly, despite my best efforts to steady it. I wanted my question to sound theoretical, but my nervous demeanor pretty much blew that.

"You?" said Nathan incredulously. "No way!" His eyes widened until they were the size of saucers. He was shocked.

I took a deep breath and paused for a few moments. Nathan just stood there looking at me, his mouth gaping open. I had the strongest desire to laugh and pretend it was all a joke, but I needed Nathan. I needed at least one person to understand.

"I am," I said flatly. I don't think I'd ever been as terrified as I was at that moment. I couldn't look Nathan directly in the eyes for a while. I gazed down at the soft, brown earth—wondering if I'd just made the biggest mistake of my life. When I lifted my eyes once more, Nathan peered into them deeply, as if he was trying to read them.

"You're not kidding, are you?" he said quietly.

"No," I said.

Nathan had a real strange look on his face. Part of it was disbelief, but I couldn't make out what else he was feeling. He almost looked afraid, but that wasn't quite it. I, on the other hand, was terrified. I felt like a doomed man waiting for the executioner's ax to fall.

I was a mess. Admitting to Nathan that I was gay took more out of me than I can describe. My lower lip started to tremble and I actually started to cry. Everything I'd been going through just seemed to bear down upon me all at once. I turned away from Nathan and sat down on the grass with my head in my hands. I felt so embarrassed about what I'd just told him. I felt so embarrassed about crying in front of him. The more I tried to hold them back, the more sobs welled up in my chest and forced their way out.

"It's okay," I heard Nathan say from behind me.

He walked around in front of me and pulled my chin up so I was forced to look into his eyes.

"It's okay that you're gay, Ethan. You're my friend."

I wanted to hug him close, but I didn't know what he'd think of that, especially after what I'd just told him. Feeling his acceptance was enough, however. It made me feel like I didn't have to handle things alone anymore.

I felt a little ridiculous sitting there in the grass, especially with Nathan looking down at me with a concerned look on his face. Nathan looked a little frightened, but I don't think it had anything to do with me being gay. I think he was a little shaken up to find that his hero was only an ordinary boy after all. Nathan had always looked up to me. I know he had kind of a hero worship for me. It was probably better that he know I had problems and weaknesses too. It's kind of hard to be friends with a hero, but it's not so hard to be friends someone who's just an ordinary guy.

Nathan extended his hand and nodded to me. I took his hand and he helped me to my feet. I smiled and he smiled back. I could tell that the fact I was gay really didn't bother him. That made me feel even more comfortable around him than I had in the past. Nathan was always pretty easy to talk to, but I'd always hidden part of myself from him, just as I'd hidden it from myself.

"Thanks, Nathan," I said, meaning more with those two words than I ever had before.

"There's nothing to thank me for," he said. "I'm your friend."

His words made me feel so good I was about ready to cry again. There is no way he could've known how much his acceptance meant to me.

CHAPTER 21

Growing Fear

My fear of being outed by my unknown tormentor increased exponentially the next day. Not long after I arrived at school, I heard something that make me sick to my stomach and frightened me to my very core. Some guys had worked Mark over in the locker room after soccer practice. No one seemed to know who'd done it, but there were at least three of them and they'd beaten him nearly to death. He was in the hospital. I didn't know how bad off he was, but I hoped he'd be okay. I looked around for Taylor to ask him about it, but he wasn't at school. I had a pretty good idea where he was—with Mark.

Everyone was talking about it. Hell, everyone was always talking about Mark and Taylor. Most of the guys just referred to them as *the fags.* I hated hearing that. It made me furious. There wasn't much I could do about it, however. I was already pushing it by being openly friendly with Mark and Taylor. I felt like a real coward for not being more supportive. After all, they were my own kind. I just didn't have the courage to stand up for what I believed. It made me feel weak and useless.

The truth was, I was scared. I'd seen how my classmates treated Mark and Tay. I didn't think I could take that. I was still trying to come to terms with the idea that I was gay. I wasn't ready for much more. Opening up to Nathan took a supreme effort. I just couldn't handle what would happen if I stood up for Mark and Taylor too much. I may have had my reasons, but I still felt like a coward and a traitor.

Mark getting his ass kicked really shook me up. I knew that it could easily have been me. If the guys who beat up Mark knew I was gay, I'd be just as much of a target. I was strong and could usually handle myself pretty well in a fight, but Mark was strong too. It hadn't saved him. No one could stand up to two or three guys at once, not in real life. The thought of getting beat up scared me more than I ever thought it would. I'd never feared that before.

Terror was the word of the day. I was terrified right down to my socks that afternoon right after wrestling practice. I met Jon in the gym and we walked to my locker. His car was in the shop and he needed a lift home. We talked about what had happened to Mark. Jon was pissed. I had no doubt he would have kicked the crap out of the guys who worked Mark over, if he could've found out who they were. No one had a clue, however. It had become the biggest secret in school. Someone had to know of course, but those who knew weren't talking.

I opened my locker and there it was, another note. I bent down and picked it up while Jon went on about the whole situation with Mark. I opened the note and read it. The words sent a shiver up my spine:

You're next faggot.

I knew exactly what the note meant. I don't think I'd ever been so frightened in my entire life. I was glad Jon was with me. I figured I was safe when I was with him. At least he'd help me if someone came after me. I folded the note with trembling hands and stuffed it into my pocket.

"Are you okay, Ethan?"

"Huh? Oh, yeah. I'm just kind of shook up over what happened to Mark."

"Yeah, it's terrible, isn't it?"

It was a rhetorical question if there ever was one.

"You want to go see him?" asked Jon.

"Yeah, but I can't, not now. I have to work. I will this weekend for sure."

"I'll go with you when you do," said Jon. "Can you drop me off at the hospital? I want to see how he is."

"Sure," I answered.

I drove Jon to the hospital, and then headed home. My heart was pounding in my chest. I felt like I was doomed to live in fear for the rest of my life. I just couldn't shake the terror that pursued me.

❧ ❧ ❧

I was still thinking about Mark, and my latest note, as I changed into my work clothes. I paused and looked at my naked body in the mirror. I flexed my right arm and my bicep bulged. I tensed the muscles of my chest and watched as my pecs flexed. I could bench over 200 pounds, more than any other guy in the whole school. I knew most every wrestling more. I was seventeen and at my physical peak. I knew none of that would save me if a bunch of guys jumped me, however. I'd fight, but there wouldn't be much I could do alone against a gang. No matter how strong I was, I'd still get my ass kicked.

I was afraid, but I'd be damned if I was going to live in fear. My Uncle Jack said something once that came to my mind just then: "A coward dies many times before his death". I don't think Jack came up with that all on his own, but I knew what it meant. I was determined to die just once.

I knew I couldn't keep myself from thinking about that last note, but I was going to do my best. It was probably just a bluff anyway, something to scare me. If I let it get to me, as I already had, then I was letting my tormentor win. The less I thought about it, the less of a victory he'd have. If it wasn't a bluff and I did get beat up, well, I'd just deal with that when it came. One thing was for sure, anyone who jumped me could expect one hell of a fight. I wouldn't hold anything back.

I walked to the barn and performed all the little tasks I did every day of my life, twice a day really. I smiled to myself as I passed Henrietta on her nest. Every morning I carefully gathered her eggs and put them in a little paper bag for Nathan to take home to Dave. I could've sent any of the eggs, but I always took special care to make sure Dave got the ones from his chicken. Dave had come to visit Henrietta several times. That boy had a real affection for his hen. Watching him with her was observing pure love. I gave Henrietta a pat on the back and went on my way.

After I finished my chores, I joined Nathan at the fencerow yet again. I didn't think too much about how we'd been working on it forever. I had too many things on my mind. I grinned when I saw Nathan. He was the one person I really felt at ease with. I didn't have to pretend in front of him. He smiled when I drew near. It was clear he was glad to see me too.

We worked a good, long while without saying too much. We'd talked over what happened to Mark at lunch, so there wasn't much more to say. I was less talkative than usual because I was thinking my own thoughts. I wanted to tell Nathan everything, but it was hard and I couldn't quite figure out how to do it, or how to begin. Finally, I just started in. I'd done enough hesitating.

"Nathan, there are some things I want to tell you. If it bothers you, just tell me, and I'll stop, but I've just got to talk to someone about it."

"Okay," he said, peering at me with his bright eyes. He intently listened. Nathan was always a good listener.

I spilled my guts about my love for Jon. I told Nathan everything. I told him how deeply in love I was with my best friend and even about how I dreamed about him. Nathan didn't say anything. He just listened. I could tell he was uncomfortable, but he didn't ask me to stop. He didn't say anything until I was finished.

I felt guilty dumping it all on Nathan. The more I talked, the more uncomfortable he became. He looked like what I was telling him made him sick to his stomach. I guess that shouldn't have surprised me. How could he possibly understand the heartaches of a boy in love with another boy? I thought of what I wanted with Jon as beautiful, but I knew most boys my age would be disgusted by it. To Nathan's credit, he didn't utter a single disparaging word. Whatever negative thoughts he had about the whole situation, he kept to himself. Instead, he did his best to try to help me. He was a true friend.

"That's rough," he said. "It's hard to love someone so much and not be able to tell him."

"Exactly," I said. "But…"

"But what?"

"I'm thinking about telling him."

"You are?"

"Yes, I just feel like I'm going to explode inside. I don't think I want to live my life wondering what could have been."

"Do you think he's gay, though? What if he's not?"

"I've asked myself those questions a thousand times, Nathan, and more. I've been watching him for a long time, and I kind of think he is."

"What makes you think so?"

"Well, for one thing, him and Brandon are about the only guys who really take up for Mark and Taylor. Jon takes a lot of shit for that, but he doesn't back down. Maybe it's more than friendship. Maybe he has other reasons, too. And then there's Brandon. You ever notice how tight those two are? I kind of think those two have something going."

"I don't know," said Nathan thoughtfully. "But if they do, it could be a problem. Maybe Jon already has a boyfriend—Brandon."

"That's true," I said, "And it's one of my many fears, but maybe they aren't really dating, maybe they just mess around or something. Or maybe there is nothing going on at all. Brandon does seem rather girl-crazy."

"Sounds like a lot of maybes to me," said Nathan.

"Yeah," I admitted. "There are a lot of 'maybes' and a lot of 'ifs'. I'll go crazy if I don't try, however. I think about Jon all the time. Just looking at him makes my heart ache. I just want to hold him and..."

I looked over at Nathan. He was obviously uncomfortable. I was glad I'd stopped myself. I was on the verge of telling Nathan how I wanted to kiss Jon, pull his shirt off, and...I forced myself to stop thinking about Jon's body before I got myself too worked up. Besides, it was my love for him that was the most important.

"Sorry, I didn't mean to give you too much information."

"It's okay," said Nathan. His expression didn't match his words. I had no doubt he was quite ill at ease.

"I know it will be a big risk, but what if I don't tell him how I feel and then I find out twenty years from now that Jon felt the same way about me. I've *got* to know."

I was talking to Nathan, but I was talking to myself too. The conversation, with Nathan and with myself, had made up my mind. I'd do it. I'll tell Jon how I felt about him. Suddenly, I was afraid for a whole new reason.

I looked at Nathan. He was still peering at me intently. I wondered what thoughts were going through his head. I couldn't read him. He seemed sad and lonely. Nathan always had that edge to him, but he seemed even sadder at the moment. I wished he'd open up to me as I had him. Maybe he would someday.

"There's something else I've got to tell you," I said. "You might want to keep your distance from me at school. You might want to keep it quiet that you're my friend."

"Why?" he asked, confused.

"Well, someone has been threatening me. They've been sending me notes."

I told him all about the notes I'd been getting in my locker. He had a queer look on his face. I couldn't tell if it was fear, surprise, or something else. I never could seem to read Nathan. He was an enigma.

"Shit," he said when I'd finished. "You have any idea who it is?"

"Not really. I've narrowed down the possibilities, but I'm not much of a detective. It could be anyone in our gym class really."

"Even me."

"Yeah, it could be you, but you wouldn't do that to me."

"I wouldn't!" said Nathan earnestly. I believed him. I'd already crossed his name off my list and I was certain now that I'd done the right thing.

I told him about the suspects I'd eliminated and who was left. He agreed that the list was still too long.

"I'm not going to pretend that we aren't friends," said Nathan, at the end of our discussion. "I am your friend and I don't care who knows. Even if...Even if things get bad."

"Thanks," I said, and meant it.

CHAPTER 22

The Death of Dreams

I'd made up my mind to open up to Jon, but it wasn't easy doing so. Over the next couple of days I actually started to tell him no less than six times, but I chickened out in the end. I just couldn't make the words come out. I didn't know how to begin, or how to tell him that I was gay and that I loved him. A part of me was putting it off too. I knew what I had to say to Jon could end things between us. I guess I was just holding on to what could've been the last days of our friendship.

On Sunday afternoon, Jon came over and we went together to the hospital to see Mark. Jon had been there often, but it was my first time. We met Taylor in the hall as we were making our way to Mark's room. He smiled when he saw us and thanked me for coming. I could tell he was under tremendous strain. There were dark circles under his eyes and he looked exhausted. He was still beautiful, however, Taylor was forever beautiful—like an angel.

When I first saw Mark, I almost gasped. I did my best to hide my reaction, but I'm sure my shock was plain to read upon my face. Mark wasn't wearing a shirt and his face and torso were bruised all over. The lower part of his chest was wrapped in bandages. He looked like he'd been in a car accident or something.

The sight of him created a flood of emotions within me, all roiling over and around one another. I was afraid of being beaten as I never had been before. At the same time I was so infuriated that I was ready to track down the guys who had done that to Mark and take them all on myself. I was filled with sadness and pity, too. My heart went out to Mark, and to Taylor. No one should've had to go through what they were experiencing. No one deserved to be beaten like that; not for anything, and certainly not for being gay. Poor Taylor didn't deserve the pain it caused him. I knew it must be unbearable for him to see Mark like that. I looked at Jon and thought about how I'd feel if he was laying in that hospital bed.

Mark seemed to be taking it pretty well, but he was not the same boy anymore. He was changed by all that had happened, not just the beating. It wasn't fair that the world treated him the way it did. It wasn't fair that boys like us suffered because we dared to love other boys.

We stayed a long time, and then took our leave. One thing I'd noticed about Mark was that he wasn't giving up. Even lying in that hospital bed, battered and bruised, he was still going on. It made me more determined that ever to do what I had to do.

Jon and I returned to the farm, grabbed something to eat, then rode Wuffa and Fairfax back to the cabin and the little lake. All the way there I tried to tell him what I wanted to say, but I just couldn't quite do it. I started several times, but the words stuck in my throat. I kept switching to another topic at the last second. Opening up to Jon was the hardest thing I'd ever had to do in my entire life. So much was riding on it. When I was done, Jon could be my boyfriend, or no friend at all. I'd never taken a risk like that before. Telling Nathan I was gay was nothing compared to telling Jon.

We dismounted right by the old cabin and let the horses wander off to the lake. It was a beautiful, bright October day. Jon looked so handsome in his jeans and black shirt. His muscles pressing against the shirt reminded me of the day we'd swam in the lake naked. The water was too cool now for that, however.

"So you want to tell me what's on your mind?" asked Jon.

I looked at him, realizing I'd been silently thinking for a good, long time. I remained silent. I didn't know what to say.

"What is it, Ethan? It's obvious something is eating at you. You've been acting strange all afternoon."

I swallowed hard and summoned the courage to make my lips move. I was actually terrified to speak. I knew I could not remain silent, however. To do so would only prolong the torment. My life was quickly becoming a living hell.

"I've got some things to tell you. Things that aren't easy for me to say. Things that probably won't be easy for you to hear."

I was so nervous I was trembling. My hands were actually shaking. Jon took my hands in his own and held them.

"It's okay, Ethan. I don't know what you have to tell me, but I'm your friend."

He peered into my eyes. I saw the same earnest look there that I'd seen in Nathan's eyes. It put me at ease just a bit. It was still hard to speak the words. It was still difficult to phrase what needed said.

"You're good friends with Mark, right?" I was asking the obvious, but I needed to start somewhere.

"Yes, I am."

"Well, you know he's gay." I truly had a grasp for the obvious that afternoon.

"Yeah," said Jon. "And?"

"And…I'm like him. I'm gay."

I looked into Jon's eyes. I know he could read the fear in my own. I searched his eyes for the first signs of anger, or acceptance. What I read there was understanding and friendship.

I was on the verge of tears. My eyes were so watery that my vision was blurred. I was still afraid.

"It's okay, Ethan. I don't mind. It doesn't bother me—really."

"There's more..." I said, my voice trailing off into silence.

I shifted my gaze for several long moments, watching the surface of the little lake sparkle in the sunlight. This was it. The moment had come and I was terrified.

I looked into Jon's eyes again, trying to convey how much I loved him without having to speak the words. We just stood there looking into each other's eyes for the longest time. My mind was filled with dreams, with dreams of Jon taking me in his arms and telling me that he loved me. Terror, too, was in my mind. I feared what I had to say next would make him sick to his stomach and end our friendship forever. Jon waited for me to speak. It was a long time before I could do so.

"I'm in love with you, Jon. I always have been. You mean more to me than anything."

Jon swallowed. There was a hint of panic in his eyes. His face blanched. He pulled away from me. It was a microscopic movement, unintentional, involuntary, but it spoke volumes. He looked more than anything like a deer caught in the headlights of on oncoming car.

"Ethan, I...I...I can't...I don't...I'm not gay."

Jon looked at me and I could tell he was deeply sorry. He knew his words hurt me. He knew he'd just sliced into my heart. Tears ran down my face.

"Ethan, I'm your friend. I care about you. But, I just can't love you like you want me to. I just can't!"

I knew what was passing between us was hard on Jon. I knew it was hurting him. It hurt me far more, however. My hopes and dreams were crushed. Jon stood right there and destroyed my life. Part of me hated him for that. Part of me hated him for not being what I so desperately needed him to be. It wasn't supposed to work out this way. Jon was supposed to tell me he loved me too. He was supposed to become my boyfriend. I'd taken the biggest risk in my life and it was all for nothing.

All I got for my troubles was damnation. All my hopes and dreams were gone.

I turned on my heel and bolted. I left Jon. I left the horses. I left everything. I ran back through the woods and between the fields—my heart filled with anguish, my mind consumed by pain. My entire world came crumbling down around me. I ran all the way home and cried my eyes out on my bed, soaking the pillowcase with my hot tears. Jon didn't try to follow when I ran. I think he knew I couldn't handle the sight of him right then. I wasn't sure I ever wanted to see him again.

❧ ❧ ❧

The next day at school, I couldn't bear to look at Jon. I just didn't know how to act around him. He knew I was gay. What's more, he knew I was in love with him. The knowledge that he was not like me, that he could never love me back, didn't make me stop loving him. I wished I could just shut off my feelings, but I couldn't. My love for Jon was still there. I wanted him every bit as much as I always had. I wanted a life with him that could not be. The pain was unbearable. I felt crushed and humiliated.

I guess things didn't turn out nearly as bad as they could have. Jon could've slugged me in the face and called me a fag. He could have told me he never wanted to see me again. He could've told everyone what I was. He did none of those things, however. He didn't hate me for what I was, he just couldn't be what I wanted.

When our eyes met for the first time after I'd run away from him, I read concern there. Jon was worried about me. That made me feel a little better, but I was still hurting inside. I didn't try to talk to him. I just wasn't ready for that. I didn't know what to say. I couldn't look into his eyes for more than a moment. He knew too much.

I sat near Jon at lunch, but not right by him. He looked at me from time to time and smiled. I guess it was his way of letting me know that we were still friends. I weakly smiled back, but it wasn't a happy smile. I felt like I'd never be happy again.

I avoided Jon before wrestling practice. I just couldn't talk to him, not yet. I'm sure he understood. He probably needed some time too. After all, what do you do when your best friend tells you he's gay and he's in love with you? It must have disgusted and disturbed him.

If Jon had been gay too, everything would have been different. He wasn't, however, and I couldn't change that—neither could he. Part of me wondered if there was a way it could be changed. Part of me hoped that Jon would just decide he wanted me too. I tried to dismiss that hope; it was false and could only bring me pain.

There was still an anger in me, an anger with Jon for not being gay. I knew that my anger wasn't reasonable. Jon couldn't help being heterosexual any more than I could being homosexual. It wasn't his fault and I wasn't being fair. Still, the emotion was there. It pained me to look at Jon with hatred in my heart. I despised myself for it and for being stupid enough to hope he could love me as I loved him. That hope yet lingered. It refused to die.

❧ ❧ ❧

After wrestling practice I hurried home, changed, and got to the farm work. I was eager to see Nathan. I needed to talk to him. Nathan was the only one that I could share my life with. I'd almost sought him out the evening before, but I didn't want to just show up at his house. I didn't think he'd like that, not with the way he was so secretive about his home life. I tried looking up his phone number, but it wasn't listed. I don't think his family had a phone. I'd wanted to talk to him at school, but I just couldn't. It was too risky. He knew something was up. He could read it in my eyes. He hadn't said anything about it, however. He probably guessed what was up, or at least had a good idea.

I found Nathan stretching out fence. I tried to smile at him, but my smile wouldn't come. Instead, tears welled up in my eyes.

"What's wrong, Ethan?" Nathan dropped what he was doing and walked over to me.

"I told him," I said, in a hoarse whisper. "I told him I loved him."

I looked at Nathan. I'd never seen a face so etched with concern. He really, really cared.

Nathan did something next I would never have suspected. He crossed the small distance between us and put his arms around me. He hugged me close as I bawled my eyes out on his shoulder. I held onto him tightly. I needed someone to hold me just then. I loved Nathan for being there for me. I just held onto him and cried.

After a few minutes I calmed down. Nathan and I sat on the grass while I told him what happened.

"I made such a fool out of myself. I'm so embarrassed about it all now."

"Why? Because you had the balls to take a real chance? Because you reached out to someone you love? Not everyone has that kind of courage, Ethan. A lot of us would like to be that brave."

I smiled wanly. When did Nathan become so wise? He didn't seem like a little boy anymore, in some ways he was far more mature than me.

"I know it hurts, Ethan, but at least you know. You don't have to wonder any more. You did what you had to do. You told me yourself you couldn't live without knowing. Jon is still your friend. All you've lost is a future that just couldn't be. All you've lost is something that wasn't really there in the first place. I know it's hard, but maybe it had to be this way."

"You're amazing," I said to Nathan, my eyes still filled with tears. I knew he was a boy with problems, problems that probably made mine pale by comparison, and yet he put them all aside because I needed him. Nathan was the best friend I'd ever had. I guess I had two best friends.

"Me?" he said.

"No, the guy standing behind you. Of course you!" I laughed a little. It was a real laugh. I felt a lot better.

I knew Nathan was right. I'd been saying much the same thing to myself. Part of me wouldn't listen, however. Part of me kept hoping that my dream could yet come true. I guess it was a kind of denial. The pain of what had happened was just too much to bear, so I held onto a dead hope, praying for a miracle.

We talked a little more and our conversation edged away from my troubles. Nathan got me talking about wrestling and pulled my mind away from all that haunted me. I knew I'd never forget his kindness.

"We'd better get back to work," Nathan said finally. "I'd like to get paid and I don't think your uncle will pay me for sitting on my butt."

"He sure won't," I said.

We jumped up and started to work on the fence. There was something familiar and comfortable about the whole scene. It was something real and dependable to hold onto while the rest of the world was spinning out of control. I wished I could just go on working by Nathan's side forever.

I sought Jon out the very next day and made it a point to talk to him. We didn't discuss what had passed between us, but it was clear that Jon had no hard feelings about it. I apologized to Jon for the way I'd acted, for running away from him, and for not talking to him. He told me he understood. I was glad we could at least talk again, even if the words did not come easy. Our friendship was forever changed, but it had survived a trial that could have torn us apart. My dream was not realized, but then neither was my greatest fear.

I wasn't angry with Jon any more. There was no reason for me to be. He'd been nothing but a good friend through the whole thing. I guess I should've been happy. After all, a good friend was worth a great deal. I had a hard time being happy, however. How was I supposed to be happy when things had gone so wrong?

Jon had moved past what had happened between us. I was having a much harder time. I just couldn't quite let go of what I wanted with Jon. I just couldn't quite give up on my dream, even though I knew it would only bring me pain. I tried to be rational. I tried to tell myself that I just couldn't have what I wanted with Jon. The truth was, however, that I just couldn't let it go. I wanted it so bad, I just couldn't believe that I couldn't make it come true—somehow.

CHAPTER 23

The Loss of Friends

Nathan and I stood above the graves, looking down at the two fresh mounds of earth covered with flowers. The events of the last few days seemed so unreal that I felt as if I'd be in a waking dream, or more properly, a nightmare. It didn't seem possible that our two friends could be buried under the earth. One day we were having lunch with them at school and a few days later they were gone.

All the horrible events were still fresh in my mind—the frantic call from Brandon, the terrifying search of the old Graymoor Mansion, racing around town desperately trying to find Taylor before it was too late, then finding him—sitting leaned up against a soccer goal behind the high school—dead.

The vision of Taylor sitting there, pale and lifeless, was burned into my mind forever, as was the vision of Brandon when he'd discovered we were too late. He'd held Taylor's lifeless body in his arms, rocking back and forth—wailing. I sank to my knees not two feet away, sobbing with a grief that I'm sure will never go away. I gazed at Taylor's serene features as Brandon held him. He was beautiful even in death. I couldn't believe he was gone. I gazed at him until my own tears blinded me. The events of that night were so horrible it didn't seem possible that they could be real.

Nathan had cried so when I gave him the news the next morning. He wasn't the only one either. Taylor's loss hit almost everyone hard. It was weird to lose Taylor like that. He was there one minute and gone the next. When we'd searched for him, I was sure we'd find him—distraught, but alive. I was wrong, however, terribly wrong. Taylor was so young, his death was such a tragedy. I was overwhelmed with grief. I couldn't bear his loss.

Along with the sadness, I felt myself growing angry, too. I knew why he'd killed himself, or at least I had a good idea. He'd done himself in because everyone around him made his life a living hell—just because he was gay.

I was there when Mark arrived at school. It was so pitiful. He didn't even know what had happened. I could see the fear in his eyes, however. I think in his heart he did know. That bastard Devon told him, told him like he was glad. I watched as Mark flew at him in a rage and nearly killed him. I wished he had killed him. Devon deserved to die. It took several guys to pull Mark off of him. They shouldn't have done it. They should have let Mark beat him to death.

Brandon took Mark away—it was the last time I ever saw him. By the next morning, Mark was gone, too. He'd walked to the soccer field and blown his brains out at the exact spot where we'd found Taylor. I was sorry to lose him, but I didn't blame him. I think I'd have done the same.

Nathan and I went to the funeral and the burial. Mark and Taylor's parents had their funerals together, and buried them side-by-side. At least they did that much. It was just too bad they hadn't been more understanding when their sons were alive. Maybe then they wouldn't have had to die. Only too late did Mark and Taylor's parents realize what they'd done. I saw them looking at each other over the graves during the burial. They had tears in their eyes, even Taylor's dad who had kicked Tay out of the house only hours before his death. Despite everything, I couldn't help but feel sorry for them. They were obviously suffering from tremendous grief. I wondered what it must be like for them, to lose a son, and know that they were largely responsible for it. I'm sure they'd handle everything quite differently if they had it all to do over again. I felt sorry for them; they'd be suffering for their narrow-mindedness for the rest of their lives.

A lot of my classmates showed up for the funeral and burial. A lot of them were the same ones that had said such awful things and had made Mark and Taylor's lives hell. I think a lot of them realized just what they'd done. They had blood on their hands. They had killed those boys as surely as if they'd shot them dead. I knew some of them were sorry. I knew some of them weren't.

I had blood on my hands, too. I'd never uttered one negative comment about Mark and Tay, but I hadn't done nearly enough for them. Brandon and Jon had stood up for them. They'd taken all kinds of shit for it, but they didn't care. They supported them in every imaginable way. I should've done the same, but I was too cowardly. Yes, I'd been kind to Mark and Taylor. I'd sat by their side at lunch. I'd let them know that I was still their friend. There was so much more I could've done, however. I should have fought for them like Brandon and Jon, but I was too afraid of being found out. I was too frightened that I might receive the same treatment as Mark and Taylor. I'd betrayed them. Brandon and Jon weren't gay, but they'd been true friends, while I, a gay boy, had stood on the sidelines and allowed a tragedy to befall those sweet boys. I'd failed them and I'd failed myself. I knew that no matter how long I lived, I'd never be able to forgive myself for not being there for them when they needed me the most.

There was a chill in the air as Nathan and I stood in the graveyard. Fall had truly come at last. The early November wind stole the heat from my body. The cloudy skies seemed to fit what had happened. It was if the entire world were mourning a great loss. A few yellowed leaves fell upon the fresh earth of the graves of our friends. As if on cue, it began to rain. It was barely more than a sprinkle, but it was as if the clouds were crying. I found myself crying, too.

I looked at Nathan beside me. His face was filled with sadness, his eyes with tears. He was a compassionate soul with a soft heart.

"This shouldn't have happened," he said.

"I know, but it did. We can't change it."

"I wish we could," said Nathan.

"Me too."

"At least they can be together now and no one will ever bother them again."

"Yes," I said, "That's true. At least they have that."

I knelt and placed some flowers on each of the graves and bid my friends farewell.

* * *

It was as if a dark cloud hung over everyone's heads at school for the next several days. The hallways often seemed more like a funeral parlor than a school. Jon, Brandon and all the other friends of Mark and Taylor were torn up and grief stricken. I could find joy in nothing. I felt as if I were dead, too.

Devon hardly dared to show his face. Everyone had heard what he'd said to Mark on the very day he died. Everyone knew how he'd treated both Mark and Taylor and a lot of people considered him largely responsible for their deaths. Even most of his friends drew away from him. Being associated with Devon was no longer cool.

Just a few days after the burial, one of Devon's former friends talked and pretty soon everyone knew who had worked Mark over in the locker room a handful days before his death. Devon was even more unpopular after that. When Brandon and Jon found out they hunted down each one of those guys and beat the shit out of them. They worked Devon over so hard that the guys who were there said they thought Jon and Brandon were going to kill him.

The deaths of my friends had made a change at our school. It was days before I heard anyone utter the words "faggot" or "fairy" or any of the other gay put-downs that I usually heard on a daily basis. I think everyone has very aware that words had the power to kill. The loss of both Mark and Taylor hit everyone hard.

While they were alive, everyone focused on the fact that they were gay. Once they were gone, everyone remembered instead their kindness, their prowess on the soccer field, and their dedication to their friends. Why did it take a tragedy to make people open their eyes?

CHAPTER 24

Opening My Eyes to Reality

Just when I thought things might be getting safer for boys like me, I got another note in my locker. I unfolded the crisp, white paper with trembling hands:

> So your faggot friends took themselves out. Running out of allies, huh? You're alone now faggot. You do exactly as you're told or every faggot-hater in this school is gonna know your name.
>
> Maybe you should off yourself like your butt-buddies did. All you fags deserve to die.Two down, one to go.

Reading that note made my blood run cold. It instilled terror in my heart, but even more, it inspired anger. Whoever was writing those notes had to be one of the same people who had treated Mark and

Taylor like shit. Even their deaths didn't phase him. I despised whoever wrote those notes more than ever. How could anyone have so much hate inside of him? And for such a stupid reason? I was gay—big deal. I had half a mind to walk into the locker room the next day and demand that whoever had been writing me those notes step forward. It's what I should've done. The truth was, however, that I just didn't have the courage to admit what I was in front of everyone. Despite all that had happened, I didn't think I could deal with everyone knowing I was gay.

My list of suspects had grown narrower. Two of the guys who had worked Mark over so violently, Jeremy and Alex, were in my gym class. As soon as I found out they were the ones who helped beat Mark, I moved them right to the top of my list. I was getting closer to the truth, but the closer I came, the more frightened I became. I hated those two for what they'd done, but I feared them for what they might do. Whoever sent me those notes was as full of hate and spite as ever. If it was one of those guys, I had no doubt that he still had evil in his heart.

The official wresting season was over. I was sorry to see it end, but only the season was finished—wrestling wasn't over for me. What was to come was even more exciting than any match I'd been in so far. I finished the season undefeated, but I wasn't alone. It had never happened before at our school—no one had ever went undefeated for the entire year, but I had done it, and so had Zac. I was thrilled with what I'd accomplished. I'd hardly dared hope for it. Okay, I'd hoped, but actually achieving my goal was more than a bit of a surprise.

I was a little apprehensive about what was to come. Only one name could go up on that banner. That was my dream, to have my name on the wrestling banner as the greatest wrestler of the year. Going undefeated should have clinched it for me, in any other year it would have, but Zac had gone undefeated, too. There was to be one final match. Zac and I were to face each other on the mat and the entire school would be watching. The date was already set. There'd be a special schedule, like there was when we had a pep rally just before the end of the school day, only this time everyone was coming to see Zac and me battle it out. Hundreds of people would be watching. I'd never wrestled in front of such a crowd in my entire life.

I wasn't expecting such a tie. To be honest, I wasn't expecting to go the entire season without a defeat. I was also surprised that it was Zac, and not Steve, who had gone undefeated. Steve had met up with some tough competition at the wrong time, however, and it'd cost him. That's the way it went in wrestling. Anything could happen.

I tried not to let myself get overconfident, but I knew I could take Zac. He was in a slightly higher weight class than me, but even that didn't matter. I'd wrestled him in practices and I knew his fatal flaw; he was predictable. Zac had some awesome moves and incredible upper body strength, but he had a tendency to try the same moves in the same order. That wasn't a drawback with most opponents as they didn't have the chance to learn Zac's flaw. I'd watched him plenty, however, and had wrestled with him enough times that I'd recognized it.

I wasn't taking any chances. I wanted to win so bad I could taste it. I would definitely take advantage of what I'd learned about Zac, but I'd also be ready in case he turned out to less predictable than I anticipated. I was confident I could take him. Zac had tremendous strength, but I was stronger. He had considerable talent, but I had more. I knew anything could happen in a wrestling match, but I knew I had a good shot at emerging the victor. I knew Zac feared my wrestling abilities—it was plain to read in his eyes. I don't think he was at all enthused that he'd be facing me on the mat.

A lot of guys were betting on our match. I had a ton of them come up and tell me they had money riding on me. That made me feel even more confident, although it put extra pressure on me, too. I didn't think about the bets too much. Even if Zac beat me, it wouldn't be my fault if those guys lost money. It would be theirs for betting. I didn't intend to lose, however; I was gonna win.

❧ ❧ ❧

There was one thing more important than my upcoming contest with Zac, and that was Jon. Despite all that I knew, I just couldn't quite give up my hope for a life with him. Some little part of me just kept on hoping that he'd come to me and tell me he was willing to try. I guess I hoped that his love for me was so strong that it would grow into something more. I wanted his love as my friend to turn into love as my boyfriend. I knew I was deluding myself, but I just couldn't let go.

My mind was filled with thoughts of Jon as I joined Nathan to work on the eternal fencerow. Like my problems, the fence just kept going on and on. I knew Nathan probably wouldn't be too excited about me talking about how much I loved a boy, but I needed to talk to someone and there was no one else.

I was right, Nathan seemed uncomfortable listening to me, but listen he did. I loved him for being such a good friend.

"I wanted Jon more than I've ever wanted anything," I explained. "Why was I made to love him so when I could never have him? If you love someone that much, they should love you back. It just shouldn't be possible for them not to love you. It isn't fair!"

I was getting really worked up. Too much was going on in my life and it was becoming more than I could handle.

"I know you loved him and still love him," said Nathan. "I know it's not fair. A lot of things in life aren't fair. But this is the way things are—you can't alter reality. No matter how bad you want things to be different, wanting it won't make it happen. You did all you could with Jon. It just wasn't meant to be. I know it isn't fair, but that's the way life is."

I looked at Nathan. He was almost as upset as I was. He seemed rather impatient with me as well. I suddenly felt more than a little foolish for whining about my life in front of him. Life had dealt harder blows to Nathan than it had me, and he kept on going. He didn't even complain. He just took it and went on.

"I just wanted him to love me, Nathan. I just want someone to love me. I thought Jon was the one. I really thought he was the one. I just need someone to love me."

Tears welled up in my eyes as the emotions came out. I was telling Nathan things I'd never told him, or anyone. He could see my very soul.

Nathan took my hands and held them between his. He peered directly into my eyes, unblinking.

"Sometimes, what you want is right in front of you, Ethan, if you just have the eyes to see. Sometimes, you're looking so hard at something else, that you can't see what's been there all along."

There was a pleading quality in Nathan's voice that made me look into his eyes. There was a connection between us, a communication beyond words. I had no doubt that his words, wise as they were, meant even more than they seemed. He peered ever more deeply into my eyes as if he was searching to touch my soul. Our thoughts became one and at last I could understand the message in his eyes. I'd been blind to it for so long, but finally I could see. Nathan called to me in my mind, saying *SEE ME!*

I hugged Nathan close and actually cried on his shoulder. He wrapped his arms around me tightly and ran his fingers through my hair.

"I love you, Ethan." His voice was so sweet and sincere it made my heart melt.

We hugged even tighter. I felt like I never wanted to let go. After several long moments I released my vice-like grip. I took a step back and looked into Nathan's child-like eyes.

"I'm so sorry, Nathan." There was true regret in my voice.

Nathan began to cry. His eyes dropped to the ground, he covered his face, and just bawled his eyes out. I knew he'd misunderstood me. I knew I'd said the wrong thing. I knew he thought that I didn't love him. But that wasn't what I was sorry about. I was sorry for being so stupid—for not seeing him. I was sorry for being so wrapped up in Jon that I couldn't see that what I wanted was staring me right in the face. I loved Nathan with all my heart. I just didn't know it until he made me see. I took his chin in my hand and made him look at me.

"You don't understand, Nathan. I'm sorry I've been so stupid. I'm so sorry I wasn't smart enough to see you, to know that I love you, too. I do love you, Nathan. I really do."

Nathan clasped me in a hug that threatened to squeeze the life right out of me. He looked up into my eyes. He was still crying, but he was smiling through the tears.

"Do you really mean it? You really love me?" asked Nathan as if he were almost too afraid to ask for fear of rejection.

"I really mean it, Nathan," I said. The realization that I loved him engulfed me. How could so powerful an emotion remain hidden? It didn't seem possible, but it had. I did not know how long I'd loved Nathan, but I loved him with all my heart.

"Does this mean you'll be my boyfriend?" said Nathan. His innocence touched my heart.

"Yes it does, Nathan, if you'll have me."

He hugged me close again like he'd never let go.

"I'll have you," he said and snickered. He hugged me tighter. "I love you, Ethan."

CHAPTER 25

Dreams Do Come True

I finished up the last of the farm tasks I had for Sunday and headed back to the house. I showered then walked to my closet and tried to decide what to wear. I'd never given my appearance that much thought before, but suddenly I cared very much about how I looked. It was mid-November and the air had taken on a real chill, so I picked out a short-sleeved white shirt and a blue flannel shirt to go over it. I tucked the shirt into my jeans and left the flannel shirt unbuttoned. I was pretty satisfied with the effect.

I walked to my dresser and searched out the cologne that someone had given me for Christmas long ago. I sprayed just a little on my chest, right below the collar of my shirt. I hoped Nathan would like it.

I looked out the window and saw Nathan drawing near. My heart fluttered in my chest just a little and I felt nervous. *Ease up, Ethan, you see him every single day.* I took a deep breath, then nearly laughed at myself for acting like a giddy schoolgirl. I guess I did have good reason to be nervous. I was going on my first real date. I'd dated Kim of course, but that wasn't real. This date *mattered.*

I loved Nathan so very much. How could I have been so ignorant of my own feelings for so very long? It totally blew me away. Once Nathan made me realize I loved him, I couldn't imagine how I'd been so blind to that love for so very long, but before that moment I was clueless. Maybe I did know why I'd been blinded to my love for Nathan, after all. I'd been so obsessed with Jon that I didn't give other guys a single thought. I noticed them physically, but not emotionally. I'd felt myself drawing closer to Nathan. I'd felt the relationship between us growing—becoming more intimate, but I thought of my feelings for Nathan as love for a friend, not a boyfriend. If it hadn't been for my obsession with Jon, I'd have realized what was happening—I'd have realized I was falling in love. I smiled to myself. Nathan had forced my eyes to open. He'd made me see what was really there. Because of him, I was truly happy for the first time in a long time.

Nathan walked into my room, looking very sharp in some of the clothes I'd given him all those weeks before. He smiled at me shyly. He was so sweet and *so* cute. I'd noticed how he looked before of course, but I looked at him with new eyes. Nathan was a very handsome young man, with light blond hair and an innocent, kind face. I could still read the ever-present sadness in his eyes, but he was smiling. Nathan seemed happier than I'd ever seen him. He was excited and it showed.

It was amazing. So much had changed and I'd come so far. I'd gone from denying what I was to embracing it. Nathan had changed from merely a boy who just happened to work on the farm, to my friend, and then to my boyfriend. My whole world was transforming and it was wonderful. I felt like a butterfly coming out of its cocoon. My dream had not been destroyed, it had merely taken a new course.

"Where are we going to go?" Nathan asked.

"First, we're going to have lunch. I'm starved!"

We walked out to Jack's old green Ford pickup and I drove Nathan to *The Park's Edge*, a great restaurant that I freaking loved. It was the same place I'd taken Kim, but I didn't give her a moment's thought. All I thought about was Nathan. I gazed lovingly at Nathan over the menus. I knew I was in trouble, but it was the good kind—I was head over heels in love with that boy. Nathan's eyes met mine and he grinned at me. He was always a cute boy, but when he smiled he was beautiful. I reached across the table, took his hand for a moment, and gave it a little squeeze. We gazed into each other's eyes and I felt filled with love.

We released our grasp as the waitress neared, but the feeling was still there. Nothing could take it away. I was so happy it was hard to stay still in my seat. I ordered hot artichoke dip, pasta with eggplant and mushroom, and a big piece of chocolate cake. Nathan just couldn't decide so I suggested he just order the same. I'd eaten at that restaurant a lot, so I knew what was good. He took my suggestion and we smiled at one another again as the waitress departed.

We talked all through lunch with the ease of long time friends. There was something more than friendship there, however. There was an undercurrent of deep emotion, and desire. I knew I had a big dopey grin on my face, but I didn't care. I was too happy not to smile.

I wonder if this is how Mark and Taylor felt, I thought to myself. *Is this what it was like for them when they were together?* Sadness engulfed me for a moment. I couldn't think of my two friends without grieving for them. I pushed the memories of their recent deaths out of my mind and thought instead for a moment of how much in love they must've been. I could understand them a little better now, because of my love for Nathan. They'd endured hell on earth for their love and I knew I'd do the same if I had to—love was worth it.

I looked at Nathan's lips and thought how very much I'd like to kiss him. I wanted to just take him in my arms, hold him close, and kiss him forever. Nathan and I had known each other quite a long time, and yet such thoughts had never entered my mind before. When Nathan first started working for Uncle Jack, I'd been in denial over my sexual preference. After that, I'd been too obsessed with Jon to think of anyone else. I'd noticed that Nathan was a good looking boy, but I'd never given it any more thought than that, well, not much anyway. Sometimes a bit of lust stirred in my heart, but now it was different—now there was so much more. I loved Nathan and I wanted him, but my desire was but a part of what I felt for him.

I gave my desires more thought as we sat there. Nathan's handsome face and slim torso filled me with sexual yearning. I loved Nathan's smooth, slim body. I liked that he was smaller than me. We had completely different body types and I found that exciting. Maybe opposites really did attract. I wanted to just scoop Nathan up and ravish him right then and there. I forced my thoughts to other matters. I wanted to take things slow with Nathan and do everything just right. In time, it would all come. Waiting would not be easy, but I wanted Nathan to know I loved him and that I wasn't just out to seduce him. I did crave sex with him, but I desired his love even more.

After our late lunch Nathan and I strolled through the park in town, but found it a little too open and crowded. I led him along a remote path and we admired the yellows, oranges, and golds of the fall leaves. Soon, they'd be only a memory. Already, most of them were laying on the ground, creating a vibrant carpet of golden hue. In a couple more weeks at most, the trees would be bare. For the moment, however, Nathan and I walked through a fall paradise.

We walked past the school and across the soccer fields. We paused for just a moment at *the* soccer goal, the one where'd I'd found Taylor, the one where Mark... The memories were too fresh in my mind. Were they really gone? Nathan reached up and wiped away the tear that rolled down my cheek. He gazed into my eyes. My shoulders began to shudder and my tears flowed freely. Nathan drew me close and hugged me. I let out the pain I was feeling. I cried onto his shoulder, my body racked with sobs. In a few moments, I raised my head and looked into Nathan's eyes. He wiped my tears away once more. Nathan understood.

We left the soccer fields behind and stepped onto the path that led through the forest. The leaves were even more beautiful here than they had been near the park. The sun above cast a golden glow all around us. I took Nathan's hand and held it as we walked. The emotions bound within me at that moment mixed in a way I'd not experienced before. There was deep sadness in my heart and yet I couldn't remember ever having been so happy. The loss of my friends created a sadness with depths I'd never known before, but the simple pleasure of holding Nathan's hand was a joy beyond anything I'd imagined. It was almost too much to bear, this mix of sorrow and joy. I clung to Nathan's love and it stabilized me. I wanted to just go on holding his hand forever.

I stopped on a little hill where the path took a turn. We were well hidden from anyone who might be coming down the path in either direction. My heart fluttered in my chest and I could tell Nathan was nervous too—he trembled ever so slightly. He looked so sweet and innocent as he gazed up at me. I drew near to him, faced him, and gently pulled him to me. I leaned down, drawing my lips closer and closer to his own until at last they met. I kissed him lightly, running my lips across his, savoring his sweet taste and the feeling of love.

Our lips parted, only to search out one another again. We kissed more deeply, our lips parting, our tongues entwining. I held Nathan tightly in my arms and became lost in his. The moments stretched into an eternity of bliss. All the pain I'd suffered in my life seemed worth it, just for that kiss.

We drew apart and smiled at one another. It was our first kiss and I know that each of us would remember it forever.

"We'll have to come back here and carve our initials in that tree," said Nathan, pointing to a giant oak just to the north of the path. "Maybe inside a big heart. Every time I see it, I want to remember this day."

"I have something else that will help you remember," I said.

I reached in my pocket and pulled out a small box wrapped with paper. I handed it to Nathan.

"Open it," I said.

I watched as Nathan unwrapped my gift and opened the lid of the box. He drew out a gold chain and held it up to the light.

"Oh my gosh," he said, looking at the chain, then back at me. "You shouldn't have bought me this, it's too much!"

"No. It's not," I said. "Not at all. It's just a reminder of how much I love you, and that I'm your boyfriend." I smiled. Nathan smiled too. There was a tear in his eye.

"Here," I said, taking the necklace and fastening it around his neck. I stood back and looked at him. "You look really sexy wearing that."

Before Nathan had a chance to answer, I kissed him again. I took his hand in mine once more and we walked further down the forest path. I don't think I'd ever seen him so happy in all my life.

I don't know how much time we spent walking in the woods that day. Time seemed to have no meaning there. If was as if each moment was eternal. The golden leaves that surrounded us made it seem like we were in a magical world. It was almost as if it all existed just for us. We lingered in our world for the entire day.

That evening, I took Nathan to see a movie. It was almost as I'd dreamed when I was there with Kim, except it was Nathan at my side instead of Jon. I found that I didn't care. In fact, I was glad I was with Nathan and not Jon. My love for Nathan grew with each passing moment and I couldn't even imagine not being with him. Perhaps my love did not grow so fast as it seemed, however. Perhaps it was just coming out of hiding. I'd loved Nathan for a long time, but that love had disguised itself as love for a friend when it was really something far greater. I guess it didn't matter, my love for Nathan was finally in the light of day.

Nathan and I held hands throughout the entire film and sat as close together as we dared. I wanted to put my arm around him, but a lot of guys from school were there and it just wouldn't do. It seemed so unfair that I couldn't put my arm around my boyfriend when they could put theirs around their girlfriends with such ease. I didn't let it bother me. Nothing could ruin such a wonderful night.

I offered to drive Nathan home, but he said he'd rather walk home from my house. I didn't press him. I knew only too well that he didn't want me near his home. I had no real idea why, but I knew it had something to do with his parents. I just wished he would let me help with whatever was hurting him. We were so much closer than we'd ever been, but he still wouldn't open up to me and tell me what was wrong.

❧ ❧ ❧

I sat talking with Jon before wrestling practice the next day. It seemed like old times. Well, not quite—I was talking to him about my new boyfriend. That sure wouldn't have happened a few weeks before for any number of reasons.

As I shared my happiness with him, I grew happier still, for Jon was genuinely happy for me, and not just because it shifted my romantic interests from him. I realized just how good of a friend I had in Jon. I hadn't lost a boyfriend when he'd turned me down, I'd gained an even better friend.

"I'm just so sorry I acted like I did," I explained to him. "I'm sorry I stayed away from you. I'm sorry I was angry. I didn't have a right to act like that. You didn't do anything wrong."

"I understand," said Jon. "If I were in your shoes, I would probably have done the same. It must've been hard talking to me after what passed between us. I don't think I'd have had the balls to talk to you for a long time if our roles were reversed. I'm not mad. I was a little hurt at first, but then I did some thinking, and I understood. Besides, that's all in the past. We're friends, and that's all that matters."

Jon sighed.

"What's the matter?"

"Well, I was just thinking. I know you have problems, but I almost wish I was you. I wish I could be in love like that. I've never been in love."

"You'll find someone," I said. "I happen to know you're a very sexy guy, and quite a nice one, too. Some girl will grab you up before long."

Jon laughed a little at that.

"I hope so. I could use some grabbing."

It was my turn to laugh.

"Here," said Jon pulling a thick stack of papers out of his gym bag. "I want you to have this."

"What is it?"

"Brandon gave it to me. It's something Mark wrote before he died. I thought it might help you. I'm sure Mark would want you to read it."

I felt tears welling up in my eyes at the mention of Mark. I forced them away. I did not want to cry. I took the papers and carefully put them away, wondering just what Mark had written.

"We'd better get going," said Jon. "See you later, Ethan."

Minutes later, I was in the locker room. I had Mark's papers in my gym bag and opened my locker so I could put them there for safekeeping during practice. I cringed when I found another note there. Each one was more vicious than the last. I felt a nervous shiver in my chest as I picked it up and stuffed it in my pocket. I walked to the restroom and closed myself in a stall before taking it out to read.

> What are you willing to do to keep your secret, fag? Just how much is it worth to you? I hold your pathetic life in my hands, you know that, don't you? You're my bitch now, queer, and don't you ever forget it! Just how good have you become at sucking cock, faggot? Maybe we'll soon see.

The words made me uneasy, to say the least. I felt like my nerves couldn't handle much more. Why did he have to keep stretching things out? What did he want? Why didn't he just tell me? I was afraid I knew the answer—he wanted me to squirm. I was squirming all right. He'd called me his bitch and I knew what that could mean. I nearly retched when I considered the possibilities. I had Nathan now and I loved him. I wanted a physical relationship with him alone. What would I do if my tormentor demanded I be his sex slave? That's what his latest note seemed to hint at. At the very least, he'd demand that I blow him. Once I did it, how many more times would he want it? I couldn't bear the thought of it, not only for the disgust it raised within me, but because I knew it would mean betraying Nathan. I couldn't live with that.

I violently ripped the note into tiny pieces, as if it were my tormentor, then flushed it down the toilet. I gripped the top of the stall door and leaned there for a few moments, calming my ragged breath. I knew my tormentor might well be waiting the locker room. I didn't want him to see how badly as I was shaken. Would this nightmare never end?

That night, I pulled out the stack of papers Jon had given me. As I began reading I realized it was a diary of sorts, it was a record of all the things that had happened to Mark and Taylor—all the emotions and turmoil that Mark had experienced. He'd written about everything from the very day he'd met Taylor. He'd even mentioned me.

I was glued to the pages. I almost felt like Mark had been writing about me instead of himself. So much was familiar: the fear, the desperate longing, the pain, and the love. I was glad Mark and Taylor had found each other. It was clear from what Mark wrote that they were deeply in love. I was happy that they both had a chance to experience that before they died. At least they had that. The rest of their lives were certainly a nightmare. I didn't move from my chair until I'd read it all.

By the end, I was crying. Jon was right, it did help. It made me understand Mark and Taylor more clearly. More importantly, it made me understand myself.

I desperately wished that I'd opened up to Mark before he died and told him I was gay, too. I wished I'd taken the time to tell him that I was there for him. Most of all, I wished I'd supported him and Taylor, instead of being a coward. Maybe I could've saved them. It was too late for that, however. It was too late for a lot of things. Mark had been a good friend, but I knew if I'd had the courage to open up to him that we could've been much, much closer. The loss of Mark was incalculable. I bowed my head and cried for the loss of what could have been.

CHAPTER 26

Love in the Candlelight

The next afternoon it was back to work on the farm. There was something comfortable, familiar, and safe about it. When I was anywhere else I felt like I was on the verge of being exposed; it was as if my tormentor could rise up and denounce me at any moment. The farm, however, felt like a place where evil could not come. I knew a big reason why I felt that way was that Nathan was there.

Working by Nathan's side had taken on a whole new meaning. I'd long enjoyed the closeness and friendship between us, but suddenly there was so much more—there was love. I must have looked at Nathan hundreds of times a day just thinking about how much I loved him. I felt like I'd loved him forever. I knew that I would love him always.

When Nathan looked at me I could see my own feelings reflected in his eyes. We'd developed a closeness that was more intimate than anything I'd ever experienced. Every once in a while, out of the blue, we just hugged each other close. I would've never thought that hugging could mean so much.

Our hugging did create an awkward situation. We were standing at the edge of the pasture, holding each other tightly, when Nathan's little brother came out of nowhere. Nathan and I were so wrapped up in each other we'd been oblivious to everything else. We hadn't been kissing, as we tended to do quite a lot, but our noses were pressed together and we were smiling and gazing dreamily into each other's eyes. Dave looked at us oddly, like he couldn't comprehend what was going on.

I must admit Dave catching us like that terrified me. I thought that Nathan would probably sink right into the ground with embarrass-ment. He didn't, however. He surprised me. He stood right there calm and collected. We faced Dave, but Nathan kept his arm around my waist.

"What are you guys doin'?" asked Dave, wide-eyed and confused.

Nathan pulled his arm from my waist, kneeled down so he was eye level with his little brother, and took Dave's hand in his.

"You don't understand why me and Ethan were hugging do you?" said Nathan.

"Not really," said Dave, eyeing me.

"Well, Davy, you know how boys my age date girls right?"

"And boys my age date girls, too, " said Dave, "I'm not a little kid."

"I know that, Davy," said Nathan mussing his hair. "I'm just trying to explain something and it's not easy."

Dave nodded.

"Well, some boys date boys instead of girls, Davy. They aren't interested in girls, they are just interested in other boys."

"You mean gay?"

"Yeah, that's right."

Dave peered into his brother's eyes, looked at me, then back at his brother.

"Ethan is my boyfriend, Davy. Both of us are gay."

Dave swallowed hard and looked back and forth between us again.

"But I thought that was bad. The boys at school say…"

"It's not bad, Davy. Do you think Ethan and I are bad?"

"No way, Nathan. I think you and Ethan are awesome!"

I had to smile at that.

"Don't listen to the boys at school. Ethan and I love each other, there's nothing bad about that."

Dave looked thoughtful for a moment.

"You guys kiss? And do the other stuff?"

"We kiss," said Nathan. "And we hug like you just saw. We haven't done the "other stuff" yet, but we will."

"That's okay," said Dave. "You guys can do what you want." He paused for a moment, looking somewhat fearful. "I like girls."

"That's great!" said Nathan.

"I thought you might be mad," said Dave.

"Why would I be mad about that?"

"Well, I thought you'd be mad because I was different from you."

"Dave, you are a wonderful little brother. I'd never get mad because you are different. Differences are what make the world such a wonderful place."

As I stood there listening, I wondered when Nathan became so smart. I guess I should've realized by then just how intelligent he was. He'd sure helped me with my problems.

Nathan explained everything to his little brother with wisdom that seemed far beyond his years. I'd never have been able to handle such a situation so well.

"Just one thing, Davy. You can't tell anyone about us. It could get us in a lot of trouble."

"But why? If it's not wrong, then why would you get in trouble?"

"Some people think it's wrong, Davy, like your friends at school. If the wrong people knew about us, they'd hurt us, Davy. You understand?"

"I won't tell anyone, ever!" said Dave and hugged his brother close. "I love you, Nathan."

When Nathan stood, he had tears in his eyes, as did I. I found myself wishing I had a little brother like that. I was proud of the way Nathan had dealt with the whole thing. Dave accepted it all. It was clear it didn't bother him one bit.

"Did Henrietta lay today?" Dave asked me. I smiled. I wished everyone could accept Nathan and I the way Dave did, and as quickly.

"Go look in the refrigerator and see," I told him. If Henrietta laid an egg, I always put it in the refrigerator in a little bag for Dave.

"Okay! I have to go check on Henrietta, too!" he said, "But, I'll be back."

He ran off to the house, happy and carefree. I knew Nathan had to work very hard so Dave could have a life like that. It made me more proud and in awe of Nathan than ever. I pulled him to me, hugged him tight, and kissed him passionately.

Dave was back in just a few minutes to show Nathan the egg that his hen had laid that day. He was grinning from ear to ear. That boy seemed to be able to find happiness in just about anything. I wondered how much Nathan had to do with that.

Dave ran for home, carefully carrying his egg in the little bag. The sky was beginning to dim and the shadows of evening were long on the grass. I pulled Nathan to me and kissed him again. When our lips parted, I took him by the hand and led him away from the fencerow.

"Where are we going?" asked Nathan.

"You'll see," I said. "I have something to show you."

I led Nathan through the fields, never letting go of his hand. His touch gave me a sense of closeness. His hand felt so comfortable and warm. We walked on, following the little path into the woods. I couldn't help but stop for a moment and kiss Nathan yet again. I was so in love with him. And to make it even better, he was so in love with me.

I led Nathan to the little cabin by the lake. The moon had come out and lit up the lake like thousands of sparkling diamonds. The old log cabin looked beautiful in the blue light.

"Oh my gosh," said Nathan. "This is beautiful."

I pushed open the door and led Nathan inside. It was dark, but I lit an oil lamp and a few candles and the cabin was soon filled with a warm, romantic glow. The cabin was not as Jon had seen it. I'd been busy cleaning it up and getting it ready for Nathan.

"I love you so much," I said, hugging Nathan close. He nuzzled against my neck.

"And I love you," he said. His words flowed over me like pure joy.

Nathan gazed into my eyes and his lips neared mine. We kissed tenderly, then with greater passion and hunger. When our lips parted at last we gazed into each other's eyes, searching, communicating without words. Nathan was trembling slightly, but it was not from fear. I smiled at him—I love him so much it hurt.

I placed my hand on his chest and rubbed it through his shirt. I slowly ran my hands down over his abdomen, then pulled his shirt over his head. I stepped back and took off my shirt as well. We drew together again and necked in the candlelight as our bare chests pressed against each other. I was filled with a desire fueled by love. It overpowered me, guiding my actions.

I fumbled with Nathan's belt and finally worked it loose. My fingers unbuttoned his jeans and pulled down his zipper with the awkwardness of a virgin. I pushed his jeans to the floor. Nathan kicked off his shoes and socks and stood before me in his boxers.

Nathan reached out and removed my jeans. He didn't stop there, however. He slowly pulled down my boxers, revealing my nakedness. Soon we were both naked. We stood there gazing at each other for a few moments. Nathan was a beautiful young man. The sight of him filled me with both love and desire. I pulled him close and we necked while our naked bodies pressed together. His hardness against me sent me to new heights of arousal.

I pulled Nathan down with me onto a pallet on the floor. Our lips never parted as we sank onto the soft, feather filled mattress. Our hands began to roam and we explored each other's firm, young body. All those weeks of farm work had toned Nathan's body and thickened his muscles. He'd grown from a boy into a beautiful young man.

Our hands were replaced with lips and tongues. We made slow passionate love in the candlelit cabin, sharing everything, loving each other with our bodies as we did with our souls. I knew it was as it was meant to be. It was not what I was expecting—it was a thousand times more powerful and wonderful. We weren't having sex, we were making love and that is an entirely different thing. We gave ourselves to each other, body and spirit. It was the most wonderful night in all my life.

Two hours or more later, we lay together, Nathan's head resting on my chest. The candles had burned low and the golden light was subdued. I held Nathan in my arms, enjoying the warmth and love. I wanted to lay there with him forever. I smiled to myself. I always wanted to do everything with Nathan forever. I guess it just showed how very much I loved him. I knew then that we'd always be together—nothing would tear us apart. No matter what happened, we had each other, and that's all we really needed.

❦ ❦ ❦

The next day after school, I walked to the fencerow to join Nathan at work. He greeted me with a smile, a kiss, and a hug.

"I feel so safe when I'm with you," he said as I held him. "When I'm in your arms I feel like nothing can hurt me." I hugged him tighter, knowing I would protect him from anything and everything.

Our night together had brought us closer than ever. I felt like we were one. Every moment with Nathan was pure joy. Despite everything that was hanging over my head, I still found happiness with him.

I could still sense the sadness in Nathan. His problems had not disappeared. I knew, however, that having me in his life helped him a great deal. It sure helped me to have Nathan. When someone loves you, it's possible to handle anything.

CHAPTER 27

Dark Secrets Uncovered

Early Saturday morning I was in the barn cleaning out the horse stalls when I heard something overhead. I didn't know what it was, but it didn't sound like a barn noise to me. I put down the pitchfork and climbed the ladder into the loft. I stepped out onto the carpeting of hay and found a startled Nathan looking up at me. It was clear he'd spent the night there. His little brother was still fast asleep, nestled in some blankets up against the hay bales. Nathan looked at me with fear in his eyes—the fear of discovery.

"What are you doing up here, Nathan?"

"We were, uh, just kind of camping out."

Nathan was edgy, nervous, and downright frightened. He wasn't scared of me, however, he was just plain afraid. I had a good idea why.

"You can tell me the truth, Nathan. It's me, Ethan. When was the last time you went home?'

I knew he didn't want to answer, but I didn't let him off the hook. I'd respected his privacy all along. I hadn't asked him the things I knew he didn't want me to ask. I minded my own business. If he was too scared to go home, however, he needed my help. Letting him keep his secret wouldn't help him. It would only allow what was going on to continue. I loved him far too much to let anyone, or anything, hurt him.

"Tell me," I said firmly.

"Four days." The panic in his eyes was frightening.

"Four days?" I asked incredulously. I counted backward in my mind. The night we'd made love together in the cabin was six days before. He'd been staying away from home almost that entire time.

"Yes," said Nathan. "Four days."

"What happened, Nathan? Why can't you go home?"

He looked away and wouldn't answer. He looked at his little brother sleeping and almost cried. I walked over to him, sat down beside him, and took his chin in my hand. I gently but firmly made him look into my eyes.

"Tell me, Nathan. Tell me what's wrong so I can help you."

"You can't!" he said, tears running down his cheeks "You can't help me, Ethan."

"Tell me."

"You'll hate me for it. You'll think I'm nasty. You won't be my boyfriend anymore. You won't love me anymore!" He was bawling. I pulled him to me and hugged him close. He cried into my shoulder. I petted his hair.

"Nathan, nothing is going to change how I feel about you—nothing!"

He cried even harder and I just kept holding him. After a good long while he calmed down and sat back in the hay.

"Has someone been hurting you? Has someone been doing something to you? Your dad?"

Nathan was still sobbing. I wanted to let up and leave him be. I knew my questions were hurting him. I also knew that stopping wasn't the right thing to do. If I truly loved him, and I did, I had to find out what was hurting him.

"Tell me."

"Not my dad," he said. "Although he doesn't do anything to stop it."

"Who?"

"My mom."

"What does she do, Nathan? Does she hit you?"

"Sometimes, but that's not it. She makes me...She makes me do things," said Nathan in a hoarse whisper, as if the words were too terrible to speak out loud.

Nathan started bawling. I knew I was on top of a secret he'd been keeping for as long as I knew him. I knew he was on the brink.

"What, Nathan, what does she make you do?"

"She makes me...She's makes me.. She touches me where she shouldn't. She..." He was sobbing uncontrollably. "Please don't make me tell you! Please, Ethan, don't make me say any more!" He completely broke down in front of me. I held him close while he bawled his eyes out. I felt for him so much that I cried too. Anything that hurt him, hurt me. It was a long time before Nathan quieted down. I just held him and rocked him like a baby. He held onto me tightly, like he would never let go. Finally, he spoke again.

"I had to get out of there. I had to get Dave out of there."

"Has your mom...Has she been bothering Dave?"

"No, but she would have. I've seen that look in her eye when she looks at him. I know what it means. I had to take him away. I couldn't let it happen to him."

He looked at Dave who was still sleeping peacefully as if he hadn't a care in the world.

"Dave doesn't know about any of this," he said. "You can't tell him!" His tone was filled with panic.

"I won't," I said. "Calm down, Nathan. It's going to be okay."

"They don't love me. My parents don't love me. They don't care about Dave either. I don't want to go back there."

"You don't have to go back," I said. "Not ever."

"I don't have anywhere to go, Ethan. I don't have anything. I don't have any money. How am I going to take care of Dave?"

My soul cried for Nathan. No wonder sadness always hovered over his head. No wonder he'd never been able to be truly happy. He'd been supporting the weight of the world on his young shoulders.

"You're wrong, Nathan. You have me. I love you, and I love Dave. I won't let anything happen to you. I'll take care of you. We'll take care of Dave together. You're staying with me. You're living here from now on. You don't ever have to go back."

"But your Uncle Jack…"

"I'll talk to him, Nathan. Don't give it another thought. My home is yours now. It's ours."

Nathan didn't answer. He just cried some more. I held him until he calmed down some, then left him with his brother while I went to talk to Uncle Jack.

❧ ❧ ❧

I found Jack running the combine in the big cornfield at the far edge of the farm. He stopped when he saw me coming. He knew it was something important. I never interrupted him when he was working unless there was great need.

I told him about Nathan and Dave sleeping in the barn and about why Nathan was afraid to go home. I didn't tell him exactly why, only that Nathan's parents abused him. Uncle Jack listened gravely, showing little emotion. Uncle Jack rarely showed any emotion.

"I know this is asking a lot, Uncle Jack. I know this is your farm and not mine. But could they stay here with us? They can't go home and they don't have any place else to go."

"This isn't my farm, it's ours, Ethan, as much yours as mine. You work here every day just like I do. I couldn't run this place without you. When I'm gone, it will all be yours. And as far as Nathan and his brother are concerned, I'm not about to turn them away. They can stay here as long as they like."

"Thanks, Uncle Jack!"

I gave him the biggest hug he'd probably ever had in his life. Uncle Jack smiled and hugged me back. For him, it was an emotional outburst of unparalleled dimensions.

I thanked him again and again until he told me to get lost so he could get some work done. It was typical Uncle Jack behavior. I ran back across the fields to the barn as if I could fly. I climbed up into the loft to find Nathan talking to his little brother.

"Gather your stuff guys, it's time to show you your new home."

"Just like that?" asked Nathan, bewildered.

"Just like that," I said.

I beamed at Nathan and he was so happy he practically started crying. Dave looked a little confused. Nathan explained it to him.

"Remember what I told you, Dave? How it's not safe for us to live where we did anymore?"

Dave nodded.

"We're going to live with Ethan now. Do you like that?"

"I sure do!" Dave jumped up and grabbed his things.

I marveled at how quickly Dave adjusted to the situation. I know that Nathan had been sheltering him, but I think Davy knew there was something wrong at home, even without his brother telling him. Dave was a sharp boy. I was sure he'd picked up on a lot of things. I'm sure he knew that his parents didn't care about him. I looked at the brothers. How could anyone not care about them?

The boys followed me to the house and I took them upstairs. I led them into the extra bedroom.

"Here Dave, this can be your room."

"My own room?" he asked incredulously, looking around as if he were in a palace. "This place is nice."

"Nathan will be right next door, with me."

Nathan looked at me and smiled, then a wave of concern washed over his face.

"Is that okay with you?" he asked Dave. "You'll be okay in here by yourself won't you?"

"I'm not a baby, Nathan. Now, if you two will get out of *my* room, I want to look around."

Nathan and I laughed. It was clear his little brother would be more than fine. We left Dave to explore and headed for my, I mean *our*, room.

"I'll make room for your stuff in the closet and I'll clean out a couple of dresser drawers for you. You want top or bottom?"

"Ohhh, I'm pretty sure I like bottom, big boy, although I've never tried it," said Nathan. He giggled, but turned red. I couldn't believe he'd said that. I laughed out loud.

"Not that! I mean the drawers. You want bottom or top?"

"Ethan, I don't have any stuff. What I'm wearing and these blankets are it."

"Then we'll buy you some stuff and, until then, I'm sure you can find something of mine to wear."

"You've done too much already, Ethan."

"Hey, this isn't just for you. I have ulterior motives. I want you here. It's not every guy that gets permission for his boyfriend to move in so easily."

Nathan laughed.

"I notice there's only one bed." He raised his eyebrows and looked at me thoughtfully. I smiled at Nathan. This situation was going to have more than a few perks.

"If you want your own we can get you one."

"That won't be necessary." The wicked gleam in Nathan's eyes made my heart flutter in my chest.

"Now, what was that you said about wanting to try bottom?" I asked, arching my eyebrows. I pulled Nathan to me and kissed him deeply.

My whole world really had changed. Suddenly I felt like I had everything I'd ever wanted. It all happened overnight. I had the greatest boyfriend in the entire world, and he was living with me! I even had a little brother, who felt a lot like a son. Nathan and Dave weren't the family I'd always assumed I'd have, but that was fine by me. They were better.

None of my plans had worked out like I'd intended, but what I ended up with was even better. I'd wanted Jon as my boyfriend, instead I had Nathan. I'd planned on getting married and having a son, instead I got Dave. I found that I was much happier with what I received than I would've been with what I'd wanted. I felt like someone was looking after me, giving me what I really needed, instead of what I desired. My reality had become more wonderful than my dreams.

CHAPTER 28

My Tormentor Revealed

After wrestling practice I went to my locker once again. There, laying on the bottom of the locker, was another note. I unfolded it with the same apprehension I felt every time I found a note in my locker. It was almost as if the note itself could hurt me. The notes had been getting more and more threatening. As I read the words on the latest note, however, the message was different from all the rest:

Look behind you.

I knew someone was there. I could feel him. The moment had come. At last I'd know who had been tormenting me for all these weeks. Despite my fear, I didn't hesitate for a moment. I spun on my heel and faced my tormentor—it was Zac.

I'd never been able to cut my list of suspects down enough to discover my tormentor, but Zac was not the one I expected to see. It wouldn't have surprised me one bit to see Alex or Jeremy standing there, they were on the top of my list, but Zac...I just couldn't believe it! I'd never heard him utter a single anti-gay comment. When all the guys were on Mark and Taylor's asses, I never noticed Zac getting in on it—not once. He even seemed friendly toward them and me. It just didn't make any sense.

"You?" I asked, incredulously, my mouth gaping open in surprise. I simply couldn't believe it. I was wondering if this last note had anything to do with the others. It was typed like all the rest, but maybe that was a coincidence. Maybe Zac just put it in my locker to be funny. Maybe he knew nothing about my tormentor.

"Surprised, faggot?"

Those two words ended my doubts. It didn't seem possible that Zac was the one. I'd nearly crossed him off my list because he was such an unlikely candidate, but there was no denying reality. Sherlock Holmes said something that seemed to fit. I couldn't remember the exact words, but it went something like, "When you eliminate the impossible, whatever is left, however improbable, must be the answer." Zac was about as improbable as he could be, but without doubt, he was the one.

Zac was enjoying my shock. He stood there with crossed arms and gloated, "You are just a big, dumb jock, aren't you? All this time and you couldn't figure it out. You're not only a fag, you're stupid, too."

I ignored his insult. It hardly mattered.

"But why?" I asked. "Why have you done this to me? I've never hurt you. Is all this just because you think I'm gay?"

"I don't think you're gay, Ethan, I *know* it."

We stood there starting at each other for several moments. I wanted to tear him limb from limb, but I knew I couldn't—not unless I was willing to kill him to keep him quiet. I wasn't.

"You want to hurt me, don't you, Ethan?" smirked Zac. "But you won't. You'll do whatever I say, won't you, faggot?"

I swallowed hard. A little part of me wondered if I shouldn't just jump him, but, unless I was willing to carry it to the end, unless I really was willing to kill him, I couldn't. I wasn't the kind who could kill like that, not even to save myself from the horrors that were sure to come.

"Get on your knees," said Zac with a commanding tone.

I just stood there thinking, *No!* I remembered only too well one of his last notes. I knew what he was about to make me do and it sickened me.

"Do it, bitch!"

I sank to my knees and looked down at the floor.

"Look at me. Look at me!" he commanded.

I did as I was told. Hatred glared in my eyes, but I was his. Zac took a step forward until his crotch was inches from my face. He reached down and pulled down his zipper. I trembled. I didn't know if I could bear the shame of it. Zac unfastened his belt and popped the button on his jeans, then he slugged me.

"You'd really do it, wouldn't you, faggot?"

I rubbed my cheek where he'd hit me. I tasted blood. I looked up at him, wondering what kind of sick game he was playing with me.

"I don't want you blowing me, queer. Unlike perverts like you, I like girls. What's between us has nothing to do with you being a homo, Ethan. You fags really have a chip on your shoulder don't you? Everything has to be about your sexual orientation. Everything that goes wrong does so because you're gay. Everyone that doesn't like you feels that way because you're queer. What the fuck do I care if you're gay? Big fucking deal! I don't care what you do in your spare time, faggot."

I stood up. "If you don't care that I'm gay, then why do you call me faggot?"

"Because you are one, because I can, because you don't like it, and because you can't do shit about it."

I just looked at him. I hated guys like him. I hated those who took advantage of others just because they could.

"I don't give a shit if you're a faggot or not," said Zac. "You care, however. You don't want anyone to know. I'm willing to bet you'll do just about anything to keep me quiet. You'll do anything I want to keep your little queer secret. You were sure ready to suck me, weren't you? Or did that just turn you on?"

I wanted to pound him, but Zac was scaring me. My heart was racing and I was practically trembling. I didn't know what he had planned. There was a growing fear in the back of my mind—a fear that Zac wanted something very personal from me. I felt almost like a rape victim as their attacker closed in. That line of thought seemed irrational, however, I didn't think Zac was the least bit interested in me sexually. He said he wasn't. He'd hadn't made me blow him a few moments before, but maybe that was just part of the mind game he was playing with me. I didn't think he wanted sex from me, but, then again, I never dreamed he was the one tormenting me either. Anything could happen and there wasn't much I could do about it. I was afraid. Some guys were more than willing to use other guys, attracted or not. Some guys just got off on the control. The very thought made me want to sink into the earth and just disappear.

Zac drew closer and took my chin in his hand. I involuntarily shrank back from him. His touch repulsed me. I half expected him to grope me. I was so afraid that my breath was coming hard and fast. Zac smiled and it wasn't a friendly smile at all. He knew he had me by the balls and he was enjoying every second of it.

"I just want you to do one little thing for me, Ethan." He paused for several agonizing moments as he glared into my eyes. I lived in terror of his next words. "I want you to lose when we wrestle. You do that, and I'll forget everything I know about you—everything."

The revelation hit me like a brick upside the head. I felt like I must have been blind not to see it coming. What could Zac have possibly wanted from me more than that? It was absurdly simple, like a riddle once solved. He wanted to win that match and he knew he couldn't take me. Part of it still didn't make sense, however. One thing just didn't fit.

"You've been sending me these notes for weeks. It couldn't have all been for just this. You couldn't have known we'd be tied at the end of the season."

"Wrong, Ethan. I knew you'd be undefeated at the end. I've watched you. I've wrestled you. I was confident I'd make it, too. Maybe I'm a little conceited, but I know I'm good. There's only one guy that could beat me, and that's you. And besides, if we weren't tied at the end, I knew I'd be able to come up with something I wanted from you. Either way, I'd get something out of it. And besides, it has been a hell of a lot of fun watching you squirm."

"So this is how you want to win?" I said. It was my attempt at psychological warfare. It didn't bother Zac one bit.

"Nice try. How I win doesn't matter, Ethan, just so I do. No one else will know about this except you and me."

"And if I refuse?"

"If you refuse, I'll tell everyone what I know. I'll tell everyone how you lust after Jon. I'll tell everyone about the time you groped me in the locker room, how you tried to rape me."

"I never did that! I've never touched you!"

"You know that. I know that. But no one else knows it. I can prove you're gay, Ethan. After that, most people will believe just about anything. That won't be the end of it either, Ethan." Zac paused and grinned at me evilly. It sent a chill up my spine. "After I've let you suffer for awhile, something *very* bad will happen to you. You'll just disappear and your beaten body will be found days later. I know plenty of guys who'll help me do it, as soon as they find out you're a fag. Remember what happened to Mark, do you, Ethan? The same thing will happen to you, only this time, the boys will finish the job."

I wanted to kill Zac where he stood. I actually took a step toward him. I was enraged.

"Bad idea, Ethan," said Zac. I halted.

"I want to thank you for helping me out, Ethan. You've become pretty tight with that boy, Nathan, haven't you? He your butt-buddy now?"

I didn't answer.

"It doesn't matter. If I expose you, everyone will assume you two are getting it on. Everyone knows you're close, kinda like Mark and Taylor. You were friends with them, too, now isn't that interesting? It's just more proof that you're a faggot."

I kept my expression neutral. If Zac guessed that I cared for Nathan, he'd use it against me. Worse, he might threaten Nathan himself. At the moment, he seemed only to suspect that Nathan and I might be sleeping together. I doubted Zac could even comprehend the concept of love.

Zac made my blood run cold. It seemed beyond belief that anyone could be so evil, and yet, I knew he wasn't bluffing, at least not about exposing me and making up lies. I doubted he'd have the balls to kill me, although I wasn't sure about that either. He just might. I didn't really think so, but I'd been wrong about quite a lot recently. At the very least he'd probably get some guys to jump me and beat me senseless. That alone was enough to instill fear in my heart.

"And how do I know you'll keep quiet if I let you win?" I asked. "What's to stop you from telling everyone after the match? How do I know I can trust you?"

"You don't, but then you really don't have a choice now, do you? Besides, I'm more than willing to keep my end of the bargain." Zac grabbed the front of my shirt and pulled me toward him until his lips were practically touching my own. "I want this, I want it bad, and I'm willing to keep quiet about everything if I get it."

Zac seemed sincere. I had the feeling I could trust him to keep his part of the bargain. I was still wondering a lot about whether or not he'd really have the balls to kill me if I defied him. A death threat was certainly the kind of thing that tended to stick in one's mind.

As if on cue, Zac slammed me against the locker. My head banged into it painfully. He stared directly into my eyes with a look that could kill.

"You let me win and I forget about everything. If I lose—you die unpleasantly. Don't think I won't do it, fucker. I want this. I want to win bad and no one will miss a little faggot like you."

He shouldered me and stalked off, leaving me quite bewildered, not to mention frightened.

CHAPTER 29

The Decision of a Lifetime

I no longer had to wonder about the identity of my tormentor, or his motives. In a way, it was a relief to know who he was and what he wanted. A lot of the stuff I'd imagined had been pretty horrible. Much of what had been going through my mind was even worse than Zac's threats. I'd tried to push all my fears away and live my life, but my tormentor and his notes were always on the edge of my thoughts, lurking like a nightmare that I just couldn't shake.

I wasn't sure what I was going to do. After all the shit Zac had pulled, after all he'd done to me, I wanted to win my match against him more than ever. He didn't deserve to win, that was for sure. No one like that deserved to come out on top. I still had all my old reasons to win as well. Wrestling meant the world to me and I had a chance to be the best—just once.

Such a victory had a terrible price tag, however. If I defeated Zac, he would expose me without a doubt. He'd try his hardest to ruin everything for me and he just might succeed. I wasn't ashamed of what I was, not at all, but at the same time, I wasn't ready for my friends and teammates to know about me. Maybe someday I'd tell them all, but I just couldn't do it—not yet. I was caught between what I wanted most and what I feared the most. I was confused and afraid.

Zac's threat to kill me preyed upon my mind, too. There was something in his eyes as he threatened me with an unpleasant death, something about the way that he looked at me, that made me fear he wasn't bluffing. I could take Zac if it came down to a fight, but I knew he wouldn't be alone. I thought about what had happened to Mark in the locker room, about how Devon and his buddies had beat him senseless. That could easily be me. If Devon found out I was gay, I knew it would be me. Zac wouldn't have to look far to find somebody to take care of the job.

Devon and the others were just waiting their chance. They'd taken a lot of shit for what they'd done to Mark. One of them had cracked under pressure and talked. The next day he'd been found beaten to a pulp. It didn't take a genius to figure out who'd done it. The pack had turned on one of their own. It didn't save them. Brandon and Jon had hunted them down one by one and kicked their asses for what they'd done to Mark. They were incapable of learning, though—the just payment they received only seemed to increase their rage.

Neither Devon nor his buddies had ever shown the least regret for what they'd done. They even seemed to blame Mark for the way everyone looked down on them. They didn't take any responsibility for their own actions. If anything, they were hungry for revenge. Mark was dead, they couldn't go after him again. Taylor was gone, too. Devon's little gang was just itching to take out their frustrations on someone. I could see it in their eyes whenever I looked at them. If they found out I was gay, they'd be after me for sure. Only secrecy protected me from guys like that.

I was in hell. What I wanted most was right there for taking, but doing so would likely cost me everything. I turned it all over and over in my head, but I couldn't come to a conclusion. I just couldn't figure out what to do. I needed to talk to someone and I knew just who it was I needed.

I walked toward Nathan and the fencerow. We'd nearly finished our work there and would soon be helping Uncle Jack with the harvest. To say I'd be glad to be finished with the fencerow was an understatement. I was heartily sick of doing the same work day after day after day. I don't think I could have withstood it if it wasn't for Nathan. When he was at my side, there was nothing in my mind but thoughts of him.

When Nathan started working for Uncle Jack, I didn't know him at all. It was anything but love at first sight. We took a little while to warm up to each other. He was so distant and quiet that conversations were difficult in the beginning. And, of course, I was plagued by problems that I couldn't mention. As we worked side by side, however, we grew closer and closer until we became friends. During our first days together, I would never have dreamed for a moment that Nathan would become my boyfriend. Of course, back then I hadn't even admitted to myself that I was gay. Even later, when I'd come out to myself, I'd never thought of Nathan as a potential boyfriend. It's odd how life takes so many twists and turns and never seems to end up where one would expect. Despite the cloud of doom that hung over my head, I was glad life had put me where I was, at least where Nathan was concerned.

I can't begin to describe how wonderful it was lying beside Nathan each night. Hearing his soft breath, feeling his warmth, and just being aware of his presence filled me with contentment and joy. Being so near his smooth, firm body did make me restless at times. It awakened powerful desires within me, desires that I didn't have to resist for the first time in my life. Those desires were magnified beyond description by my love for Nathan. It wasn't just his sexy little body that drove me crazy, it was my love for him. I loved him more than anything. When we made love together it was powerful and wonderful beyond description.

I reached Nathan and found he'd nearly finished. We were actually on the verge of completing the long line of fencing! I almost felt like celebrating. I would've probably been jumping up and down in a frenzy of happiness over the completion of the fence if there wasn't so much hanging over my head.

I hugged Nathan and gave him a passionate kiss. He tasted so sweet and pure that my worries were driven from my head for a moment. They descended upon me quickly again, however, as I thought about what lay ahead.

"Nathan, I've got a problem." That was an understatement if there ever was one.

I filled Nathan in on all the details. His eyes grew wide in amazement when I told him Zac was behind it all. Nathan was clearly worried and upset—his eyes were fearful and his features were etched with concern.

"What are you going to do, Ethan?" he asked, nervously.

"I don't know. I'm not sure yet. There's so much to consider."

"Ethan, why don't you just let him win? I know how important this is to you, but you know you're a better wrestler than Zac. Do you really need to beat him to prove that? Can't you just let him win?" There was a pleading tone to Nathan's voice that touched my heart. I knew he loved me and couldn't bear to think of me getting hurt. It made me want to throw the match just for his sake. At the same time, I didn't want to knuckle under to Zac's threats. His kind didn't deserve to win.

"This is about a lot more than just wrestling, Nathan."

"I know it is and that just makes it harder, but I don't want you to get hurt, Ethan. I…I just don't want to see that happen to you."

I smiled at Nathan.

"Thanks," I said. "I know that would be the easy way out, and it may be what I end up doing, but I don't want to let him win like this. It isn't fair and it isn't right. I shouldn't have to give up what I want so badly because of someone like Zac."

There wasn't much more to say about it, so we both fell silent. I could tell by the look in Nathan's eyes that he wanted to plead with me to let Zac win. I could also tell that he didn't do it because he knew just what all this meant to me. I loved him more than ever for it.

The November wind was chill, but still I managed to work up a bit of a sweat. The breeze cooled my dampened shirt, but my working muscles kept me warm. The beautiful leaves had all fallen and lie on the ground, brown and lifeless. Winter was coming. I felt as if all things were drawing to a end, but to what end, I did not know.

My lips were silent, but a battle raged in my mind. The decision I had to make tormented me. I turned it over and over in my head, weighing the consequences, considering the results. If I defied Zac, could I handle what would happen? Could I take being publicly outed? Could I stand living in fear for my safely and my life? Could I withstand the taunts and derision? If I knuckled under to Zac, could I live with that decision? Could I go on day after day knowing that I had given up a dream out of fear? Could I live with myself knowing that I'd been a coward, that I just wasn't strong enough to stand up for what I was? There was no easy answer. Each path was plagued by consequences and doubts. I just wished it was all over and done.

My problems never left my thoughts until Nathan and I prepared for bed. I watched as he slipped out of his jeans and pulled his shirt off his slim torso. He filled me with a desire that threatened to overwhelm me. Nathan pulled off his boxers and slipped under the sheet. The brief glimpse of his firm little butt only served to heighten my desires.

Before Nathan had become my boyfriend, I'd always fantasized about a different type of guy. I'd always been drawn to very well-built young men. Something about a muscular chest and bulging biceps really attracted me. I guess I was attracted to the strength, as well as the beauty. Nathan wasn't that type of boy. He had muscle certainly, and was gaining more, but he was very slim—almost too thin. He wasn't at all like the guys I'd drooled over, and yet, once I fell for him, he was more attractive to me than any of them. I loved Nathan with all my heart. In my eyes there was no one more beautiful, sexy, or enticing. The mere sight of him took my breath away.

Nathan's eyes were on me as I undressed and I could read desire in them. I read something else there too, something that brought me far more pleasure than his obvious interest in my body—love. Nathan loved me just as I loved him. There was nothing more important to me in all the world.

I slipped off my boxers and crawled into bed beside Nathan. I leaned up on my elbow and gazed at him laying beside me. I pushed his blond hair back out of his eyes and looked upon his face. He was more beautiful to me than any boy in the world.

"You'll never know how much you mean to me, Nathan. You've made my life worth living."

"I love you, Ethan," he said.

"And I love you, Nathan."

I pulled Nathan to me and hugged him close. I could feel his smooth skin against my own. I could feel his heart beating in his chest. His slim muscles pressed against my own, heightening my arousal. My intense love for him made me want him all the more. My lips sought out his and I kissed him gently. I kissed his lips, his cheeks, his forehead, his neck, and his chest. I didn't seem to be able to stop kissing him. Always my lips returned to his own and our tongues entwined. We kissed each other far into the night, reveling in the closeness, intimacy, and love. As long as I was in his arms, my troubles could not touch me.

I lay there late at night while Nathan slept beside me. He looked so sweet and innocent asleep that I didn't understand how anyone could wish to hurt him. I'd make sure no one ever did. I listened to his soft breath. I smiled. Everything about Nathan brought me joy. This was what love was meant to be.

I closed my eyes, but was still aware of this presence beside me. Being near Nathan had long brought me peace, but his presence was even more powerful and meaningful now. There was a world of difference between a friend and a boyfriend. A friend can be wonderful beyond the power of description, but a boyfriend was all that, and so much more. Nathan instantly filled a void in my life that had always been there. When he held me and told me he loved me, he made all the pain I'd suffered in my life worthwhile. There could be nothing greater than the love that was between us. I thought for a moment about Mark and Taylor. I understood now what they had together. They had paid a terrible price for it, but I knew that I would pay any price for what I had with Nathan. It was worth it, no matter what happened.

I felt foolish for having pined so after Jon. How much time had I wasted chasing after a straight boy? I'd been so obsessed with Jon that I'd never considered that someone else could make me happy. I thought my dream had died when Jon told me he couldn't love me the way I wanted. I hadn't thought for a moment that there were other possibilities. Nathan had done the impossible. He had given me back my dream. More than that, he'd made my dream come true.

I didn't know why I had been so blind. I didn't know why I'd been unable to see Nathan the way I saw him now. It seemed almost impossible that I could've been so stupid. Obsession is an unpredictable and unfathomable thing, however. I'd been obsessed with Jon and it had blinded me to everything else. I'd considered Nathan a friend. I'd cared about him, worried about him, but I'd never once seen him with the eyes that I was seeing him with now.

My eyes had been opened at last, however. I loved Nathan so dearly it almost hurt. The depth of my feelings for him was immeasurable. Nathan fulfilled my dream, and he'd done even more. He'd given me back my friendship with Jon. It was as if he'd come along and made everything right again. It was as if he'd healed all my wounds with his love.

I opened my eyes and gazed upon Nathan. The covers were pulled down to his abdomen, leaving his smooth, firm chest bare. The sight of him filled me with desire. I'd noticed long ago that he was attractive, but I hadn't really been attracted to him, not until we fell in love. When I thought of his sensual lips all I wanted to do was kiss him. I wanted to caress and feel his firm young body. My desire for Nathan intensified with each passing moment. *Down, Ethan,* I thought to myself and laughed quietly. My Nathan needed his sleep and I needed to have just a little self-control. I contented myself with just looking at him with love in my heart.

I thought of the tough life that Nathan had led and it made me love him all the more. I wanted to make sure his life was a good one from now on. Nathan had experienced enough of pain and suffering. He deserved better, and, if I had anything to say about it, he was going to get better—much better—his little brother, too. Together, Nathan and I would make sure Dave grew up in a home where he was loved and cared for. We'd take care of him. That thought made me feel good inside. Nathan had given me everything—even a son. I fell to sleep with that happy thought in my mind.

Nathan complicated the decision I had to make. I wondered if perhaps I should throw the wrestling match for his sake. When Zac outed me, things would get pretty rough and part of that would fall on Nathan. He would suffer because I was suffering. When everyone found out he was living with me, the fag label would fall on him, too. If Zac made good on his threat to kill me, what would happen to Nathan then?

I wanted to be someone Nathan could be proud of, however. I'd felt like such a traitor when Mark and Taylor were first outed. I didn't stand by them. I didn't stand up to those that taunted and tormented them. I'd been too great a coward to do what I knew was right. I'd made up for that later to some degree, but I'd never really stood up for what I was. It made me feel like a coward. If I threw my wrestling match, it was only further proof of my cowardice. When would I be able to stand up for myself and not live in hiding? When?

If I threw the match for Nathan's sake, how would that make me feel about him? Would I resent him at some point in the future? Would I blame him for preventing me from realizing a dream? I didn't think I would ever feel that way. After all, it was Nathan who had made my dreams come true. But what if I felt differently later? I didn't want anything to ever come between us. If Nathan ever found out I threw the match just for him, he'd be very upset. If I let Zac win for Nathan's sake, I knew that I could never let Nathan know the truth.

I had another decision to make that was much closer to home. What about Jack? Nathan and I lived under the same roof—his roof. It was only a matter of time before our intimacy became known to him. Uncle Jack was old but far from stupid. It wouldn't take him long to notice the way we looked at each other. It wouldn't take him long to catch us holding hands or kissing. He probably already wondered about us sleeping together. After all, it wouldn't have been that hard to go out and buy Nathan his own bed.

I didn't think we'd have a problem with Nathan's parents. Nathan had been living with Uncle Jack and I for days and they didn't so much as call. For all they knew he and Dave were dead. Apparently, they just didn't care. I couldn't believe that someone could be like that; so unfeeling, so uncaring about their very own flesh and blood. I was glad Nathan and Dave were out of that place, it was a house without love.

I feared Uncle Jack would not react well if I told him about us. He didn't seem the type that would tolerate gays, especially under his own roof. I was afraid when Uncle Jack found out about me that it would change everything. When he found out about Nathan and me, it would be a hundred times worse. I knew Jack loved me, but I also knew what could happen. A lot of boys lost their father's love when their homosexuality was revealed. I knew a lot of boys lost their family and their home. Uncle Jack wasn't my father. Even though we had a strong father-son bond, I knew it could vanish in an instant when he found out I was gay. The thought of losing his love hurt me. The thought of having to leave the farm hurt me as well. I could easily lose all that I knew.

The next day, I discussed what to do about Uncle Jack with Nathan and together we decided to tell him. There wasn't much of a way we could hide it from him, and he deserved to know the truth. If he kicked us both out on the street, then we'd just have to deal with that. To say we were apprehensive about the possibilities was a vast understatement. Regardless, both Nathan and I felt that we had to tell him. We couldn't live a lie. It wasn't fair to Jack and it wasn't fair to us. We had to be true to him, and to ourselves.

We were nervous about approaching him all day. The opportunity didn't come until night, when Nathan and I sat with Uncle Jack at the kitchen table. He'd just come in from the fields and was having a late supper that Nathan had made for him. I made a few tries at telling him about Nathan and I, but at the last second I switched to another topic. I didn't know how to begin, or what to say. Finally Jack looked me straight in the eye.

"What's eating you, boy?"

I swallowed hard. The moment had come. It was now or never.

"I have something to tell you, something you probably won't like."

"You two didn't tear up the tractor did you?"

"No sir."

"The truck?"

"No sir, nothing like that."

"Then what is it, Ethan?"

"It's about me. It's about us. I, uh, I don't like girls, Uncle Jack. I mean, I do, but..., uh, I don't like them like that. I, uh...I'm gay, Uncle Jack."

"We're gay," said Nathan, taking my hand. Despite the gravity of the situation, and the sheer terror, I felt Nathan's love flowing through me and it helped to steady me.

Nathan and I waited for the explosion that was sure to come. Uncle Jack just sat there calmly, but he could sit calmly through a tornado. It didn't mean anything. I was trembling with fear.

"I see," said Jack. "Anything else?"

"Well, uh...no."

"Okay," he said and got up from the table.

"Okay? That's it?" I asked. I simply couldn't believe it.

"What more is there?" asked Jack. "Look, Ethan, I want you to be happy and if this is what you are, then fine. If you and Nathan make each other happy, then all the better. Just be careful." There was a worried look in Jack's eyes. He knew as well as everyone that life was not easy, or safe, for gay boys.

"Now, I'm going to bed. You two mind cleaning up?"

"No, sir," I said astounded.

"Good night then, boys, see you tomorrow."

Nathan and I sat there speechless. Never in a million years would I have guessed Uncle Jack would react like that. I expected anger, maybe rage, perhaps acceptance after a time, but what we'd told him didn't phase him a bit! It was like it didn't matter to him, like it didn't change the way he felt about me at all. I was astounded and clearly Nathan felt the same. We just sat there stunned for the longest time.

Jack's lack of reaction made me wonder something in the back of my mind—had he known all along? Had he long ago figured out that I liked boys? Had he guessed that Nathan was more than a friend? Had he seen us in the fields hugging and kissing? Jack was shrewd. I wouldn't put it past him. I was just amazed that he was so accepting.

"Well, I guess that's that," said Nathan finally and smiled as he squeezed my hand.

We stood and I hugged Nathan close right there in the kitchen.

"I love you so much, you know that?" I whispered in his ear.

"Almost as much as I love you," he answered back.

I pressed my lips to his and kissed him. I'd never been so content in all my life. Our lips parted and we smiled at one another.

"I sure liked that," said Nathan.

"Me too, now we'd better get these dishes done or we'll be in trouble!"

Nathan laughed and all my cares seemed to disappear in an instant.

Every time Zac looked at me in school, he had a smug look on his face that made me want to punch his lights out. The crap he was pulling seemed even more reprehensible because of the recent deaths of Mark and Taylor. They had died because of people like Zac. Their deaths had touched a lot of people. I noticed that a lot of guys who were down on gays before weren't so vocal about it anymore. After Mark and Taylor died, I didn't hear the world "fag" nearly as often. It just wasn't cool to use that as a put down. Others hadn't learned a thing, however, or just didn't care. Zac was one of those. I both hated and pitied him for it.

My problems with Zac were far from over, but, for the most part, my life had fallen into place, and all because of Nathan. One wonderful gift that Nathan had given me was a restored friendship with Jon. I felt at ease around him once again. With Nathan as my boyfriend, I was able to largely put aside my feelings for Jon. I must admit I still found him attractive and still experienced stirrings of desire when he was near, but all that was under control. It was merely my body reacting naturally to his good looks. I had Nathan now and he's all I'd ever need or want.

The anger I'd felt toward Jon was gone, too. I'd realized he'd done nothing wrong. He couldn't help being heterosexual anymore than I could help being homosexual. Having Nathan as my boyfriend took care of the intense emotional need that had been unfulfilled for so very long. With that taken care of, I could enjoy my friendship with Jon. Things were as they had once been. It was almost as if the conflict had never existed. Jon understood and I realized that Jon had been a very good friend all along. I felt very lucky to have such a wonderful friend in Jon and such a fantastic boyfriend in Nathan. Thanks to Nathan, I had the best of everything.

CHAPTER 30

Wrestling with Demons

The day of the wrestling match drew ever closer and before I knew it, it had arrived. The gym was packed to the rafters, but I was most aware of the presence of Nathan, Dave, and Jon. Even Uncle Jack was there. That surprised me a lot. Jack had never come to one of my matches before. He was always far too busy working on the farm.

I stepped out onto the mat and faced Zac. The muscles in his chest, shoulders, and arms tensed and flexed. I didn't give his body much consideration, however, instead I looked into his eyes. Zac was arrogant and self-assured. I hated the smug look on his face.

"Ready to lose, fag boy?" he said quietly.

I didn't answer him. He didn't deserve an answer.

We took our places on the mat. The whistle blew and the match began. We collided in the center. Zac seemed stronger than I remembered. I could feel his muscles tense and flex under my hands. He was a powerful young man, but I had even greater power. I got a firm grip of his upper torso and tried to force him down to the mat. From the position I was in, I just couldn't take him down. There was just no way to get him off his legs. Zac struggled to break free, but couldn't, until he managed to get me a bit off balance. He broke away and smiled at me. It wasn't a nice smile at all.

We circled each other and Zac dove in. I shifted my position, but he was ready for it. He'd read my stance, he knew there was only one way for me to go. He slammed me face down on the mat. He struggled to turn me onto my back. It was a contest of sheer power—a contest that Zac could not win. No matter how he strained, no matter how he shifted his body for leverage, he couldn't force me onto my back. I tensed my muscles and pushed outward with my arms and chest. I broke his hold and jumped to my feet. We circled one another yet again.

I was a mass of indecision. After all the pondering, all the debating, I still didn't know whether I should throw the match or not. I was wrestling with both Zac and myself.

The first period ended and I took the defensive position. As Zac wrapped his arm around my waist, he leaned over and whispered so that only I could hear.

"You're doing good, faggot. Keep it up. Make this look like a real match. As soon as you let me win, you're free."

The whistle blew and Zac's arm tightened around me like a vise. His other sought to force me down. I surged upward and broke away from him. He couldn't stop me. I scored a point for an escape, but I didn't even bother to keep track. Points didn't seem to matter. I had too many other things going through my head.

As we wrestled, my mind was filled with thoughts that had nothing to do with the match. Sounds and images flooded my consciousness. I heard Zac's threats in my mind and read his notes yet again. I saw Nathan's look of concern when I told him about my troubles and his look of joy on that day long ago when I'd given him some of my old clothes. I saw Uncle Jack riding the tractor in the distance, toiling to make ends meet. I saw Jon as he turned me down, and as he hugged me when I told him about Nathan and me. I saw Mark and Taylor, too, the way they looked at each other with such love. I saw them laying in their caskets and I saw their graves. One image after another played through my mind, unbidden, and beyond my control.

Zac slammed me onto my back. I wasn't quite sure how it had happened. I had no memory of the seconds that led up to it. My own mind had worked against me—unintentionally. Zac pushed my shoulders closer and closer to the mat.

"This is it, faggot. Make it look good."

My back went ever closer to the mat, down and down. Everything moved in slow motion. Moments lasted an eternity. It was if I could see it all from above; Zac on top of me; Nathan, Jon, Dave, and Uncle Jack cheering me on at the top of their lungs; the crowd shouting and waving. I felt my left shoulder touch the mat, my right growing ever closer. The referee put his head on the mat to see if I was pinned.

The world still moved in slow motion and thoughts still flooded my mind. I was intently aware of all my surroundings. I could feel the presence of Nathan and those close to me. I could even feel the presence of Mark and Taylor. Somehow, I knew they were there. I focused my thoughts and my energy. I surged upward, channeling all my strength into lifting both Zac and myself off the mat. Zac fought hard against me, pressing down with every bit of his weight and strength. His face contorted with strain and rage. I struggled against him, inching myself right up off the mat, a nearly impossible move. I pushed Zac back further and broke free!

Zac was enraged. If looks could kill, I would've been dead on the mat. I'd never seen such a look of hatred before in all my life. It didn't frighten me, however. My fear left me as I became true to myself. I made my decision. I knew what I had to do.

The world shifted from slow motion and time passed at an accelerated rate. I pounced on Zac and slammed him down on the mat. I pinned him down while he fought me with everything he had. His muscles bulged and he strained his guts out, but he was impotent against me. The referee put his head to mat once more and a moment later slapped it hard as I pressed Zac's shoulders against the mat. It was over. I'd won.

I stood up and looked around me as the crowd cheered. I looked straight at Nathan, Jon, Dave, and Jack and smiled at them. They smiled and cheered back. Nathan was crying, but I knew he was happy. I could read it on his face. He was crying tears of joy. Our eyes locked, both of us knew just what this moment meant. Everyone in the gym knew I'd just accomplished something. They didn't realize, however, that I'd achieved something far greater than becoming the best. I'd overcome my greatest fear. I'd been true to myself. I was proud not only to be a kick-ass wrestler, but a gay boy as well.

"You'll pay for this, fucker. You're dead," Zac hissed at me, then stalked off to the locker room. I followed him a few moments later, my back reddened by the hands of my teammates smacking me in congratulation. Much of the team was waiting on me in the locker room and the rest followed me in, along with a few others.

Once again, if looks could kill I would've dropped dead. Zac glared at me with such baleful hatred that it was beyond belief.

Zac started to speak, but I cut him off.

"Zac has something he wants to tell you all," I said. "But I'm going to tell you instead."

The locker room grew deathly still. The tone of my voice let all there know that something serious was going down. I noticed that Nathan and Jon had stepped into the locker room and were listening intently. My heart pounded in my chest and I trembled slightly. I remembered, at just that moment, that this was the very spot where Mark and Taylor had been outed. I was following in their footsteps. I hoped they'd be proud of me.

"I've been hiding something from all of you for a long time. I've done it mainly because I've been afraid—afraid of what you might think of me, afraid of losing your friendship. Some of you standing here will hate me for this, but I hope most of you will understand, or at least try to understand. I'm the same guy you've known all along, nothing has changed. There's just one thing you don't know about me. I'm gay."

The absolute silence continued in the locker room. Zac glared at me, hating me for cheating him out of his moment. Some of those standing there looked at me in shock, others didn't seem so surprised. Nathan came to my side and held my hand, announcing in silence what I had just proclaimed in words. Jon stood by me, as I knew he would. I waited to see what would happen next.

Steve leveled his gaze at me, then spoke hesitantly.

"So this means I don't have to compete with you for girls, huh?"

"I guess so," I said, a slight smile creasing the corners of my mouth. My heart leaped at his implied acceptance.

"Then I'm all for it!" yelled Steve.

That made pretty much everyone laugh. It broke the tension and the silence. I had a real good feeling. I had a feeling things had changed some in Verona, Indiana. Maybe my friends and classmates had learned more from the deaths of Mark and Taylor than I guessed. The locker room slowly cleared out as my friends and teammates congratulated me. Not one of them failed to shake my hand. Not one of them turned on me. I was so relieved and so happy that I nearly cried.

Zac was a different story, of course. He looked mad enough to chew on barbed wire. He quickly changed and left, shouldering his way past our teammates. He glared at me with pure hatred as he departed. It sent a chill up my spine.

"What was that about?" asked Jon, watching Zac stalk out of the locker room.

I waited until Nathan, Jon, and I were alone in the locker room to answer. When there was no one else around to hear, I told Jon all about the notes I'd received and Zac's threats.

"That fucking piece of shit!" said Jon when he'd heard the entire story. "I've got more than half a mind to track him down and fuck him up."

"No," I said, "Don't. He's not worth it."

"You'd better watch your back, Ethan. I wouldn't trust him."

"Don't worry. I'll be watching. I don't trust him as far as I can throw him."

"I'll be watching him, too," said Jon. He meant it. Jon was pissed. I knew I wouldn't have to worry about Zac when Jon was around.

I pushed Zac out of my mind. I wasn't going to allow him to torment me a moment longer. He no longer had a secret to hold over my head. I'd told my teammates and soon it would be all over the school. By the next day everyone would know I was gay.

I felt good about myself. I'd finally stood up for what I was. I knew there would be problems ahead, but problems were life—no one, gay or straight, was without them. I pulled Nathan to me and hugged him close. I loved him more than I could express. Whatever came, I knew he'd be at my side.

CHAPTER 31

My Boyfriend

I pulled the truck up near the farmhouse, creating a small cloud of dust. Dave got out and ran inside, but I took Nathan by the hand and led him off toward the fields. Much of the harvesting was done and great open spaces lay where there had been tall stalks of corn. We walked past the just finished fence. Nathan and I had completed it that very day. It seemed to go on forever. No wonder it had taken so many weeks to get it set in place.

I led Nathan beyond the fields, enjoying the closeness and his love. We walked along the little path that led into the forest. The very same path Jon and I had followed the day I taught him to ride. That day seemed so very long ago. It was part of another age.

We walked past the old cabin. Nathan and I smiled at each other, remembering our first time there together. That was a night I'd never forget—neither of us would. I led Nathan by the hand to the very spot where Jon and I had devoured our picnic weeks before. I pulled Nathan to me and hugged him like I'd never let him go. I felt his love flowing through me. At last I was at peace with myself. I knew who I was and what I was and I was glad to be me.

I took Nathan's chin in my hand and pulled his lips to mine. Our tongues entwined and we necked in the bright sunlight, so lost in each other that we were unaware of our surroundings. When our lips parted at last we were almost surprised to see the forest around us, denuded of leaves. It was almost as if we'd been in some far distant place where only the two of us existed.

I gazed upon Nathan, my heart filled with love and desire. I slowly pulled his shirt over his head, baring his slim, firm torso. He shivered in the cold air as I ran my hands up along his sides and over his smooth chest. Nathan was so beautiful, so kind and loving. I was glad that I'd never made love with another. Touching each other, bringing each other physical pleasure was something special between us, and only us. It was an expression of our love.

Nathan smiled at me and shyly pulled my shirt over my head. He ran his hands over the muscles of my chest. His touch was gentle, a loving caress. We moved slowly, unhurried. We both knew we had all the time in the world and we wanted to make our time together last. I knew we'd always be together, but that didn't make any one moment less special. Instead, it made our time together more precious, because we knew it would never end.

I pulled Nathan to me and kissed him yet again. His soft sweet kisses filled me with love and contentment. While our lips gently wrestled, I fumbled with Nathan's belt and the button on his jeans. Moments later his jeans slid down over his slim hips and fell to his ankles. I kneeled in front of Nathan and grasped the hardness in his boxers. He closed his eyes as I removed the last of his clothing, leaned forward, and created pleasure for him that I'd never created for another.

As the sun dipped below the horizon, I held Nathan in my arms. We lay together naked in the grass, watching the shadows darken. I was never so much in love. Nathan snuggled against me and lay his head on my chest. I ran my fingers through his hair and told him how very much

I loved him. It filled me with happiness and contentment to hear him echo my words.

We'd lain by the lake for hours, making love, resting in each other's arms, making love again. It had grown nearly dark before we arose and dressed. Even then we stood there and kissed one another until it had become nearly too dark to see. Neither of us wanted the moment to end. At last I took Nathan's hand in mine and led him back the way we had come. I don't think that I'd ever really understood what it was to be happy until Nathan and I had fallen in love. We were so in love with each other that nothing else seemed to matter.

CHAPTER 32

Lessons on the Soccer Field

Nathan laughed as he shot the ball past me yet again into the goal. The ball caught a glint of moonlight as it slammed into the net.

"Hey, I'm a wrestler, not a soccer player!" I yelled at him. "I told you I was no good at this."

"Wimp!" he yelled back, still laughing.

I was right, I was no good at soccer. Nathan made me look like a total incompetent. I missed the ball half the time when I tried to kick it and I couldn't get a shot past him to save my life. I didn't really care. Both of us were having a blast. We'd been playing soccer since the late afternoon and couldn't make ourselves stop. We always had fun together. Nathan was the greatest boyfriend in all the world.

Nathan came toward me with the ball yet again. He looked so cute wearing nothing but a pair of sleek black soccer shorts. I loved him in those shorts, which is why I'd bought them for him. I guess they were a present for both of us. He got to wear them and I got to see him in them. I think I got the better end of the deal.

We were all hot and sweaty and out of breath, despite the fact that the shadows had grown so deep that it was difficult to see and a chill was rising in the air. I felt its cold prickle my naked skin. It felt good in contrast to my heated body.

It had been a great day and all because I'd spent it with Nathan; working by his side in the morning, taking a long walk with him in the afternoon, taking him to our special place to eat, then playing with him on the soccer fields. It had to be one of the best days of my life.

All that was laid waste instantly, however, when I looked up and saw Zac coming toward us. He wasn't alone either. There were four other guys with him. My heart pounded in fear when I saw them. I knew who they were. I'd have known even if I couldn't see their faces. It was the same group that had beaten Mark so severely in the locker room that they'd nearly killed him.

Nathan stopped when he saw them coming. There was terror in his eyes. They were practically upon us before we even noticed them. It was far too late to run. I tried to calm myself, but I was shaken with fear. I knew this day would come sooner or later, but now that it was upon me, it seemed more terrifying than anything I'd dreamed.

"Hey, faggots," said Zac, "it's pay back time."

Almost before I knew what was going on, Zac, Jeremy, and Alex rushed at me and grabbed my arms. They didn't start punching me as I expected, they just held me back while Devon and Rob grabbed Nathan. I wished they were punching me instead. Watching Devon and Rob overpower Nathan was harder to bear than any pain. They didn't hurt him, they just held him, and tied his wrists above his head to the goal post. I fought against the three holding me. I jerked them around like rag dolls, my muscles bulging, but I couldn't quite break free. Whenever I managed to break away from one of them, the others just held on tighter until the third regained his grip. Nathan was securely tied before I had a chance to do anything about it.

Zac and the others shoved me away. I started to move toward Nathan, but Devon whipped out a nasty looking knife and held it to Nathan's throat.

"If you come any closer, things get nasty for your boyfriend," said Devon.

Nathan was trying not to show his fear, but his eyes were wild with terror. I could barely keep myself from attacking Devon. My entire body was tensed and ready. I wanted nothing more than to rush him and tear his fucking head off.

"Go ahead, faggot!" said Devon, "Come after me! Just give me an excuse to cut him! Yeah, come on!" His eyes were alight with a wicked gleam. I knew he'd like nothing better than to cut Nathan's throat.

I stood where I was, feeling impotent and controlled. Zac took a step toward me.

"Now let's talk," said Zac. He smiled at me wickedly. He was loving every second. He and Devon were two of a kind. He slugged me hard in the face. I just stood there and took it. Zac grinned, then spoke.

"We could easily kill you both, but hey, I'm not greedy. I'm sure Devon and the others here figure your boyfriend deserves to die just because he's a fag, but my quarrel is with you. I'm even going to give you the chance to just walk away, Ethan. We'll let you leave and we won't follow. That will be the end of it."

He smiled so evilly that it turned my blood to ice.

"Of course, Ethan, if you leave, I can't make any promises about what will happen to your boyfriend. Devon and his buddies don't really like fags so if they don't get to do some work on you, they just might take out their frustrations on Nathan here."

"You bastard!" I screamed at him and started to rush forward. Devon held the knife closer to Nathan's throat, however, and I backed off.

"That's a good faggot," said Zac. "Now, are you going to leave, or are you going to stay?"

I stood right there. He knew damn well I wasn't about to leave while they had Nathan. My mind was racing while I tried to think of some way to get him away from them. There had to be some way for us to get out of there.

"Well," said Zac in mock surprise, "I guess you aren't as big a pussy as I thought you were. That's okay, I like it this way better. This will be twice as much fun with Nathan here to watch you die."

I was truly afraid, but I tried not to show it. I didn't want to give Zac the satisfaction. I still wasn't sure if he meant what he said. I didn't really think those guys would have the balls to kill me. Still, there were things worse than death. I knew at the very least that I was in for the worst beating of my life. I knew Zac would beat me so bad I might end up dead, even if he didn't mean to kill me.

"Just don't say I didn't give you the chance to walk away," he smirked.

I was tensed and ready. They wouldn't get me without a fight. I'd do as much damage as I could before they got me. Maybe, if I was lucky, I could take all five of them. I knew the odds of that were pretty slim, however. I could see the smirk on Zac's face. I wanted to slap it off him.

They circled me like a pack of wolves on a bear. I couldn't watch them all at once. I was hoping I could take a couple of them out. I was ready. If I got my chance I'd slug one of them so hard it would knock him out, maybe kill him. I wasn't going to hold anything back. If I could take out a couple of them, I might have a chance.

They knew that's what I'd be trying, however. They had to know. It was my only hope. I was far more powerful than any one of them, but I didn't stand a chance against all five. Even two on one would've been hard. Five on one was just about impossible.

They kept constantly moving, darting in, feinting. One would distract me while another tried to lay his hands on me. They weren't trying to hit me. They were trying to grab me. I knew if they got on me it was all over.

I wondered why they didn't just order me to stand still while they tied me up. They had Nathan. I had to do whatever they wanted. Maybe it was a game to them. They knew they could take me—with five on one the outcome was close to certain. Maybe they were willing to take the pain I'd deal out for the pleasure of taking me down. Perhaps they had some twisted need to feel superior—to know they'd taken out a gay boy. Maybe they wanted to be able to brag about how they'd whipped my ass. Perhaps they were just stupid. Who knew? I wasn't about to give them ideas. At least this way, I had a chance, slim though it was.

All five of them rushed me at once. I fought them, but they were ready. I couldn't even land a punch on Jeremy, who was right in front of me. My arm was knocked away in mid-swing by Zac flinging his entire body upon it. I was knocked to the ground. They were all over me. Zac had his knee on my chest, bearing down on me with all his weight. He slugged me hard in the face. The others grabbed my arms. There were two of them on each arm before I even had a chance to fight my way free. They had a firm hold on me. I flew into a rage, but I couldn't break away. They pulled me to my feet and held me firmly while Zac circled around in front.

"Turn him this way so Nathan can see. I want him to have a good view."

I struggled against those holding me, but with two on each arm I didn't have a chance. A picture of Mark laying in his hospital bed flashed in my mind. I almost wished that they would just kill me quickly so I wouldn't have to go through a beating like Mark had. I wasn't a coward, but I was afraid.

Zac was enjoying every second of my helpless state. He just stood before me and glared at me without saying a word. He looked me up and down as if taking stock, deciding what he wanted to do to me first. The waiting was horrible beyond description.

Zac smiled and I found his smile more frightening than his glare. He was doing his best to make me squirm and it was working. No matter how hard I fought it, there was terror in my eyes. To be honest, I'd have done just about anything to get out of there. I was on the verge of panic.

Zac got up real close to me and spoke quietly, but loud enough that everyone could hear.

"I warned you, Ethan. I told you. You just had to do one little thing to avoid all this, but you wouldn't do it. No, you had to be the tough guy. You had to defy me. You're going to pay now, Ethan. Why did you defy me, Ethan? Did you think I was bluffing? Did you really think I'd just let it go?"

"No," I said. "I knew you and these losers would come after me."

That answer earned me a slug in the face.

"You think I was bluffing about killing you?" snarled Zac.

I didn't answer right away. I wasn't sure what I believed.

"You did, didn't you? You didn't think I'd really do it."

Zac got so close to my face I could feel his hot breath on me.

"Well you were wrong, faggot. You are going to die. By the time the sun comes up, you'll be a nothing more than a bloody corpse laying on the soccer field."

I swallowed hard. I knew he meant every word. It was hard to imagine how someone so evil could even exist.

"Get away from him you fucking bastard!" yelled Nathan.

Nathan tried his best to get loose, but they had tied him too well. All he could do was stand there and watch. It made it all a hundred times worse. I didn't want Nathan to see what was going to happen. Zac just laughed.

"How sweet. Your boyfriend's worried about you, Ethan. Too bad he can't do anything to save you. He's just another useless little faggot."

I had to bite back the words I wanted to hurl at Zac. I wanted to tell him how Nathan was twice the man he was. I was afraid to say anything, however. I was afraid that if I did so, Zac would hurt Nathan.

"You know, I think this is the very spot where Taylor died," said Zac. "And where Mark blew his brains out. Yes, it is, isn't it? How appropriate. This is the place where fags die."

I'd never hated anyone so much in all my life.

"Say goodbye, fag," said Zac.

He aimed a sharp blow at my stomach. I tensed my abdomen, but it still hurt. He punched me again quickly, and the pain was more intense. I grunted. Zac smiled. He slugged me in the face so hard it snapped my head back. It hurt more than I'd ever imagined it could. Zac jabbed me in the ribs, then the nuts. Nathan screamed at him to stop. He was crying and hysterical. He just kept screaming at Zac to leave me alone. I was afraid Zac would start in on him just to shut him up. I couldn't give it much thought, however, the pain made it hard to think clearly. I was in more pain than I'd ever experienced in my entire life and Zac was just getting started.

"Having fun yet, gay boy?"

Zac pulled back his fist for another shot, but it never fell. Zac's face snapped back as someone punched him hard from the side. In the growing darkness I couldn't even make out who it was. It was all a blur. Only when I heard his voice did I know it was Jon.

I made out Brandon's voice, too, as he smashed into two of the guys holding me and took them to the ground. I broke free and turned on my attackers. We were outnumbered five against three, but Zac, Devon and the others found themselves outmatched. A rain of blows fell on me. It was if my attackers were desperate to inflict as much damage on me as they possibly could. My arms were free at last, however, and I gave much better than I took.

I knocked Alex out cold with a punch to the face. He fell to the grass and lay there as if he was dead. Jon punched Rob hard in the stomach. He doubled over and Jon kept right on punching him. Rob cowered before Jon, then fell on the earth, moaning and holding his stomach.

Brandon beat Jeremy senseless and it wasn't long before he was laying on the grass moaning, too. Both Alex and Jeremy were great wrestlers, but they weren't that tough in a fistfight. It wasn't just a normal fight either—Jon, Brandon, and I were beyond pissed. We were enraged at what they'd done to Mark, and what they were doing to Nathan and me.

Zac and Devon were much harder to subdue; they fought as if they were fighting for their lives. Perhaps they were. Neither of them would give up, no matter what we did to them. They just kept coming back for more. Finally Brandon got Devon from behind and held him with one arm across the throat and the other pinning Devon's arms behind his back. A few moments later I was able to pin Zac in much the same way.

Jon untied Nathan and I almost cried with relief that he was okay. I'd been so afraid for him, so terrified of what they might do to him. I held Zac while Jon tied him up with his very own rope, then he and Brandon tied up Devon and the others, too. It wasn't long before they were all sitting on the grass neatly bound. It was very thoughtful of those boys to bring enough rope for us to tie them all.

A lump rose in my throat when I realized how much rope there was. No one would need that much rope, unless…

I wrapped my arms around Nathan and held him close. I took his head in my hands and looked into his face. He was still a bit wild-eyed, but he was fine. I kissed him passionately and mussed his blond hair.

I turned my attention to our prisoners and the smile faded from my lips. I hated them. I hated them all.

I grabbed Zac by the collar and jerked him to his feet.

"What else were you planning on doing with this?" I hissed at him. "Huh?" I shoved the coil of rope into his face.

He clamped his mouth shut and glared at me.

"I can make you talk!" I snarled at him. "You will tell me, one way or another!"

I could tell Zac was shaken by that. His henchmen were, too. They were in fear for their lives. They should have been. Those bastards deserved to die. At that moment I was ready to kill them all.

"Tell me!" My face was mere inches from his and I could read the terror in his eyes. He was cracking. His angry glare was replaced by fear. He knew he'd better talk or I'd put him through pain he'd never experienced the likes of before.

"The rope was to hang you with and your little boyfriend," he said quickly. He was almost desperate to get the words out. I'd never seen anyone so terrified before.

"Shut up, Zac!" yelled Devon. "Don't tell him anything!"

Brandon grabbed up the knife that had been held to Nathan's neck. He pounced on Devon, painfully pulled his head back by the hair, and held the knife against his bared throat.

"That was your idea, wasn't it?" Brandon hissed at Devon. "You were going to kill them, like you killed Taylor and Mark!"

"I didn't kill them!" screamed Devon in a panic.

"Didn't you?"

"They killed themselves and you know it!"

"And why, Devon? Huh? Because of you and bastards like you! Well, you're not getting a chance to pull shit like that again!" He pulled Devon's head back even further.

"Brandon, stop!" I yelled.

He looked over his shoulder at me. His eyes were so filled with anger and hate that I had to fight to keep from taking a step backward. Devon's eyes were wild with terror. He knew he was about to get his throat cut.

"Don't do this," I pleaded with Brandon. I'd been on the verge of killing Zac myself. So close it was terrifying to even think about. Seeing Brandon mere moments away from committing murder cleared my head, however.

Brandon slowly shook his head, his eyes filled with hate. I understood the hate—I felt it too. To be honest, I wanted to kill Devon and Zac as much as he did.

"Don't do this. Don't become one of them. If you kill him, that's all you'll be. That's not what we're about. I know what he did. I know what he was going to do. But that doesn't make this right."

He turned his face back to Devon and brought the knife closer to his throat. Devon screamed and cried and begged for his life. I watched in horror at what was about to happen. Brandon was out of his mind with grief and rage. His entire body trembled. There were tears in his eyes. I knew he was reliving it all; finding Taylor's dead body, learning Mark had blown his brains out. Brandon had snapped.

I kept speaking to him, desperately trying to stop him.

"I know Mark was your friend and Taylor, but they wouldn't want you to do this. Don't throw away your life for revenge. They wouldn't want you to do this, Brandon."

That made him pause.

"You can't bring them back, Brandon. You can't undo what's already been done. Killing Devon won't change anything. Please. Mark and Taylor wouldn't want you to do this, Brandon. They wouldn't. Please."

Brandon's head bowed. The knife fell from his hands, and he started crying. Tears filled my eyes as I watched him. I could only imagine the pain. Jon held Brandon as he cried. It was a good long while before anyone said anything.

"So what do we do with these losers?" said Jon finally, turning to me.

I looked down at them, all neatly tied up. We could have done anything we wanted to them. We could have beaten them, tortured them, or even killed them. My friends and I weren't that sort, however. We were better than the boys before us would ever be.

"We let them go," I said

I stared down at all of them. All I read on their faces was fear, mixed with relief. I didn't blame them. After what had happened, I think I would've pissed my pants if I were in their place.

"If any of you EVER give Nathan or me, or anyone else any shit, the four of us will hunt you down and make you very sorry. Before we're finished with you, you'll be begging for us to kill you," I said. The tone of my voice left no doubt I was dead serious.

"And," added Jon, "If anything happens to either Ethan or Nathan, we know just who to look for. You hurt them and we'll finish what Brandon started."

Brandon grabbed Devon by the shirt and pulled his face to within mere inches of his own.

"Just give me an excuse, Devon. Just say one fucking thing about any of my friends again and I'll cut your throat. Don't think for a second I won't do it."

I don't think I'd ever seen such a look of sheer terror on anyone's face as I saw that night of the faces of Zac, Devon, Alex, Jeremy, and Rob.

Brandon and Jon untied each of them while Nathan and I stood there and watched. I held Nathan close. I was so glad he was safe.

Each of our prisoners beat it out of there fast as soon as he was released. I grabbed Devon's arm for a moment before he departed. He looked into my eyes.

"How does it feel, Devon, knowing that a gay boy saved your life?"

Devon looked more humbled than I'd ever seen him before.

"Thank you," he said meekly, then walked away.

When the last of them were gone, Nathan and I thanked Brandon and Jon a couple of hundred times. Without them, we knew we'd both have been dead. I'd never really thought that Zac would have the balls to kill me. I'd been wrong. What's more, he'd planned to kill Nathan, too.

"We should've called the cops," said Jon.

"Maybe we should have," I said, "but I just want all this to end. I don't want to spend the next several weeks answering questions. I just want this to be over."

Jon nodded.

"I just wish we could have saved them," said Brandon quietly, looking at the soccer goal where Taylor and Mark had died.

"I know, Brandon," I said. "I know."

I held Brandon as he cried.

❦ ❦ ❦

The next day, Nathan and I walked hand in hand out to the soccer field, to the very spot where both Taylor and Mark had died, to the very place that we had nearly met our ends. There was a chill in the air, but it was sunny and bright. It seemed such a different place from the night before. It was hard to believe what had happened. The night before was like a bad dream, a nightmare. It had been only too real, however. It was an eerie feeling, coming that close to death.

We laid wild flowers before the goal and stood there in silence for a few moments, remembering our friends.

"I hope you guys are happy, wherever you are," I said looking into the sky. Somehow, I knew they were.

I turned to Nathan and hugged him close. I kissed him and felt his love flow through me. We stood there holding each other. We loved each other more than anything. It had been a long hard road, but having Nathan in my life was worth it all. I took Nathan's hand in mine.

"Let's go home," I said.

CHAPTER 33

Do Not Open Until Christmas

Nathan and I had trudged only a few hundred yards through the deep snow, but already our cheeks were rosy and our breaths created small clouds of white in the frosty air. When we returned, it would be time for hot chocolate in the kitchen, but until then the cold would seep through our gloves and up under our coats. I shivered slightly, but I didn't mind the cold—it was nearly Christmas.

I took Nathan's hand in my own as the snow crunched beneath our feet. Before us was an undisturbed blanket of sparkling white, covering the fields where in warmer weather, corn and beans reached for the sun. All of nature was dormant now. The trees were sleeping and even the deer didn't leave their warm beds for long at a time.

"How about that one?" asked Nathan, pointing to a great pine in the near distance. It was beautiful, half covered in snow.

"Not unless we set it up in the barn," I laughed. "It's got to be at least ten feet tall."

"I'd have thought it was six, tops!"

"Everything looks smaller under the open sky, so keep your eye out for a little tree. One that looks too small will probably suit us just fine."

Nathan squeezed my hand and smiled. I raised his gloved hand to my lips and kissed it. My heart was full of joy when I was near him. Just having him in my life was the greatest Christmas present of all.

We strolled along from tree to tree. None quite suited our purpose. Most were far too large, like the first, while others were misshapen or just didn't have quite the right look. The tree we selected had to look just so.

As our feet broke though the snow, my mind drifted to the beautifully wrapped box that sat upon my dresser. The paper was red with small decorated Christmas trees all over. Taped to the top was a white label, with the words "Do Not Open Until Christmas" written across it. I'd received it in the mail almost two months ago, but I'd dutifully obeyed the instructions even though curiosity consumed me from inside.

What could it be? I wondered. It wasn't a large box. It was some twelve inches square. I'd measured it myself. It wasn't heavy, but it wasn't light. It didn't rattle when I carefully shook it. It defied all guessing. I'd spent many an hour pondering it, for it wasn't just any box. It was precious to me beyond price.

I yearned to rip away the bright paper and see what was inside. And yet, a part of me never wanted to open it and reveal the secret it held. A part of me want to keep it wrapped forever, so that the unveiling would always be in the future, an event to be anticipated with sadness and joy. As long as the box remained unopened the story went on without ending. When the contents were at last brought into the light of day, the tale would be finished. The last connection would be revealed. That cherished Christmas gift was like the last chapter of a book I never wanted to end. As long as it held its secret, there was more to come.

Nathan halted, and looked into my eyes. He leaned in toward me and pressed his lips to mine. Every kiss was like the first, so filled with wonder and love. I hugged him close and nuzzled in his warmth. We held each other, kissing and smiling. We leaned back and gazed into each other's eyes. I read love in Nathan's and knew that the same shown in my own. I kissed his forehead and his cheeks. I loved him more than life itself. I knew I didn't deserve him, but neither did anyone else, so I figured I might as well have him for myself. We hugged each other tight and our lips met once again. His lips tasted as sweet as a peppermint candy cane.

Nathan took my hand once again and led me through the snow. The shadows were beginning to lengthen and the snow took on a golden glow. In only a few steps more we both lifted our heads and spotted it, our perfect Christmas tree. It was sitting on a small hill, in the shadow of its larger cousins. We approached it and found it was of an ideal height. It was just a bit taller than me.

Nathan stood back while I took my ax in hand and swung for the trunk. It wasn't long before the tree began to tilt, and then fell upon its side. Nathan and I both lifted the trunk from the ground and pulled our tree back toward the farmhouse.

A icy wind bit our faces and our fingers became numb. Our breaths rose up in great clouds of white steam as we toiled to draw our tree closer to home. When I thought we were close enough, I stopped and gave a shrill whistle. For a few moments there was no answer, but soon we heard a neigh and moments later Wuffa came thundering in our direction. Before we knew it, the great horse was before us.

"That'a boy," I said, smoothing his flank.

While I attached a rope to his harness and our Christmas tree, Nathan greeted Wuffa and fed him a carrot he'd brought along in his pocket. In less than a minute, we were on the move. Wuffa pulled the tree along without effort, while we walked by his side. Nathan hummed "Oh, Christmas Tree" as we grew ever closer to our destination. Wuffa seemed pleased to be helping. I could almost detect a smile.

Wuffa walked right up to the house, without direction of any kind. We untied the tree and followed him back to the barn. There we took off his harness and fed him and Fairfax a special treat of oats. They whinnied their approval as Nathan and I trudged toward the house.

We pulled the tree inside and set it up in a stand with minimal loss of pine needles. We placed it before a large window so it could be seen from the outside when it was ablaze with bright lights. We were as eager as small children to decorate the tree, but we were chilled to the bone. We pulled off our coats, scarves, boots, and gloves and made our way to the kitchen. A scent of chocolate permeated the air. Uncle Jack had hot chocolate waiting on us, with tiny marshmallows on top. He pretended to be gruff, but he was an old softy inside.

We sat and sipped cocoa with him while feeling returned to our fingers. The wind was blowing outside and it had began to snow once again. It felt so cozy and warm in the farmhouse with a winter storm howling just beyond the walls. We'd returned just in time.

While Uncle Jack made the annual trip into the attic for Christmas ornaments and lights, Nathan and I stirred up some Christmas cookies in an old milk crock. We used my mother's recipe for sugar cookies and cut out Santa, angel, and Christmas tree shapes with cookie cutters we found in a drawer. We baked them in the oven, and then decorated them with red and green sugar. In only a few minutes the scent of Christmas cookies mingled with that of pine and filled the whole first floor. Nathan and I sampled our handiwork, then found our way to the living room to transform our tree into something more.

I helped Nathan as he wound the lights round and round the tree. I was glad we had the new kind. I remembered the old ones. If one bulb was burned out, none of them would work. Not so with our lights. I liked the smaller bulbs, too. There were just right, like little stars, shining in the night.

Nathan had a bit of trouble as he neared the top of the tree. I put him on my shoulders and he finished wrapping the lights on the uppermost branches. I could've just done it myself, but it was more fun to hold my boyfriend on my shoulders while he finished the job. We were both giggling before we were done. Nathan plugged in the lights and the tree was ablaze with a rainbow of colors.

"Ohhhh," said Dave, as he stepped into the room.

"So there you are," I said. "I feared you might miss out on decorating the tree."

"I was out with Henrietta, making sure she was snug and warm."

I smiled. Nathan's little brother loved Henrietta, his pet hen, more than anything.

"Well, you're just in time to help us," I said.

We opened the boxes sitting near the tree and began pulling out ornaments of all sizes and shapes. Some of them were plain balls in blue, red, yellow, or green. Others were shaped like Santas, angels, snow-men, or sleighs. We found hooks in the bottom of the boxes and together decorated our tree. We invited Jack to help, but he said he'd leave it to us young guys while he took a short winter's nap upstairs in his room.

I ran up the stairs and pulled my portable radio from the closet shelf. I paused for a moment to look at the brightly wrapped box with the "Do Not Open Until Christmas" notice on top, and then returned to the living room. I plugged in the radio and soon "Deck The Halls" played gently in the background.

As each ornament was placed just so on the tree, its beauty grew. I loved Christmas and there was something special about a gaily-deco-rated tree. This year, it was all the more special, because Nathan was by my side. It was our first Christmas together and hopefully the first of many, many more.

My lip began to tremble as I pulled a silver ornament out of the box. It was a pinecone, fashioned out of thin, fragile glass. The stem was a pipe-cleaner and it had holly leaves of foil and two small, red, wooden holly berries. My eyes watered as I gazed at it, holding it in my hand.

"Are you okay, Ethan?" asked Nathan in a quiet voice. Dave looked at me out of the corner of his eye, and pretended he didn't see me crying.

"Yeah. I was just thinking of my mom. This ornament was always on our tree. I can remember her holding me up so I could hang it. I miss her so."

Nathan crossed the short distance between us and took me in his arms. He hugged me and kissed my forehead.

"Let's hang it right in the middle, so it'll show better than all the rest," he said.

Nathan followed as I walked to the tree and hung the ornament full of memories upon a sturdy branch. We stepped back and admired it.

"I think your mom would like it there," said Nathan, as he kissed my cheek. I smiled and we returned to decorating the tree.

As the radio played "Silent Night", "Silver Bells", and "I'll Be Home for Christmas" we finished placing bulbs on the branches. There wasn't room for an ornament more. We took out a box of icicles and carefully draped them on the tree. I felt like my heart was glowing warm in my chest. I wanted to freeze time and be trapped in that moment forever. Snow was falling outside, Christmas music was playing, and I was decorating the tree with the boy that I loved. Nothing could ever be better than that.

When the tree was finished, we grabbed a plate of cookies from the kitchen and sat side by side on the sofa. We gazed dreamily at the tree, while we munched on angels and snowmen. We just sat there in silence, luxuriating in the beauty and comfort of the moment. We sat there until we grew sleepy, and then climbed the stairs to bed. Nathan and I tucked in Dave, almost as if he were our son, and then slipped into our own room. There we lay next to each other and snuggled, while the wind whipped the snow about outside.

I awaked in the night. Nathan lay naked and warm beside me, breathing softly in his sleep. He was like an angel himself. I looked to the window and saw the snow drifting down in the moonlight. There is nothing quite so beautiful as falling snow, except for my Nathan, of course.

My gaze drifted to the package that sat upon my dresser. *Just a few more days now*, I told myself. *Just a few more days until what is inside is revealed at last.* I drifted off to sleep, dreaming dreams of Christmas that I had not dreamt since I was a little boy.

❦ ❦ ❦

Christmas Eve arrived at last. In our home, we unwrapped presents not on Christmas morning, but late on Christmas Eve. It was a tradition started in the days when we all went to Grandmother's on Christmas Day. The tradition continued, even though Grandma was long gone. I liked opening presents on Christmas Eve. It spread Christmas out over two days, instead of just one.

After supper, Uncle Jack, Nathan, Dave, and I gathered around the tree. I felt content within the arms of my little family. In previous years, it had just been Jack and me. Those were good years, but Nathan and his little brother made our family complete. As was tradition, we unwrapped gifts one by one. I gave Nathan a red sweater, with tiny little reindeer all over. He put it on and looked so very handsome in it. I also bought him some records, a pair of wooly house shoes, an assortment of candy, and the cassette recorder he'd been wanting. Nathan giggled with delight when he opened it and hugged me tight.

Nathan gave me a book on wrestling moves, some flannel boxers, a big box of chocolate turtles (Yum!), and a camera that spit out photos and developed them right before your eyes!

Dave made out the best of all on presents. All of us spoiled him. Jack got him a new Monopoly game (the old one was about worn to bits), a model car, a book on chickens, and a cool little airplane on a wire that really flew. Nathan and I put our money together and bought him an electric train set and some candy. Dave squealed when he unwrapped the train and hugged us both tight. He wanted to set it up and start playing with it right then and there.

Uncle Jack was the world's hardest person to buy for. He didn't need anything and didn't want anything. Nathan gave him a couple of boxes of chocolate covered cherries (his favorite) and I got him a nice flannel shirt. Dave gave him another box of chocolate covered cherries and a card he'd made himself. Together, we'd pooled our money and bought him something extra nice. We watched as he unwrapped and opened the small box. He smiled when he pulled out a beautiful Case pocketknife. We knew he wanted it. We saw him looking at it in the hardware store. We knew he wouldn't buy it for himself. He'd think it was a waste of money since he already had a perfectly good knife.

"Boys, this is far too expensive a gift for you to be giving me." I could tell he was touched, more by the sacrifice and thought than the knife itself.

"Nothing is too good for you," I said, hugging Jack.

"We love you," said Nathan, as he squeezed him about the waist. Dave jumped up into his arms and hugged him tight.

"I love you boys, too," he said, and, if I wasn't mistaken, a tear rolled down his cheek.

"Now," said Jack, clapping his hands together. "It's time to take you upstairs and show you what I bought you all for Christmas."

Nathan and I knew where our gift was hidden. A spare bedroom had been locked up for days. We heard Jack moving around in there from time to time, but we had no idea what was up. We had many theories about what might be in that room, but we didn't really have any clear notion of what was inside. We followed Jack up the stairs, wondering what it could be.

"I only got you boys one gift and it's for the two of you to share. I doubt you'll be disappointed, though. And you can use it too, Dave."

Our anticipation mounted as Jack fitted key to lock. The door swung wide and Nathan and I gasped. There in the middle of the room, sitting with a big red bow around it, was a beautiful chrome weight machine! It wasn't just a weight machine. It was a home fitness center.

"Oh my gosh!" I said out loud, running to it. "It's got butterfly arms, a leg press, and lat bar and everything!"

Nathan ran his hand admiringly along the bench. I could tell he was every bit as excited as me. We'd been working out with an old padded bench and a set of cheap plastic weights. The machine standing before us was like something out of a professional gym. It must have cost a *fortune.*

Both Nathan and I clasped Jack in a bear hug and told him it was the best Christmas present ever. Dave was less excited. He was more interested in his new train set.

"I think I'll go downstairs and admire my new knife," said Jack. "I'll leave you boys to check out your weight machine."

"Thanks again, Jack!" said Nathan.

"Yeah, thanks!"

Jack smiled and left us to ourselves. Dave left, too, no doubt to set up his train. Nathan and I tried out all the different exercises. I couldn't wait to start working out on that machine on a regular basis.

Later, we returned downstairs and talked with Uncle Jack while Dave played with his toys. Jack went to bed about ten and Dave turned in, too; the little guy was exhausted with all the excitement of the day. Nathan and I sat there and looked at the tree. A little before eleven, we climbed into bed ourselves and kissed each other until we fell asleep.

I awoke by Nathan's side on Christmas morning. I just lay there looking at him, until he awakened as well. We snuggled under the comforters for a few minutes, then sat up, and stretched.

As we dressed I looked at the package sitting on my dresser. It was Christmas Day at last. I could open it now and see what was inside. Nathan's eyes caught mine and he knew I was thinking about the present and the secret it held inside.

"Let's wait until after breakfast," I said. Nathan nodded. I wanted to rip the package open without delay, but a part of me wanted to preserve the mystery—for just a little longer.

We hurried downstairs into the kitchen. Uncle Jack and Dave had already left. There was a note on the table saying they'd gone to check on Mrs. Pearson, an elderly lady who lived in town. Jack kinda looked after her, doing odd jobs, running her to the grocery, and just keeping her company. She was *really* old and alone, and poor, too. Jack never mentioned it once, but I knew he'd been helping her with her heating bills so she could keep warm, and probably with a whole lot more. Jack was like that. He cared about people, but he never let on. I thought Jack was very thoughtful for all that he did for her and for going to visit her on Christmas day.

"I'm making you blueberry pancakes for Christmas breakfast!" announced Nathan.

"Need any help?"

"You can fry some bacon, and set up the table, but that's it!"

I smiled. Nathan whipped up batter and added blueberries, while I set about frying some bacon. The aroma of the kitchen was heavenly. We grinned at each other now and then, with big, dopey smiles that only those in love can manage. Sometimes it amazed me how content and happy I was just being with Nathan. We could be fixing breakfast, like now, or out toiling on the farm, and it was just the same. As long as Nathan was near, I was happy.

In minutes, we were devouring blueberry pancakes swimming in syrup and butter. It was delicious. I'd even managed to get the bacon just right; kinda chewy, but not underdone. We ate and talked and laughed together. It was a beautiful Christmas morning.

After we cleaned up after ourselves, I asked Nathan to wait for me by the tree. I ran upstairs and grabbed the package from the top of my dresser. I'd kept it there, since the day I'd pulled it out of a box the mailman had delivered in early November. My hands trembled slightly as I held it. It was such a beautifully wrapped package—a last Christmas gift from a dear friend.

Nathan and I sat in front of the Christmas tree. Its beautiful lights and decorations made it look magical. I held the package in my lap and just looked at it for a few moments. I read the note taped to the top once again, "Do Not Open Until Christmas". I'd yearned to rip it open so many times, but I'd managed to restrain myself. I looked at Nathan. He smiled and nodded his head.

I ripped the beautiful wrapping away and slowly opened the box. I reached inside and pulled out a note, a thick sealed envelope, and a threadbare stuffed rabbit. I passed the bunny to Nathan and he held as if it were a great treasure. I held the handwritten note in both hands and read it out loud, my voice quivering with emotion.

> *Ethan,*
>
> *I won't be around for Christmas this year, but I wanted to give you something that's very special to me. I know it's old and ratty, but it's my most treasured possession of all. Taylor gave me this rabbit not long after everyone found out about us. He said it would watch over me, when he wasn't there. It was his very first toy and he kept it near him always. I know we never discussed such things, but I kinda think that maybe you're like Taylor and me. I wanted someone to have his rabbit who would keep it and not just throw it away. I know it doesn't look like much, but he valued it above all else, and so did I in turn. Keep it for us, will you? I'll rest easier knowing it's in your hands.*

In the envelope you'll find the money I was saving up for college. I won't be needing it now. I want you to take some of it and buy Brandon that leather jacket he's always looking at in the store window downtown. I'm sure you know the one. Everyone does. The one he's always drooling over. Don't tell him it came from me. I don't think he could handle that. Just buy it and have it sent to him anonymously. I want you to keep the rest for yourself. Do whatever you want with it, but use at least some of it for fun. Buy yourself something, or throw a wild party, or whatever, just do something fun and cool, and remember Tay and me.

Merry Christmas,
Mark

Tears streamed down my face, and Nathan's too. I screwed my eyes shut, then sobbed. It had been nearly two months since Mark and Taylor died, but it seemed like yesterday. I always liked Mark and Taylor. I just wished I'd done more for them when I had the chance.

Nathan opened the envelope and pulled out a big stack of bills.

"Whoa!" he said, "There must be nearly a thousand bucks in here!"

When we counted it out, it was more than two thousand. Mark must've been saving that money for years. I knew he mowed lawns and did odd jobs in the summer, but…wow.

I knew the leather jacket Mark was talking about. I'd seen Brandon eyeing it myself. It would cost about $200. There'd be a whole lot of money left over.

"I don't really feel comfortable spending all this money," I said.

"That's what Mark wanted."

"Yeah, but still..."

"Well, he didn't say we had to spend all of it on something fun, just some of it. How 'bout next year were throw a kickass party on Taylor and Mark's birthday. We'll invite all their friends and have a blast."

"I think they'd like that," I said, "but what about the rest? The only thing I wanted bad is a weight machine, and Jack already gave us that."

"You could take a couple hundred bucks and buy yourself somethin' nice, somethin' you really want. Then, how 'bout..." Nathan paused, looking very thoughtful, then smiled. "How 'bout usin' some of it to put a plaque up on the soccer field, a memorial to Mark and Taylor. It could say somethin' like...Um...This field is dedicated to the memory of Mark Bailey and Taylor Potter. They died here all too early because of hatred and intolerance. May the future learn from what happened and not let it happen again."

I looked at Nathan with tears in my eyes. Sometimes, he amazed me.

"Nathan, that's a wonderful idea! And we could take whatever is left and set up some kind of fund, maybe like a scholarship for gay boys or something, in Mark and Taylor's names. It wouldn't be much at first, but we could let it build up interest until someday it could pay some boy's tuition for college every year."

"Awesome!" said Nathan.

"But, about me buying myself something..." I said, "We're *each* takin' out some money to buy something fun."

"Mark gave the money to you, not me," said Nathan.

"And I'm giving it to you. Besides, if Mark knew you were my boyfriend, he'd want you to have it, too. He loved Taylor more than anything, just like I love you."

Nathan hugged me and we kissed. I felt warm inside. Our first Christmas was one I'd remember forever. In years to come, I'd remember the swirling snow, our first Christmas tree, hot chocolate, gaily decorated cookies, and a last holiday gift from a friend, marked "Do Not Open Until Christmas". It really was a Merry Christmas. I knew all the others would be too, as long as Nathan and I were together. In the end, that's all that mattered.

The End

You can read more about Ethan and Nathan in *A Better Place* and other novels in the Gay Youth Chronicles.

About the Author

Someone Is Watching by Mark A. Roeder is the second novel in the continuing series *The Gay Youth Chronicles*. Roeder is also the author of *The Vampire's Heart* and numerous columns on collecting. He currently lives in southern Indiana. More information about his novels can be found at markroeder.com. Roeder is always happy to hear from readers and attempts to answer all emails. He can be reached at markaroeder@yahoo.com.

0-595-26073-X

Printed in the United States
949200003B